'A pacey, dark dive into the morality of tech. It plays artfully on the subtle tropes of social media gurus and Silicon Valley bros without being obvious. Rather than being a parallel to Twitter discourse, it's a cathartic answer to it'

New Statesman

'The deft assurance of Sperling's writing . . . an engaging takedown of the social media startup scene and the moral ambivalence of its characters'

Lunate

'Outrageous, sexy and funny. Sperling writes with the caustic economy of Waugh or Spark, but his characters have more heart, including the sock-puppets. The plot is so taut I'm still re-reading it trying to work out exactly how he brings the tension of a heist movie to 30-something bedsit London, all the while deliciously subverting our expectations. A joy to read'

Luke Kennard on *Astroturf*

'I loved Matthew Sperling's sly, subversive novel, a wickedly funny tale of how to come out on top in a fake news world'

Olivia Laing on *Astroturf*

VIRAL

Matthew Sperling

riverrun

First published in Great Britain in 2020 by riverrun
This paperback edition first published in 2021 by

riverrun

An imprint of

Quercus Editions Limited
Carmelite House
50 Victoria Embankment
London EC4Y 0DZ

An Hachette UK company

A CIP catalogue record for this book is available
from the British Library

Paperback ISBN 978 1 52940 197 4
Ebook ISBN 978 1 52940 194 3

This book is a work of fiction. Names, characters,
businesses, organizations, places and events are
either the product of the author's imagination
or used fictitiously. Any resemblance to
actual persons, living or dead, events or
locales is entirely coincidental.

10 9 8 7 6 5 4 3 2 1

Typeset by Jouve (UK), Milton Keynes

Printed and bound in Great Britain by Clays Ltd, Elcograf S.p.A.

Papers used by Quercus are from well-managed forests
and other responsible sources.

I

F OUR, EIGHT, SIX, SIX — ALICE mouthed the numbers to herself as she keyed in the code, her breath steaming in the frozen air. The entry system gave out a piercing, long beep, she felt the bolt thud, and she pushed open the door to the building that housed The Thing Factory office. Inside, she pulled the iron grille of the lift door across, enjoyed the sturdy, buckle-and-rope feel of it juddering up to the fourth floor, and searched for her swipe card with her fingertips in the bottom of her bag. When she stepped into the hallway, still looking for the card, the mural that covered the entire front wall of the office reared up in front of her. In photo-realistic detail, it showed an array of historical figures with their gazes absorbed in smartphones, iPads or laptops: in the left corner, Mesut Özil was taking a selfie with one arm draped over the shoulders of Jesus of Nazareth; in the right, Mahatma Gandhi and Stephen Hawking appeared to be Skyping the Vitruvian Man; in the middle, Mao Zedong, Abraham Lincoln and Elizabeth I were taking a conference call with Elizabeth II. Alice's business partner, Ned, had commissioned the mural from a street artist he'd met at a party. Alice thought it was pretty dreadful, but it seemed to have the desired effect. Every visitor to the office was invited to spend a minute contemplating it, and when The Thing Factory had been profiled in a magazine about start-ups, the article was topped and tailed with discussion of the mural.

The lift door opened and out stepped one of the interns, her swipe card already in her hand. 'Hello,' she said. 'Shall I get the door?'

'Thanks.' Alice followed her into the office, took off her coat and scarf and draped them over the back of one of the tattered leather sofas, and headed to the meeting room. Ned was sitting with his feet up on a desk, tapping away at his laptop. He didn't look up when she came in.

'Just a sec,' he said. 'I'm just checking the edit for the social media manager advert.'

While he flicked at the touchpad, Alice looked through the windows into the main part of the office. The Thing Factory occupied part of the top floor of a four-storey 1960s building near the corner of Kottbusser Tor, with a view across to the traffic island where the U-Bahn entrance was located. She and Ned had found the place after several weeks of viewing dingy, characterless or poorly located premises. They knew straight away that this was a place they could do something with. Alice liked the solidity of the building, so different from 1960s buildings in London; the coarse, hard-wearing carpets in the wide hallways, the tall ceilings, and the presence on the other floors of a pet-insurance company and an advertising agency. The building showed signs of its former existence as a mattress factory. Weight-bearing pillars of cast iron were distributed across the floor, marking the places where there used to be internal walls. At intervals around the wall were a series of small iron rings, the function of which someone had googled, to discover they were called safety eyebolts, for anchoring your body weight with a harness during heavy industrial work. Someone had had the idea of looping stiff garden wire through the eyebolts to hold a ring of artificial roses in place around the office wall.

Finally Ned lifted the laptop up and swivelled it towards her. 'What do you think?'

Alice sat on the edge of the desk and read the text.

We are The Thing Factory. The world's most innovative social media marketing agency. Based in Berlin's vibrant Kreuzberg district, we are having a transformational impact on social-first marketing. We are developing home-grown social channels with tens of millions of engagements and a growing number of followers every minute, and we use these channels to work with world-class brands in developing and driving strategy for social content, maximising creativity and creating unprecedented value. Now we're looking for more social media managers. Fancy joining us? Then tell us about yourself. We're not looking for bland, off-the-peg CVs. We're looking for talent, flair and originality. We want to hear your story.

'It seems fine,' Alice said, scanning quickly over the job description. She paused when she came to the final bullet point:

Other benefits of working here include: unlimited paid leave; management training opportunities; funding and support for developing your own side-hustles and passion projects; games consoles; a drinks fridge restocked daily; and many more!

'Are you sure about this leave thing?' Alice said.

'Trust me. It'll be good for the vibe. We'll move everyone's contracts over to that. No one will take the piss. In fact, I'm willing to bet that people will take less leave this way than if they had a normal entitlement.'

'Fine. Do we have a German version of the ad?'

'I'm getting one done this afternoon. It should be ready soon/after the plenary. I've just had a look at the project chats, and I think the social team should have good stuff for us.'

Alice took out her phone and opened Cubicle, the virtual office app they had started using two weeks ago. She saw the red bubble telling her that she had eighty-three new alerts since last night. 'I think I'll wait to hear about it in person,' she said.

'Cool,' said Ned. 'I sent you a message on there to say that I've set up a meeting with someone at that protein shake company. You remember we met one of them?'

'That little nerdy guy with see-through glasses frames?'

'Sebastian, yeah. He seems smart. Forward-thinking.'

'It sounds like a good lead,' Alice said – and she saw a smile play across Ned's face in a way that she found off-putting. Like he needed a pat on the head from her. It was starting to seem to Alice that even though the company had been Ned's idea originally, she was better at the job than him. They both knew that he couldn't have founded the company without her half of the start-up money, but she suspected now that he wouldn't have been able to make it work without her at all. In meetings, she could tell that she was better than he was at reading the room; that she could see the shape of a problem faster than him, and had a surer sense of the right solution; that she inspired more confidence in the staff. And the contacts book of potential clients that she'd built up in the last few months was twice as promising as Ned's, when he spent more time than her seeking them out. 'Let's go over the client leads this afternoon,' Alice said. 'We've got Daniel's Hype Session now, don't we?'

Ned looked through into the main office and nodded. 'It looks like he's ready to begin.'

'HELLO, SO I AM Daniel,' Daniel said, 'and can I just say at the beginning that it's really super exciting to be working with you all in this moment, where the possibilities of the start-up world seem so, well, exciting. So thank you for that, and for having me into your company as your finance and legal officer. Some of you know I have worked with Ned a little bit before on a project that was about the Amazon rainforest, and I don't know if I will do anything as exotic as that now, but there we are.'

Some murmurs of welcome from the team acknowledged Daniel's thanks, while Ned felt a minor inward wince at the mention of the rainforest project. Except for Alice, no one else in the company knew about that. The website had offered people the chance to buy their own patch of the Brazilian Amazon and save it from destruction, giving them a handsome ownership certificate and a pack of glossy photographs in return. So what if customers had to study the small print carefully to notice that in fact all they had bought was a single share in the freehold on the same ten square metres of barren ground that the company already owned, and that the photographs were for illustrative purposes only? Did they really think they were going to get their own plot for so little money? It seemed like a fairly harmless ruse. Still, Ned didn't exactly want everyone knowing about it. When he wound up the website last spring, he had tried to scrub all mention of his connection to it from the internet.

Daniel carried on: 'What I am wanting to do today is to show you perhaps a different side of myself. And I have some PowerPoint slides to accompany this!'

Ned had taken the idea of the Hype Session from his old job as a web developer in London, where all the team members were gathered together once a week to do team-building exercises, play games or perform charades in front of each other. Back then, Ned had found it tedious and awkward. It had felt like a waste of the first fifteen minutes of the day, and it left him feeling more alienated from his colleagues, not more bonded with them. At The Thing Factory, however, he believed he had made the Hype Session into something vibrant and engaging for his team. Instead of leading the sessions himself, Ned turned responsibility for each one over to a different person, and found that they responded well, coming up with inventive things that encouraged a feeling of trust and openness in the organisation. It could be an autobiographical sketch describing the creative path that had led them to working at The Thing

Factory, a talk on a hobby or enthusiasm of theirs, or a selection of their favourite songs or film clips, interspersed with their own commentary. These sessions were quickly becoming highlights of the working routine, richly anticipated and dissected in detail after the event, and Ned was starting to wonder whether people were investing slightly too much time and effort into their contributions.

Daniel was happily carrying on with his presentation, standing in front of a PowerPoint slide showing himself sitting cross-legged in front of some mountains. 'I have always suspected that I was a little bit "Buddish",' he said. 'Not exactly a Buddhist in the literal sense, but a very spiritually awake person. So even though I am not shaving my head or wearing orange robes or chanting a mantra, definitely I am a little bit Buddish. And there came a time in my life, just last summer, in fact, when very much I was in need of something. I didn't know exactly what, but I was feeling a sort of absence, which was also a sense of clutter, you know?'

Last summer: Ned tried to remember whether he had seen Daniel then. Maybe not, he thought. He had been busy making plans for the business with Alice.

'So it was at this low point in my life,' Daniel was saying, 'that a friend of mine told me about this really terrific organisation called, in German, One-Month Monk. And you laugh, but as soon as I heard that phrase, before I'd even seen the website, I knew that this was what I was needing: to go to Thailand, to be connected to a host monastery and to be a monk for one month.'

Daniel reached down to his laptop to move the slideshow along.

'And here we see the monastery where I was living; it's a very simple sort of place, not at all like Western temples where you will have the very rich paintings and all that sort of thing. In this photo you see also the head of the monastic order, and he's wearing the traditional Thai Buddhist ceremonial robes, so this is a pretty serious guy we're talking about.'

'He looks like a cool dude,' said a voice off to Ned's left.

'Yes, it is true there is something a little bit "accidental hipster" about him,' said Daniel, and earned a laugh from his audience. 'He could become definitely one of your memes. But this is not so important I think when you make a comparison to the role he has as a spiritual practitioner, because the main purpose of this month was for gaining spiritual insight, with the ultimate aim of attaining a state of nirvana. Which is not just a great band, but also an important religious concept. So apart from certain domestic duties, the main occupation of this month was to perform meditation. I wonder, has anybody else had any experience with transcendental meditation?'

Three hands went up. Ned tuned out for a moment while Daniel continued. Through the window out on Kottbusser Tor he could see a group of men holding a banner hung between two long canes, with a slogan written in Turkish which Ned took to be about some political issue or other. On the sunny paving area behind them, people were still eating brunch, huddled up against the cold in puffy coats and scarves. Daniel carried on and Ned wasn't really listening, but something about the way he spoke had reassured Ned that they'd made a good decision in taking him on. Ned liked people who'd had problems and dealt with them, especially when they had done it in unusual ways. Those were the kind of people he wanted around him. As he directed his full attention back towards Daniel, he found his openness winning and endearing.

'While I was in the monastery I lived by the eight precepts of Buddhism, which you can read on this slide here, and they include things like to not kill any living creature, to not drink alcohol, to not engage in sex or masturbation – that one was a little difficult for a whole month – and then various other precepts, the most unusual of which is perhaps to not sleep off the ground. So I didn't have even a bed or a mattress, I was only using a very firm wooden thing that I unrolled and slept on for this entire month, but the amazing thing was, my back has never felt more comfortable than in this period.'

Ned looked across at one of the interns, who was writing something down in a notebook. Was she really taking notes? Maybe she didn't want to forget the eight precepts. Anyway, what the fuck was a 'precept'? Honestly, it sometimes seemed to Ned as if educated Germans actually spoke better English than native speakers did.

Daniel's tone suggested he was wrapping up. 'So for me it was an important experience, because one of the insights that I gained from meditation told me what the source of the emotional blockage was. And I won't today tell it to you, because it is a little bit of a personal thing from my past, but I felt immediately like I was free to live my life and fully to be myself. And that is what is leading me here today, because it was when I got back from Thailand that I decided to stay in Berlin and seek a full-time job that would be more satisfying of my goals, and it was after I had mapped out that desire, a few weeks ago, that Ned got back in touch with me about what he and Alice were doing here with The Thing Factory. And so that is just a little sense of who I am, to introduce that side of my experience to you all, just in case you are ever thinking, wow, Daniel is such a chilled-out guy or anything like that. At this stage, has anyone got any questions they would like to ask?'

Two hands went up.

AN HOUR LATER, ALICE was with the rest of the team in the meeting room, ready for the weekly plenary, the meeting in which everyone came together to share progress on their respective projects, review their processes, and consider whether the current work cycle was going as well as it could. She sat looking straight ahead for two minutes, gathering her thoughts. Everyone was here: the seven core staff and the three current interns. Alice allowed herself a moment of reflection on how all these people were in this room, in some cases thousands of miles from where they originated, because of her and Ned, because of this thing they had conjured up. It was an enjoyable thought.

It was thrilling, how quickly life was coming these days. Moving to Berlin last summer, starting The Thing Factory, had been just what she needed: a new way of thinking about the next phase of her life. She needed to succeed at something. She'd had, she now saw, a bizarrely diffident attitude to her own abilities throughout her twenties. When she thought about the time wasted in half-heartedly trying to make it as an actor – all those months in LA punctuated by nothing but occasional days as an extra or a lighting double – it puzzled her that her life had been like that. Her life at that time didn't feel like anything she had chosen. So many of her contemporaries had accomplished things, made things happen for themselves, so that in their early thirties they were fairly high up in journalism or finance or politics. And it annoyed her how everyone had always assumed that just because she was financially secure and pretty, she couldn't possibly have any ambitions or worries of her own. Perhaps she had colluded with that assumption. But, no, she had decided that she wasn't going to do that anymore. That was why she loved the feeling of purposiveness, the fuller sense of herself that The Thing Factory gave her. She loved being good at something.

Tristan, the creative director, pushed his way into the room. He was struggling to get his headphones off while his hood was up and he was holding a takeaway coffee, an iPad and his phone. 'Just a second, hello, hello,' he said. 'Crumbs, it's a bit cold outside, innit?' He arranged his stuff on the table, then slipped into a thick Yorkshire accent and said, 'Bloody brass monkeys.'

'We *are* ten minutes late beginning . . .' Ned said. Alice flashed him a look – she could tell he was in a sour mood with Tristan – and he smiled. 'I hear that you're going to lead the sprint demo on social today,' he said.

'Hell yeah,' Tristan said, seated at last. 'The first part of it anyway, to talk mainly about home-grown accounts, and then I'll hand over. Since we were looking at lifestyle, fashion and fitness influencers last week, today I wanted to focus on the humour vertical. Look, this is amazing. You've got to see this.'

He was holding an iPad with a tabloid story open on the screen. He handed it across the desk to Alice. 'Jihadi Problems is getting mad traction,' he said.

Alice looked doubtfully at the screen. It was a *Daily Mirror* story, the page so crowded with adverts and videos that it took her a second to make it out. '*Is Homesick State,*' she said. 'What does that even mean? Is it supposed to be a pun?'

'Yeah, it's like a play on Islamic State . . . Islamic State, *Is Homesick State,*' said Tristan, then repeated the phrase to himself a few times, trying out various ways of emphasising it. 'It doesn't really work, to be honest. But read the story anyway.'

'It doesn't work at all,' said Ned.

'*Brummie lad joins sick ISIS death cult . . . but misses his PG-Tips,*' Alice read aloud. 'What the fuck? This is mad. Is this one of yours?'

'Yeah!' said Tristan. 'It's Jihadi Problems, the account I started at the start of last week.'

'Right, yes, I saw this on Cubicle.'

'It got good traction straight away,' Tristan said, 'but this has sent it through the roof. It went up on the *Mirror* online last night and I think it must be in the print paper this morning.'

'And they think it's a real account?'

'Yeah. They can't have looked very closely, because some of the tweets are just silly. But it must be more convincing than I thought.'

Alice scanned the story. 'It says here that people are calling for it to be banned. What if Twitter suspends the account?'

'It's all cool, because I phoned up Twitter and they're fine with it carrying on. It was based on some real jihadi accounts that I found pretty fascinating, but those ones tend to get shut down pretty quickly. What I want to do is keep on growing it, but gradually reveal that it's not really a member of Isis. Once people have started to realise that, I'll add "Parody Account" to the bio. But the idea was just to take the setting of Isis, since it's been so much in the news in the last year and it's so weirdly fascinating, and to find the humour in it.'

Alice handed the iPad to Ned. He looked worried, and said, 'The only thing I'd say, Tristan, is just be careful with the brand. You know? Once you start getting into Isis you're into some pretty dark shit, and I wouldn't want a Thing Factory account tweeting out beheading videos or anything like that.'

Tristan looked put out. 'No, obviously not, I'm not going to start tweeting Isis propaganda. It's pretty light-hearted really.'

'So the idea is that it's pretending to be a British jihadi?'

'Yeah, and the joke is that he's just moaning about everyday stuff. Like, for example, he has this thing about chicken; it's sort of a running joke that he's always moaning about missing his fried chicken.'

'Sounds hilarious,' Ned said.

Alice wondered if his bad mood was going to spoil the meeting. 'The tweets are very inventive,' she said.

'There's more to the chicken thing than that, anyway,' said Tristan. 'There's this thing about how in Isis they insist on boiling the chicken breasts in water to take the flavour out and make them more, like, holy or something. Devout.'

'Do they really do that?' said Alice.

'I believe so. But with Jihadi Problems, really the whole thing deflates Isis. You know, it punctures their ridiculousness by showing that even while there's a background of jihad and beheadings and guerrilla fighting and all that, this is just a down-to-earth British lad who's got mixed up in it.'

'Like in *Four Lions*,' said one of the interns.

'Sort of, yeah.'

'Are you writing all the content yourself?' Alice said.

'At the moment,' said Tristan. 'But I'll delegate it once it's bedded in. There are a couple of creators who I thought would be good for this one.'

'How many followers does Jihadi Problems have?' Ned asked.

Tristan said, 'I think it's up to seventy-four,' then leaned over the iPad, tapped a few times, and said, 'No, seventy-six thousand now. That's in nine days, more or less.'

That was why Alice knew they'd done well in appointing Tristan, even if Ned found him annoying. She'd been the one who argued for him after his interview. His understanding of social media was so instinctive and sure, it seemed like magic. When he first started, he said that he could tell if a post was going to do big numbers within five minutes of creating it, but now he had it down to sixty seconds, and if a piece of content hadn't had at least a few dozen engagements in that first minute it would be deleted, either to be retried in a revised form or let go altogether. This happened to three or four of every ten pieces of content, but of the other six or seven, all of them would get engagements in the five figures, and one would normally get into six figures. At his interview, Tristan had described the buzz he got from seeing his work disseminated online as the equivalent of making a roomful of people laugh at a stand-up spot – he had come to Berlin with the intention of honing his craft on the English-language stand-up scene – but online, he said, the feeling was multiplied and spread out. Alice had been sceptical then; after two months working with him, all her doubts were gone.

'Anyway,' Tristan was saying, 'it was a pretty busy week already before all this started. As you know, we've added something like a dozen new accounts to the portfolio in the last fortnight, and some of them are taking off big time. So we've got things like Porn Interiors, this is where we take screencaps from people's amateur porn videos and the guy that runs the account writes these really hilarious, sort of catty but ultimately quite sweet, critiques of the interior design and the home furnishings in the background of where they're fucking. It's a really simple idea, but it works brilliantly. He's now got almost two hundred thousand followers for that. It's obviously a bit top-shelf, but the nice thing is it's now getting mainstream traction as well. Lily Allen has been engaging with the content. And what we're going to launch next week is Porn Interiors SFW, which will be the same thing but with the people having sex blurred out, so the people who want to look at Twitter on their work computer can follow that one, and it'll have all the same tweets.'

'But we don't have the copyright to any of these images, right? If they're taken from screencaps?'

'I'm not sure about that, but I think the position is that it comes under Creative Commons. If you take a screencap, you've created that image, and you're free to disseminate it.'

'We need to get Daniel to check that out,' Ned said. 'We don't want to find that we build up a million followers and then Pornhub sues for infringement and it has to be taken down.'

Daniel made a note on his tablet.

'Yeah, but Pornhub hasn't got a leg to stand on with copyright,' Tristan said – 'everything on there is pirated.'

'That's true.'

'The other thing that's really taken off, and the last thing I wanted to flag up before I hand over, is Nana Says. This is an account where all the tweets are in the voice of a Nan.' (Tristan crooked his back like a little old lady and mumbled *'Ooh, hello, dearie'* under his breath.) 'The tweets are all really cutting and funny; they hit on that ability of old people to just say truthful things in a way that non-old people can't because it would be too rude, but they also quite often contain good life advice. I've put an example up on screen here. It says, "You don't need to tell me about the 5:2 diet, dearie. That's what we did when we'd filled up the coupons in our ration book." Do you want some more examples?'

'I think I get the idea,' said Ned flatly.

'Okay, maybe that's not the funniest tweet. But Nana Says has now got almost half a million followers in just three weeks, and they're all getting a lot of engagement as well, so I think it has potential to become an account with strong loyalty as we develop the character.'

'Thanks, that's great, Tristan,' Alice said. 'Before we move on, I could do with a coffee too. Shall we take ten minutes?'

There was general agreement, and people were starting to stand up and gather their things when Tristan said, 'Ned? This might sound weird. Are you, like, bleeding?'

Alice saw Ned look down at the line of blood smeared across the desk, then she noticed the bloodstains on his laptop and his paper cone of water. He looked at his hands, then put his thumb in his mouth. 'Holy shit,' he said, 'I'm sorry about that. I must have snagged my thumb on something. I didn't notice.'

'Wow, there is really blood all over the place,' said one of the German interns.

'Can you sponge that up, Ned?' Alice said.

Ned squeezed his thumb between two fingers to seal up the cut, and didn't answer.

O N HER WAY OUT, Alice had put her arm across Ned's shoulders, said in his ear, 'Let's raise the enthusiasm a little bit when we get back, yeah?', walked off, and turned back from the doorway to wink at him in a gesture so hammy and exaggerated that he couldn't help smiling. He felt a little jolt of energy. Strange how she could read his moods so accurately.

While the others were out getting coffee, Ned went around the room with a damp sponge to wipe the blood from the table, the chair, and the door's frame and handle. He even found a smudge on one of the walls. It had never occurred to him how often he touched things. Maybe it was some kind of nervous tic. It looked like he had been trailing his left hand all over the room.

Fifteen minutes later, everyone was back in the meeting room. 'Awesome,' Ned said, 'it sounds like it's been a really great week, so thanks for that, Tristan. It's really cool to see how many new accounts we're adding, and how they're flourishing in all these ways. Soon Alice and I will be able to feed back to everyone about the progress we've made in building up the potential client base. But Fola, what's new with you?'

'What's new,' said Folasade, the head of content, 'is that I've brought four new accounts in on retainer this week, all of them run by really good, energetic people. The one I wanted to tell you about is called Astrology for Bros, and as you can see from this sampler of recent content, the idea is pretty simple: it's astrological readings, real ones, but whereas most astrology is directed towards women, here the life advice that follows on from astrological readings is specifically tailored for . . . well, bros, as the account name suggests, but really you might say men more generally. This one here is a good example of the tweets. It says, "Mercury is heading retrograde for you this week, Aries bros, but don't even fucking think of skipping leg day."'

'I love it,' said Ned. He felt almost embarrassed that someone as bright and talented as Folasade was now working for him, managing silly social media accounts. Two years ago she had got a First from Cambridge after being the first person in her family to go to university, and after that she worked in a digital agency in London, before deciding she wanted to move to Berlin. At her interview she had told Ned and Alice how her parents wanted her to be a lawyer or a doctor – that was what all Nigerian parents wanted, she said with a laugh – but she was proud she had insisted on doing Modern Languages. The story was told as an example of her independent-mindedness. Ned kept to himself his nagging feeling that being a doctor would have been a better use of her abilities than overseeing all these Twitter and Instagram channels. He was aware, too, of the irony involved in being the boss of someone who was so much more accomplished than he had been at her age. But there it was, she had applied for the job and taken it, and a few months in, she seemed to love doing it. And she was good at it.

'Obviously,' she was saying, 'there's a lot more to it than just that sort of juxtaposition. It's got 317,000 followers after only two months, which is big numbers, especially since astrology could be seen as a slightly niche thing. And the thing that's clever is that it's sort of challenging and reassuring at once. Like, it will do some tweet that seems to be playing on gender stereotypes and maybe reinforcing them, but in the process it raises awareness of issues around them, and so simultaneously you sort of chuckle in recognition but you also question it.'

'Can I see more tweets?' Ned said.

'Sure,' said Folasade. 'The next one I've got lined up here is a good example of what I was just saying. "This new moon occurs with an eclipse, so don't be afraid to have a heart to heart with another bro about the things that really matter (#nohomo)."'

'Brilliant,' said Ned. 'And that got thirty-eight thousand retweets? Amazing.'

'The creator of Astrology for Bros is this guy from Manchester called Paul, I think he's just twenty-two, and Tristan and I both think he's a super-talented guy. So we've got him on a retainer now. I've asked him to prepare a pitch of three further ideas for content themes, and to come up with sample content for one of them, so we'll see what he comes back with from that. But I think he's going to be a great addition.'

Folasade spent the next ten minutes talking them through a handful of other accounts. It pleased Ned to observe how raptly everyone was listening, how much Folasade made them laugh, and how fluent she was at speaking without notes. When she was finished, Ned said, 'Okay. It looks like it's all going great. But my question with all this stuff, as you can probably guess, is when is it going to be ready to be monetised? Let's not forget that's the point of all this. It's all very well having four million followers across all these platforms—'

'Six million in total,' Tristan said.

'Sure, six million. But it only means something when we can start getting paid content to run on them. Otherwise we're just influencing people to laugh at all this novelty stuff.'

'I don't think "novelty" is fair,' said Tristan. 'There's a

serious point to a lot of the accounts. As we showed last week, the humour vertical is just one part of it, alongside the fashion and fitness verticals, and health and nutrition and activism. Anyway, making people laugh is a serious thing to do.'

Ned looked to Alice, but her attitude was hard to read.

'My point is,' he said, 'that we can't wait forever. At the moment we could go to people, we could go to all the businesses and ad brokers that me and Alice have been making contact with, and we could say, look, we have these ten million followers, these six million followers, whatever, and they're very loyal and engaged and highly targeted and all that, and we can do a coordinated series of tweets across all the platforms at once giving exposure to your hashtag. And people would see that the opportunity is out of this world. And I think we need to do it now, because what worries me is that Twitter, Instagram, all these places will change their policies on paid content, and we'll have built up this audience who we're not allowed to advertise to. And then it really will be pointless.'

'The way I see it,' Tristan said, 'is that we can hold our nerve for just a bit longer. We don't want to jump too soon and start selling services before we've seen how big this can get. Remember what they said in that Facebook movie?'

'They said a lot of things in that movie.'

'They said, making a million dollars is pretty cool, but making a billion dollars is fucking awesome. That's not an exact quote, but you see my point.'

Ned turned to Alice. 'What do you think?'

'I think Tristan's right. I think we should have faith in him.'

'Thank you,' Tristan said. 'I just think that what we're building here is this incredibly powerful tool, and we don't want to misunderestimate how much we could do with it.'

Ned turned to Folasade, who nodded in agreement with Tristan. 'Okay,' he said. 'We'll stick for now. But I'm really keen to get going on this. We're throwing a lot of money at this each month and it's got to start giving something back soon.'

'It will,' said Tristan. 'Don't worry.'

Ned put two thumbs up to signal his agreement. His problem, he knew, was that having come up with the project, he wasn't able to carry it out himself. He'd known as soon as he met Tristan that his understanding of social media went far beyond what Ned was capable of. Ned was simply too old, at thirty-three, to get it. It didn't help, of course, that Tristan was so annoying. Last week he had sent through a new design for a Twitter banner with the email message 'OMG this banner is such a babe I want to snog its face off', and several times throughout the day Ned had found himself wondering why his creative director was speaking in the voice of an adolescent girl, when he was a twenty-four-year-old man with a ginger beard flecked with grey hairs. And why did Tristan always wear horrible vintage shell suits, novelty Christmas jumpers, and flowery shirts buttoned all the way up to the top, when he surely knew that they made him look like a wanker?

When the rest of the team had dispersed and gone back to work, Ned and Alice spoke in the meeting room for a few minutes. The plenary had gone well, they said; the numbers for social were growing at a terrific rate; they both thought Tristan and Folasade were doing great work growing all the accounts. Alice paused a moment, then said, 'You seemed a bit irritable at the start. Is everything okay?'

'I'm sorry for that,' he said. 'I don't know what it is. It's a lot of things. I've just got the feeling that there's something else we should be doing. I'm not sure what it is, but I feel like I'm on the verge of a new idea, the thing that will really take us into the big time.'

'We've got it already, Ned. It's social. You've already hit on the thing that's going to make us big. That's why I came in on this, remember? We just need to keep on resourcing the project, and have faith in it.'

'But it's costing so much money. Every month, thousands and thousands.'

'Keep your nerve. That's all you need to do. In the scheme of things, the monthly development cost is nothing compared to the potential yield. We can swallow these early losses because we've modelled it forward.'

'But in the meantime we're paying a load of kids to tweet all this stuff I don't understand.'

'Don't worry, Granddad. Tristan understands it. Just count the eyeballs.' Ned smirked in spite of himself at her impression of Tristan, and Alice carried on: 'It's all about the eyeballs. Content begets eyeballs begets wonga. The classic formula.'

'Maybe I should go on holiday and come back for the wonga part.'

'Anyway, profit might not even matter. Look at Twitter. No profit, no real business plan, and they've got investors throwing billions at them because of their reach. Because of the eyeballs.'

'The eyeballs, yes, I get it.'

'You were right about the concept in the first place. You still are. It seems like you forget that sometimes, or like you've lost confidence in it.'

'Hmm . . .'

'I have a theory,' said Alice.

'Yeah?'

'My theory is that you're struggling with the fact that

you have to let Tristan run it. That's the thing you really don't like. With all the other businesses and the scams—'

'Not scams.'

'Fine, with all the other businesses, you could do the whole thing yourself, every single detail, but with this you have to trust this other person to do it. That's why you preferred the small-fry stuff you were doing, the stuff that wasn't scalable, because you could do it all yourself, in secret. You're being a meddler, when you need to be acting like a strategist.'

Ned could feel himself breaking into a smile. 'Did you get that "meddler" and "strategist" thing from one of your business books?'

'I'm right, though, aren't I?'

'It's very sexy when you're this insightful.'

'I know it is,' said Alice. 'Let's not go down that road again though.'

Ned laughed. Alice was looking at him curiously. 'Look,' she said, 'if you think you're on the verge of a new idea, why don't you spend some time next week thinking about which direction you'd like to diversify in? Put some of the team on it. We could all sit in – in fact, why don't we use the plenary time for that? Then if you fix on a good direction, we can take someone off social to work on development with you.'

'Are you sure we can spare anyone?'

'I think so, yeah. Tristan's got all the creators in order and I'm dealing with clients, so it's pretty much running itself.'

'That would be great,' Ned said. He took a bottle of Club-Mate from the centre of the table – one of the interns had the job of restocking the energy drinks in the fridge every morning and laying them out ahead of meetings – unscrewed the cap and took a sip.

'I don't know how you can drink Club-Mate so early in the day,' Alice said.

'It's pronounced *mah-ta*. Like stigmata.'

'Whatever. It just tastes like stale cigarettes to me.'

'False,' Ned said, and held the bottle up close to his face to read from the label. 'It actually has a *Geschmack von Koffein und Gerbstoffen*. A taste of caffeine and . . . something.'

'Herb stuffing?'

'I suspect that's a false friend.'

'Whatever it means, it tastes gross.'

'One day you'll understand. And then you'll know you've become a true Berliner.'

Alice shook her head, laughing. 'You're such a patronising dick.'

AFTER WORK, MOST OF the team took their regular table at The Mint Gun Club, the gay bar around the corner from the office. Over the next ninety minutes, Ned watched it fill up with beautiful people in their twenties, all tattoos and shiny teeth. Behind the bar stood a small zoo of taxidermy creatures: a huge fish, a baby boar, a yellow duckling under a bell jar. All across the ceiling, white satellite dishes had been converted into lamp fixtures. Several members of the team came here after work most nights of the week, so the bartenders knew their regular orders. Last month, just before Christmas, Ned and Folasade had drunkenly snogged in the hallway that led towards the toilets, in an incident that neither of them had mentioned since then. Now she took her lime and soda from Ned's hand, flashed him a smile and sat down.

'Wasn't Daniel good?' Alice said.

'It was really interesting,' said Folasade. 'I knew someone else who was into meditation, but Daniel made it sound more profound.'

'Yeah,' said Tristan, 'but he missed out the bit about how,

before the insight starts, it just makes your legs go numb. I got pins and needles in my balls when I tried it.'

'Trust you to lower the tone,' Folasade said. 'What do you know about it?'

'Been there, done that,' Tristan said, and then repeated the words in a Texan accent.

'You kept pretty quiet earlier.'

'He did put his hand up,' Ned said, 'when Daniel asked.'

'Oh, I didn't notice that.'

'Well, not all of us have to make ourselves the centre of attention all the time,' Tristan said, then slurped as loudly as he could through his straw.

'Says the man in the pink and yellow shell suit top.'

Everyone laughed at Folasade's joke, and Tristan mimed blowing his nail-varnish dry in response.

'I thought it was interesting,' Folasade said, 'the way that what Daniel was saying chimed with what that guy was saying about well-being the other week.'

'Yeah,' said one of the interns.

Folasade was referring to the lunchtime lecture Ned had organised for the team two weeks ago. In truth, he had been rather disappointed by the triteness of what the visiting speaker had said.

'Oh yeah, I meant to tell you all,' Ned said. 'I was doing some more thinking about that topic and I found this amazing podcast. It was a TED-Talk sort of thing, and he was saying that the main thing is, you don't achieve happiness by aiming for happiness itself. It has to come as a by-product of other things.'

'How do you mean?'

'I can't remember it very precisely, it was by some professor in behavioural economics who'd based it on loads of research and data, but when I heard it, it instantly clicked. Basically he said that happiness, or well-being, depends on getting the right balance of purposefulness and pleasure in your life. So you need to fill your time with things that either give you a sense of doing something worthwhile, or give you pleasure. But the balance between the two will be different for everyone. So, you know, for someone like Arsène Wenger, his time is one hundred per cent about trying to win football matches, he has no interests or anything beyond football. But for Alex Ferguson, he was like sixty per cent dedicated to the purpose of winning at football but forty per cent dedicated to things that gave him pleasure, like collecting wine or buying racehorses or that sort of thing. But they both have high levels of well-being because they're spending their time in the way that satisfies them.'

'But surely Alex Ferguson also gets pleasure from football, and gets purpose from his racehorses winning races,' Tristan said.

'Sure, but that reinforces my point,' Ned said. 'Anyway, it was just an example off the top of my head, it's not the example this guy used. Of course, lots of people also get pleasure from achieving their purpose.'

'I definitely agree with that,' said Richard, a colleague who had started at the company last week, after his earnest, thoughtful-seeming demeanour had impressed Ned at his interview. Ned liked him. It was the first thing Richard had said in perhaps ten minutes, and carried more weight because of that. 'It's like Daniel was saying about transcendental meditation, you wouldn't think that just sitting on the floor doing breathing exercises was something pleasurable, right? But for lots of people it's almost orgasmic as an experience. And for me there are things that are similar – like it sounds silly, but I did a Maths and Philosophy degree and when I'm working out a problem, on one level it's fundamentally boring, but the experience of being absorbed to that extent in abstract values and relationships often has something blissful and weird about it.'

'Exactly,' said Ned. 'You don't attain happiness directly but you do it through the back door—'

'Hello, that's a bit top-shelf,' said Tristan, but Ned ignored him.

'—You do it by finding the things that absorb your attention, that give you pleasure and that make you feel like

37

you're getting something done, and you get the right combination of those things in your daily life. So I think, for example, that my problem in the last few years is that I struggle a bit to do purely pleasurable things. I'm always regimenting my life and running it according to goals and timetables and to-do lists. And in a way I'm glad of that, because up to my late twenties I didn't have that sort of drive, I was just cruising along in a way that neither gave me pleasure nor much sense of purpose. But now that I have a lot of purpose, I need to put a bit more pleasure back into the mix. And that's one of the aims for the next few years, to get the balance that's right for me.'

There was a moment's silence round the table. Ned narrowed his eyes, looked up to his left and wondered whether what he had said was really true. Probably it was. When he thought about the last few years, there was hardly a time when he didn't have a project on the go, when he wasn't driven every day by trying to achieve his aims with one business or another.

One of the interns put his empty glass down and said, 'I think that makes it my round. Same again?'

Most people wanted the same again. Ned asked for another large beer.

'How did your date go last night?' Alice said to Tristan. 'I haven't heard yet.'

'Ah, yes,' said Tristan. 'That.'

People around the table were giggling.

'Well, how did it go?'

'Pretty well. Yes, pretty successfully I'd say.'

'You're being very coy.'

'Tell her what you did!' said Folasade.

'Did you sleep with her?'

'No. Well, not quite.'

'Oh yes?'

'We fooled around a bit.'

'Say more.'

'I fingered her in the *Denkmal*.'

Folasade snorted with laughter, and her drink went up her nose.

'In the *what*?'

'You know. The *Denkmal*. The memorial. We were walking in there and you know how it's very intricate, a bit like a maze where you can get lost among all the blocks? Anyway, it was all dark and atmospheric in there, and one thing led to another. It was romantic.'

'Don't you think that's a bit disrespectful?'

'I did wonder about that. But it was a very nice, tender moment.'

'Wasn't it a bit challenging when you're wearing so many layers of clothes? It was like minus two last night.'

'I guess nature finds a way. I mean, I took my gloves off, obviously.'

'Is this Anna?' Alice said. 'That really quiet girl we spoke to at that opening?'

'Yeah. She's not that quiet. She does actually talk.'

'She's very pretty. She's like a beautiful little baby bird.'

Ned rose and headed to the toilet. Something had annoyed him, he couldn't quite say what. Maybe the lack of response his thoughts on well-being had provoked, or maybe the way Alice was acting towards Tristan. Ned felt like she was playing up to Tristan, in a way that made him feel cut out. All that shit about that girl Anna . . . Ned felt obscurely slighted by Alice's interest in Tristan's romantic adventures. She never asked him about his own, and since she'd told him when she came to Berlin last year that they ought to be just friends, she acted as if they'd never been anything else. As if their history in London had never happened.

She had touched a nerve earlier, as well, with that stuff about scalability. About scams. Ned was pretty sure he had introduced the word 'scalable' to her, and now here she was, using it against him. Sure, his first start-ups hadn't been scalable. But they hadn't been scams exactly. The rainforest site just sold people something they wanted to believe in, and it probably had the effect of raising the environmental awareness of the people who bought into it, leading them on to other kinds of activism and charity. It was totally legal. Daniel had made sure of that for him. Admittedly, the sites Ned had run before that – the ones that sold caffeine tablets marketed as 'metabolic boosters' for people wanting to lose weight, or counterfeit steroids – they were a bit more dodgy. But that was a long time ago. The steroid site was getting on for three years ago. And Alice knew that Ned was only doing legitimate business now. She'd made him promise that when she agreed to go into partnership with him. So why did she have to bring it up?

When Ned came back to the table, Tristan was saying that he didn't want to go on to another bar, and Folasade was trying to persuade him to come, since he had a day off tomorrow.

'No, I want to go to bed early, have a lie-in and then go to brunch. I'll see you all back at the mattress factory.'

'Brunch?' said Folasade.

'Brunch. It's like a cross between breakfast and lunch. Very fashionable.'

'Shut up, you fool. I don't want to go to brunch, I want to go out now. Ned, you'll take me out, won't you?'

'Where do you want to go?'

'There's this new bone-broth bar in Friedrichshain that I'm keen to try.'

'What the fuck is a bone-broth bar?'

'It's, like, a bar where you drink bone broth.'

'Why would you want to do that?'

'For the collagen, apparently. It's really good for you. But when you drink the broth, it's just nice, it's like drinking a cup of really nice stock. My friend has been.'

'But surely,' Alice said, 'drinking collagen doesn't mean that you have more collagen in your body. Don't you just digest it and shit it out?'

'Look, I don't know,' said Folasade. 'But it's a big thing and I'd like to try it. All the Hollywood people are into it.'

'Well, if they're into it, I'm sold,' said Ned. He drank the last third of his beer in one go, placed the glass decisively down and said, 'Shall we?'

'This is the most Berlin thing I've ever seen,' said Tristan. 'People from a social media start-up going to a bone-broth bar.' His voice shifted into an impression of a jaded hippie. 'That's the thing about bone broth, they draw you in with the highs but they never tell you about the lows, man. Yeah, the whole life just went out of the bone-broth scene after Altamont, that shit got really dark . . .'

Ned had stood up and taken his coat down from the hooks. 'Will someone take Tristan's batteries out, please, and turn him off for the night?' Then he extended his hand to Folasade, who took it and climbed up from the bench.

As they walked to the U-Bahn, Ned resentfully played over Tristan's words in his head, until Tristan's voice was an infant's whine. *That's so Berlin . . .* Every ex-pat, it seemed to Ned, had their own story of decline: of when Berlin had been a great place to move to, and when exactly it had stopped being great. Oh, people would say, when they first came in 2004, Berlin was *really* the place for good techno and good drugs and cheap apartments, but by 2006 it had become another Hackney, ruined by rich Americans and English public schoolkids, Hugos and Hermiones who didn't even try to learn German . . . To Ned, this was nonsense. Now it was 2015 and he was in Berlin because it was such a nice place to live, because it was so useable as a city, and because of the start-up scene. He didn't give a shit about techno music. He felt freer in Berlin than he had in London, perhaps because in Berlin everyone was an outsider. It was as if the city had drawn in the most enterprising young people from all of Germany, and half of those from the rest of Europe as well, and they formed a new ad hoc society here.

Ned loved Berlin. He loved Kreuzberg, and his neighbourhood just across the canal from the office. He loved his apartment on Dieffenbachstraße, even its lack of a lift; he bounded up the five flights of stairs at a sprint several times a day, enjoying how quickly his pulse returned to normal afterwards. He loved its high ceilings, thick walls and thick wooden floorboards. He loved his mastery of the U-Bahn and the S-Bahn and the buses and the trams, and the resourcefulness of buying his *Monatskarte* and getting a whole month's travel for seventy euros – ridiculously cheap compared to London. He loved feeling at home in the rhythms of the city's infrastructure, its networks and flows of people and traffic and money. Whenever he went back to London he was struck with fresh eyes by the poor quality of everything – the pavements and roads literally breaking up, made of garbage, deliberately shitty and inferior – so that he wanted to get back as quickly as possible. He loved the Turkish bakery around the corner from his apartment, the flatbread you bought for fifty cents straight from the oven; he loved the ridiculous brunches in the bar-cafés, with four different meats, three cheeses and half a dozen bread rolls. He loved the way the dogs all walked off the lead and were so well behaved, trotting companionably in front of their owners, sniffing and pissing at trees and bins, checking back in if their owners had stopped to chat. He loved the riverbanks and the lakes, with their cheap private beaches and their nudist areas. He loved the TV Tower.

He turned to Folasade, who was sitting next to him reading a Harry Potter book in a battered hardback copy. 'Are they really any good, those books?' he said.

Folasade turned to look at him. 'What, you've never read them?'

'You forget how old I am. I was probably at university when the first one came out.'

'They're for adults too.'

'I guess it's just not the kind of thing I'd expect you to like. Isn't it all a sort of boarding school fantasy? Fucking Hufflepuff and Mugglewump and all that nonsense.'

'I'm not even going to engage with that remark,' Folasade said, looking back at her book with a smile on her face. 'Anyway, why shouldn't I like it? I used to fantasise about going to a boarding school. Do you think I should just be reading Audre Lorde and listening to Tupac?'

'Who's Audre Lorde?' said Ned.

'Ned, seriously?'

'Just kidding. No, she's great, I loved "Royals".'

'Fuck *off*,' said Folasade, cuffing him playfully around the head. 'You are ridiculous.'

They were silent for a few moments before Folasade said thoughtfully, 'I guess part of the attraction of the books is being in this other world, away from your family. I mean, my family are great, but when I was growing up it was always chaos, uncles and aunties and everyone just dropping in, staying for dinner. Staying with us. I had to share my bed once with this cousin who'd come over, and she wasn't a real cousin, she was probably like the daughter of a business associate of my dad's or something. But she turned up with no notice and then it's, oh, just budge up, Fola, and we're top and tailing, with her smelly feet in my face. And then she stayed for three months!'

'It sounds quite nice to me,' said Ned. 'You wouldn't get lonely.'

'Were you an only child?'

'Yeah, I was,' Ned said. Then they were silent until he turned to her and said, 'Are we seriously going to a bone-broth bar?'

AN HOUR LATER, ALICE was sitting in a stall in a restaurant bathroom, having left her date waiting at the table. Holy shit, she thought, was this really what her friend Abby thought of her? That she would make a good match with this guy? That they were on the same level? Abby had put them in touch last summer when she found out that Alice was in Berlin, and sent Alice a message talking him up, but they hadn't met until now. He had looked handsome in the photo, and granted, he *was* handsome. But, honestly . . . Alice took her phone from her handbag and began writing a text, getting as far as 'ABBY WHAT THE ACTUAL FUCK?'

She had known they were a bad match almost as soon as they met. Five minutes after they had sat down at the table, his phone had rung. He excused himself and took the call in the hallway while Alice looked at her phone, then he came back, refilled his wine glass and said, 'Sorry about that. Tenant problems.'

'You're a landlord?'

'I have these flats in Bristol but I've got nightmare

tenants at the moment. Never pay their rent on time. So I'm trying to get them out, but there's all this red tape. The thing that pissed me off is they never told me they were DSS. I'd never have given them the flat if I knew they were on benefits. They're real arseholes.'

'Because they're late with their rent?'

'Just the fact of being on benefits is a red flag for me. Morally, I mean. If you don't want to work for a living, why should I subsidise you to sit at home all day with a flat-screen TV out of my taxes, you know?'

'Right, yes,' Alice said, toying with her fork and wondering if she could be bothered to argue the point. She let it drop and said, 'What do you get up to when you're not chasing tenants?'

He told her about the record label he was going to start. *Zápalka*, it was called; he seemed to be waiting for Alice to ask him what it meant.

'What does it mean?'

'It's Czech for a match. A matchstick. When I thought of it, I thought, eureka, that's perfect, because a match is like the international language of how strangers meet each other in different cultures. I have this trick when I'm travelling that I never carry matches, so I've always got a perfect conversation starter with any woman I see smoking – just go up and ask for a match in their own language.'

'Don't more people use lighters than matches these days?'

'Sure, yeah. I couldn't find a word for lighter that sounded as cool as *zápalka* though.'

'When you said it, I thought it would be a South American thing. Like Zapatista.'

'What's Zapatista?'

'It's a Mexican communist group, isn't it?'

'Christ,' he said. He looked genuinely upset at the thought.

The conversation moved on. Alice told him that she'd been in Berlin for seven months, and that she was in Los Angeles for two years before that, working as an actor. She told him in vague terms about The Thing Factory. He didn't ask any questions, instead telling her how interested he'd become in Instagram. He asked her if she knew what Instagram was, as if she hadn't just told him that she ran a social media company. He'd been making a study of Instagram influencers, he said, just to confirm some theories he had. Alice declined to ask what the theories were, and he moved on to telling her which other apps he liked. He'd become interested in the sceptical movement, he said, and in the issue of free speech. 'That's the thing about me,' he said, 'I'm the kind of person who can never be bored.' Alice nodded along. 'I don't think I've been bored since I was a teenager. It's just impossible. I don't see how anyone can be bored in the age we live in. I think if you're able to get bored, it just shows that you're a boring person. There's always more albums to listen to, more films to watch, more places to travel to, more martial arts to practise, more hunting to do.'

Alice asked what sort of hunting he meant.

'Game. Big game. Birds. You name it, I've probably shot it. Can you guess how many guns I've got?'

Alice was unable to guess.

'I've got six. They're all back at my parents' house, locked up. I wanted to bring some of them out here actually, but there's all these ridiculous laws about transporting firearms across national borders. But just a few months ago in Poland I had the most amazing experience, shooting an AK-47 – out in the open, not even on a closed shooting range. A Kalashnikov. Have you ever shot a Kalashnikov?'

Alice confirmed that she had never in fact shot any gun, before they were interrupted by the waiter. She ordered her meal, wondering how much longer she would have to stick the evening out and choosing not to have a starter, then excused herself and went cringing into the ladies.

She should have known he was going to be a wanker from the messages they'd exchanged, Alice thought as she sat in the stall. There was something weirdly bland and scripted about everything he wrote; Alice wondered now whether he might be acting according to a set of rules for picking up women. Was he one of those guys?

It occurred to Alice that Abby was in Thailand. It was probably the middle of the night; she would save the text for later. It pissed her off, the idea that just because she was in her thirties and single again, people thought they should try to pimp her out to their mediocre friends. She'd had the same thing, more than once, when she told people she was breaking up with her last boyfriend – I'm sorry to hear that, they said, and she wanted to say: why were they sorry about something that was going to make her happier? Did they think that being in a relationship with somebody – anybody, even her last boyfriend, a podgy, coke-addled screenwriter who'd only ever had one film script produced, fifteen years ago, and wasn't even nice to her – was what made her a valuable person? Did they think she'd be crying herself to sleep? Did they think she should be grateful to them for setting her up with guys like this?

It made her wonder about Ned. Maybe she had thrown away the possibility of something good, when she came to Berlin and told him they should be friends and business partners and nothing more. It would have been a stable relationship with somebody dynamic and interesting. Somebody she was fond of, found attractive, was stimulated by, and had pretty good sex with. Okay, he wasn't the sort of man who could really make her abandon herself in sex, really feel like she was going to come undone, but she'd only had that with two or three people, and those men were usually bastards in a different way; they weren't able to have relationships with women who might outstrip them. And Ned had a certain low-key animal intensity that she could get on board with. In many ways, Alice liked Ned because he let her be herself. He gave her room to grow, even if that could sometimes be mistaken for not being very interested in her as a person.

It had been six minutes since she left the table. That was probably pushing it, wasn't it? Just finish your meal, she told herself, and then she could leave. She took a deep breath and left the cubicle.

ON THE OTHER SIDE of Kreuzberg the next evening, Ned sat with a woman named Rachel in Zitrone, his local bar-café on the corner of Dieffenbachstraße, eating a plate of chicken and mushroom in a creamy sauce. Rachel was picking carefully through her Greek salad, removing the rings of red onion and constructing a feta-clogged pile of them on her side plate.

'You don't like onions?'

'Normally I'm fine with them, but, you know . . .'

Ned looked blank.

'On a first date? Raw onions might seem a bit anti-social later, if you know what I mean.'

Ned knew what she meant. The date seemed to be going well. Conversation flowed easily; she was funny, and she laughed at Ned's jokes; she was interesting and pretty. The food was nice. Yes, Ned was enjoying himself. At the moment she was working part-time in an elementary school as a language assistant, she said, and she spent the rest of her time on her music. On Tinder she had used a ridiculously busty photo – she seemed to be wearing a corset or something – but in person now she looked more like an elementary-school assistant, if an unusually smart and attractive one, in a black cardigan and a high-necked black dress with a repeating pattern of hares on it. Likewise, the bravado of her flirting, the sly joke about the onions, these sat oddly with what Ned thought was a certain reserve of sadness in her, which emerged in moments when her outgoingness paused. The primary school job was perfect for her, she was saying, because as well as working with the kids and improving her German, she got to run the music club after school.

'So what sort of music do you do?' Ned said.

'I wonder if you've heard any of my songs. "Jesus in the Garden"? "Fruit Tree from His Hand"?'

Ned turned his palms upwards. 'Sorry.'

'Looks like someone hasn't been a good little evangelical boy.'

'Ha, you could say that. So you're like a Christian rock star?'

'"Star" might be stretching it. But yeah, I guess. I spend some of the year travelling round festivals in the US with my band, and with that and the royalties from the albums and radio and whatnot, I more or less get by.'

'Ha, that's awesome. How does "Fruit Tree from His Hand" go?'

'Do you want me to sing it?' Rachel started dipping her shoulders and clapping her hands in four-four time, and was on the verge of breaking into song when she said, 'Yeah, I'm not sure Zitrone is ready for "Fruit Tree from His Hand" actually.'

'I'll find it on Spotify.'

'Oi, you should buy it properly!' said Rachel, shaking her fist at him. 'If you stream it, you're basically stealing money out of my pocket.'

'How about I buy the whole album and you pay for dinner?'

'Very gallant,' she said. She looked down for a moment and said thoughtfully, 'I am proud of that song though. A lot of God-rock is just cliché, but that one comes from this great story in the Apocrypha where Jesus performs this extra miracle of throwing up a handful of seed and it turns into these blossoming fruit trees in mid-air, and then they float away down the river Jordan.'

'Jesus!'

'Exactly.'

'I didn't know He did more miracles. Bonus content.'

'It means that song's quite controversial though. Lot of people don't accept the Apocrypha. Or maybe it's not from the Apocrypha; it's some piece of papyrus they found in the fifties.'

'Full disclosure,' said Ned. 'What's the Apocrypha when it's at home?'

'Oh my god, you're such a heathen. What the Apocrypha *are* – because it's a plural noun – are the books of the Bible that aren't considered canonical, so they're not in the Hebrew Bible.'

'Oh nice. Like DVD extras.'

'Bonus content, yeah, you said that already. And another thing. Jesus didn't *do* miracles, he *performed* miracles.' She put on the voice of a sulky, slow-witted teenage boy, and said, 'Oh look, I done a miracle, shall I do another miracle?'

Ned liked being teased by her. He was enjoying himself. The Christian stuff gave him pause, but she seemed very relaxed and funny about it. It felt like they had a rapport. They shared a thick slice of cheesecake, and over the last crumbs of the biscuit base their forks clashed and got into a play-fight, each of them giving their own fork an action-figure voice ('Take that! . . . Argh, I'm pinned!'). Rachel's fork said, 'I will never surrender, you cannot defeat me!' before shifting into a tender tone and saying, 'Wait, let us end our quarrel, I love you! Mwah, mwah, mwah,' and gyrating against Ned's fork absurdly. He joined in and their forks made out with each other for a few seconds, until Rachel abruptly stopped, laid the fork down and said, 'But enough of this foolishness. Shall we get out of here?'

'Good idea.' Ned caught the waitress's eye and mouthed, 'Die Rechnung, bitte.'

'What's your fancy?' Rachel said.

'There's a good place down the street for an aperitif.'

'Hmm,' said Rachel, reaching across the table and wrapping two of her fingers around Ned's own. 'Or . . .'

Ned smiled at her.

TWO WEEKS PASSED. IN that time, Alice opened negotiations with six different companies, all of which were interested in working with The Thing Factory: two clothing companies, a tourist agency, a charity, a takeaway food app and Maximus, the protein shake company that Ned had made contact with.

When she laid out her pitch to clients, Alice felt eloquent and persuasive. Through their development of bespoke micro-influencers with high levels of follower engagement, she said, The Thing Factory could take a uniquely granular approach to brand advocacy, that would have a greater reach than traditional advertising or celebrity endorsements. Why pay Kim Kardashian to tweet about your product to tens of millions of followers, almost none of whom cared about the kinds of product you were offering (and many of whom were not real people but automated bots anyway), when instead, for a fraction of the price, you could get Thing Factory accounts to promote your message to an audience of between 50,000 and 1,000,000 followers, who had a known interest in your product type and exceptional levels of loyalty and trust in the influencer? It seemed to Alice that she hardly even needed to sell the idea; she knew that if companies didn't want to work with The Thing Factory, they were making a mistake, and it was their loss more than hers.

On the Friday of the third week in February, the temperature hit minus three degrees. Alice was sitting in the meeting room going over a strategy document when Tristan leaned into the doorway and said, 'Knock knock.'

'Tristan, hi.'

'Just wanted to remind you that I'll be away at the start of next week. Probably until Wednesday morning.'

'Oh yes, where are you off again?'

'It's this conference on social in Manchester.'

'Are you feeling mad for it?' said Alice.

'That is a terrible accent. Yeah, though, it should be good. The keynotes are on personal branding and on the effect of social on mental health. I'm on a panel about predictions for the future.'

'What are your predictions?'

'My big one is that stories will start to supersede the newsfeed. We might even see the death of the feed. It's going to be all about the stories now, after Snapchat. That's how people want to engage.'

'Gosh,' Alice said. She had looked at Snapchat once, and

found the interface baffling. 'And what's the effect of social on mental health?'

'I'll have to wait and find out. Probably it's just making us all more depressed and anxious.'

Pause.

'We might not want to admit that, given our business model,' Alice said.

'Maybe the speaker will put a positive spin on it,' Tristan said, then put up two thumbs and added, 'I'm fookin' mad for it, me!'

'Indeed,' Alice said.

'I love how you always say "indeed", instead of just "yes".'

'No, I don't.'

'You do. Anytime anyone says, like, "Would you like a coffee?", you're like, "Indeed I would". Someone says, "It's a nice day, isn't it?" and you're like, "Indeed", or "So I gather".'

Alice smiled, charmed despite herself. 'And you think that this tells you something about me?'

Tristan rested his chin in his hand for a second in a thinking pose, then said, 'I would say it shows what tremendous self-possession you have. It's like: you won't be drawn into someone else's sentence just to confirm or deny it, you always have to send it back with a bit of top spin. To make it your own, you know?'

'Ah, fuck off, Tristan,' said Alice.

'What? I'm being sincere. I think it's very admirable.'

'Go back to being mad for it. Or, here's an idea, do some work.'

'Yes, boss,' Tristan said, then turned and walked in slow motion back to his desk.

In the last few weeks, Alice had started to admit to herself that she had a bit of a crush on Tristan. He was so goofy, and yet somehow so sweet and earnest at the same time. She often found herself moved to play up to him, to tell him off, or to say something to make him laugh. The fact that Ned clearly hated him was part of it too. It kept Ned on his toes, Alice could see, if she sided with Tristan over him from time to time. She sometimes wondered what it would be like to go to bed with Tristan. Fun, she thought. He wasn't exactly good-looking, but the confidence he projected made it seem unimportant; his physical mousiness translated into energy and charisma in social settings. Yes, it would probably be fun . . .

Alice got up and headed for the bathroom in the hallway, only to find that Tristan was heading there too. They performed an awkward little tango negotiating who would go first through the doors. As they were drying their hands, Tristan said, 'You know, I wanted to tell you something.'

'Oh yes?'

'I haven't spoken to Ned about this or anything, but now I think about it, I think we probably are ready to launch. To go live with brand content on social.'

'Really?'

'I mean, I still want to build it up more as we go along, don't get me wrong. But the base is ready. It's like seven million followers now, and if we start with the right brands it will only help things grow.'

Alice was glad Tristan was telling her this aside from the rest of the team. She knew Ned would be weird about it, if it came from Tristan directly. If she presented it to Ned as her idea, and one that Folasade and Tristan were on board with, that ought to be just the ticket. It was even rather good that Ned now had his eyes on the direction to diversify in, rather than on social – it meant that Alice could drive that forward herself, start with the clients she wanted and be in control of the negotiations.

'Thanks, Tristan,' she said. 'Leave it with me for now and I'll talk to Ned about it soon.'

'So we're saying that the future is in platforms, right? The future is in Uberising more and more goods and services, taking away all the overheads and all the restrictions around connecting providers to consumers. What we need to do, then, is to work out what to Uberise next.'

Ned was in his groove, striding up and down by the windows at the side of the meeting room. The brainstorming session seemed to be going well. Everyone seemed engaged. Daniel was nodding profoundly, and Folasade had a quizzical look on her face. Ned dragged the whiteboard out from the corner, wiped it down and said, 'Can we think about that for the next few minutes?'

Ned played the part of a start-up guru with an irony that was perhaps lost on some of his colleagues. After all, what was the difference between his manner in these meetings, his mastery of specialised jargon, his sense of purpose, his conviction about the direction the future was going in and every other guy's who came to Berlin with an idea for a start-up? If anything, he was better at it than the ridiculous people he had met at that seed-funding fair last year, before Alice had come on board. Most of them only had one idea – if that – whereas he had ideas to spare. They just seemed to come to him, as if he could gather them out of the air.

'So, in everything we've been doing we've been talking about emotion, right? About the way that it's emotional reactions, and not really rational thinking, that power people's choices. What we need to do is to harness that discussion and to think about the products, the encounters, the kinds of connection between people that produce an emotional reaction. And then we can ruthlessly exploit them for our own profit, right?'

Everyone except Alice laughed, and Alice smiled indulgently.

'So where do we start with this?'

Silence.

'Daniel,' Ned said. 'Good morning.'

'Good morning.'

'Tell me, talk me through the emotional reactions you've experienced so far today, everything leading up to your arriving at the office.'

Daniel laughed nervously. 'Ahh, let me see . . .' he said. 'I felt happy when Jana texted me when I was waking up. She is in Leipzig at a social enterprise conference so we haven't seen each other this week.'

'Okay,' Ned said. 'Tell me more.'

'And then I guess I was feeling rather sexy when we were IMing while we were still in bed. Is that an emotion?'

'Now we're talking,' Ned said, and wrote SEX in large letters in one corner of the whiteboard. 'But let's come back to that in the future if we need to. I'm pretty sure that dating sites and pornography and all that sort of thing are too crowded as markets for us to do anything with. Let's leave that there. Any other emotional reactions you want to tell us about? Did anything make you feel angry, frustrated, guilty today?'

'I can't think of anything. It has not been a very emotional morning.'

'Anyone else?'

'I felt guilty this morning,' said Richard. 'Twice, actually: first when I realised I had forgotten my sister's birthday yesterday, and then when I passed a homeless guy at my U-Bahn station.'

'Now that's interesting,' Ned said. 'Did you give him any money?'

'No.'

'But did you think about it?'

'I did think about it, yeah. It's so freezing at the moment and everything. But then I thought, I'm not all that rich right now, I'm not earning much, I can't give money to everyone, and anyway, what do I really know about this guy? You know, what's he going to do with the money if I give him a few euros?'

Ned wrote HOMELESSNESS on the whiteboard, took a sip of water and said, 'Can we do anything with that?'

'You could have an app that was like a mapping app that showed where the highest concentration of homeless people were at any moment,' said another of the interns.

Ned frowned. 'What would that achieve?'

'I dunno, it just came to me. I guess it would help people who wanted to donate money go to the right part of town to do it.'

'Yeah, I don't think that really works. Let's park that for now,' Ned said.

'Anyway, how would you track the concentration?' said Tristan, laughing. 'Would we tag the homeless with GPS devices?'

There were a few laughs around the group, and the intern looked embarrassed. Ned said, 'I don't hear any bright ideas from you, Tristan, so keep it to yourself, yeah?'

'Maybe if there was an app where we could provide more information,' Folasade said, 'so that people could make better informed decisions about whether to donate money or not.'

'Now that's interesting, how would that go?'

Alice spoke for the first time: 'You could model it on a crowdfunding app. Each homeless person has their own

66

profile, and users can find out more about them and their stories and see who else has given them money.'

'I like it,' Ned said, pacing briefly in front of the white-board before writing 'Uberise the homeless?' on there and turning back towards the team. 'What sort of information would have made you more likely to give him money?' he asked Richard.

'Like, if you knew that it wouldn't just go on crack or whatever.'

'Hmm . . . I see what you mean, but I think we want a stronger storytelling element than that. There needs to be a narrative to make people give their money. A backstory, and some attainable target.'

He was looking at Alice, and she responded, 'So we make sure each user profile has the story of how they ended up on the streets. Make it relatable.'

'Yeah,' Ned said. 'But it also needs a forward-looking element. We don't just want how they ended up on the streets, we want how they're going to get out of it. How each dona-tion is going to help them out of their situation. The point of the app should be to help them get training or qualifications, so that they're asking for something specific that will help them turn their lives around.'

'Like a GoFundMe for the homeless,' said Alice.

'Exactly,' said Ned. 'Click here to give brave Joakim ten

euros towards his goal of raising whatever amount for tuition fees to become an electrician. That sort of thing.'

'And how do we make money?'

'I guess we just take an administration fee from each donation. We run it like a charity. We can make money but also do something genuinely good, and we raise the profile of The Thing Factory in the meantime for our profit-making ventures.'

'I like it,' said Alice. 'Let's Uberise the homeless.'

Ned turned towards the board and rubbed out the question mark after that phrase. 'Okay, let's see where this goes. Richard, could you write up a one-page concept description this afternoon and send that round the whole team on Cubicle? Then we can set up a project group to work on the details. And if anyone has any ideas for a name for it, shout now. No takers?'

After a pause, Richard said, 'How about Off the Streets? Or Better Future?'

Ned mimed throwing the whiteboard eraser at Richard's head and said, 'If that's the best we've got then it's definitely time to break for lunch.'

'Wait, wait, I've got it,' said Richard. 'We call it Streetwise. Get it? It's, like, a combination of being on the street and getting wise.'

Ned grinned, and wrote STREETWISE up on the board.

N ED ASKED FOLASADE TO help him draw up a development plan for Streetwise, but within a few days it became clear that German law around setting up new charitable ventures was more complicated and restrictive than they had assumed. Getting the app launched, Daniel said, would be time-consuming and administratively tricky, and would obliterate any chance they had of getting up and running without making considerable losses. They were faced with a few choices: either they set up the app at a loss, and hope to make the money back eventually through the percentage of each donation they took as an administration fee, or they raise funds for setting up the app from third-party investors, or they change the idea altogether.

Ned knew they had been on to something with Streetwise. But they shouldn't do it as a charity. And they shouldn't target the homeless, who anyway often didn't have reliable access to phones, computers or power sources. No, they had to find a different group of marginalised people to help. The more Ned thought about it, the more he thought that

Daniel's first instinct at the brainstorming session had been right. His mind had gone first of all to sex.

The matter played at the back of Ned's mind for several days, before the solution came to him. Pornography was saturated, dating sites were saturated, but escorting – now there was a possibility. The more avenues Ned went down in his unsuccessful attempts to find anyone online who'd had the idea before him, the more incredible it seemed. It was an open goal, as a business idea. In the UK there were AdultWork and Vivastreet, but those sites weren't great: their interfaces were clunky, each page had far too much irrelevant information, they didn't have good mobile apps and they were hard to navigate. In Berlin there didn't seem to be any equivalent. A client would need to track down each escort or massage parlour's individually run webpage, if they didn't want to turn up somewhere on spec, or to pick up a street walker in the red light district.

The app that Ned started to imagine over the course of the next few days would benefit both clients and service providers. It would answer clients' desires for reassurance that they weren't going to be ripped off or tricked, and it would allow escorts to set clear boundaries in advance of an appointment and give them accountability around the clients they were taking bookings from. Each user's profile, whether it was as a provider or a seeker of services, would be peer-rated and reviewed, so that escorts could use this as screening information.

Ned spent two days with Folasade working out a business model. They wouldn't charge service providers a membership fee, but they would offer a further range of paid features. People could pay for their profile to appear more prominently in the app's search results, or on its front page; they could pay to make their profiles searchable by more specific kinds of information, such as their availability on any particular day, or their preference for offering a particular service; they could pay to upload a larger gallery of photographs to their profile, or to upload video content. On the other side of the arrangement, while the site was also free for members seeking services, clients could pay by the minute to have direct camera contact with a service provider, or to get subscription access to private galleries featuring more explicit content, or to be sent items by a service provider through the post (Polaroids, used underwear, et cetera), and for each of these services the site would take a commission on all transactions, with the rest going straight to the service providers.

As well as making money, the site would improve the working conditions of escorts. No longer would escorts need to sell their labour through a brothel that skimmed off the majority of their earnings, or take bookings from clients who didn't provide them with screening details. It would help them to run their own enterprise, and it would encourage solidarity and knowledge-sharing among them, since they could check with each other through the direct message function on the reliability of different clients.

Ned hadn't had any particular views on sex work until quite recently. He probably would have said that paying for sex was for exploitative losers who couldn't get laid without it, and that the women who worked as prostitutes must be desperate, or drug addicts, or trafficked. Alice had changed his views: she told him he should say 'escorts' or 'sex workers' instead of 'prostitutes', and told him about a friend of hers from drama school who had done sex work, had enjoyed it and had found that her regular clients were often interesting, vulnerable people themselves, with all sorts of emotional needs. For Alice, the only important thing in debates around sex work was to increase the safety and dignity of the people engaged in it.

That was what Ned wanted to do. He knew that selling and paying for sex were legal in Germany. And he knew that The Thing Factory needed to move quickly. There would surely be other people out there who'd had the idea of making a user-friendly platform for sex work here. The Thing Factory had to get in on the ground floor and capture the market.

When Ned and Folasade emerged from their planning phase and presented the new idea to the rest of the team at the

72

end of the first week in March, there were some doubts about the project. Tristan thought it was a bit barmy, Daniel was doubtful about how much money it would make and Alice wanted to make sure it didn't divert too many resources from social, which had begun publishing brand-associated content for its first three clients that week. But the strongest objections came from Richard, who was against a sex-work app on moral grounds. When Richard said that he didn't think they should enable the exploitation of vulnerable women forced to sell their bodies, Ned paused a moment, cradled his fingers under his chin and contemplated how to respond. Before he said anything, he found Alice bursting into the conversation.

'First of all,' she said, 'it's not just women, is it? Some men are also sex workers, and some trans people too. Actually quite a high proportion of them are. Second, this thing about *selling your body* is meaningless. It's just rhetoric. If you sell something you give it over to someone so that you don't have it anymore, but nobody's depriving themselves of their own bodies. All people are doing is selling a service, and okay, it involves an unusually intimate kind of physical engagement. But it's hardly different in that regard from all sorts of other kind of care work and nursing that bring you into intimate bodily contact with someone else.'

'Umm, well . . .' Richard said, seeming a bit thrown. 'I just think we should regard sex as a different category of activity from ones that can be bought and sold as services. Or ones that ought to be bought and sold. I think we should try to make sex into something outside of exchange and that whole, like, economics of scarcity.'

Ned was surprised by the precision of Richard's argument. Well, he did say he'd done Philosophy at university.

'But Richard,' Alice said, 'that's just capitalism you're describing, it's not sex work in particular. We're all against capitalism, or at least we're all critical of it. But the world is what it is.'

'But does that mean that we can't change it?'

'No, we can change it a bit, but we do have to operate within its realities. People have been buying and selling sex since I don't know when. Roman times probably.'

'It's in the Bible,' Folasade said – 'that was Roman times, wasn't it?'

'Yeah, I think so.'

'It's definitely in the ballpark of Roman times.'

'We're getting sidetracked anyway,' Alice said. 'Richard has asked the question of whether we're okay as a team with pushing forward on the escort platform, so we need to decide that. I think we should do it – it'll be something that will actually help escorts run their own businesses and it will make things safer for them, so it seems to me to be unambiguously a good idea, morally as well as financially.'

Alice met Ned's eye, and he realised he had been looking at her with an especially intense gaze, his eyes widened in delight, his lips repressing a slight smile. He hadn't expected her to speak quite so ardently on the topic. He straightened up and said, 'Thanks, Alice. Are we all agreed then that we're going ahead with the venture? Do all those in favour want to raise their hands?'

Ned raised his own hand, followed by Alice, Folasade, Tristan and everyone else on the team except Richard, who looked sad. After a moment, Richard raised his hand as well.

'So that's carried,' Ned said. 'I guess we need to start thinking about a name.'

He stood up and wheeled out the whiteboard from the corner of the room, buzzing with excitement at having found his next big project.

2

'SO, NATALYA, MELODY, ROSA. Thanks so much for coming in to help us out today, we really appreciate it. I thought that to start out we should all introduce ourselves and say something about our roles, to give you a sense of where the different questions we're asking are coming from. So I'll start: I'm Ned, I'm the joint founder and CEO of The Thing Factory, and I'm the project lead for this app that we have in mind – or the co-lead, I should say. I'm also a web developer.'

'I'm Folasade, I'm the other co-lead, and on this project I'll be a UXer, which is to say that I'll deal with user experience when we're thinking about the content architecture.'

'I'm Daniel—'

Natalya interrupted to say to Folasade, 'Excuse me, how are you writing that?'

'Oh, it's F-O-L—'

'No, the word that is like USA?'

'Oh, it's basically U, like the letter U, for User, and X for Experience, so we say UXer for someone who does UX.'

'Thank you.'

'Yes, so I'm Daniel, and I'm the finance and legal officer of The Thing Factory.'

'And I'm Jaki, I've joined the team to work on this project more as a programmer than a developer, so I will do more coding and less design than a developer would do. And it's probably a good thing that I leave the design decisions to these people, who are more conscious of style than I am.'

'As you can tell from Jaki's choice of t-shirt,' said Daniel.

Ned could sense that Daniel and Jaki were nervous in the escorts' presence; there was something false about their attempted humour, as if they had been put off their stride, and were trying too hard now to seem at ease around these women. Ned really wanted this meeting to go well.

Natalya smiled politely and said, 'It is nice to meet you all. I am Natalya, which is a professional name that I use for the purpose of working as a webcam performer and escort.'

'I am Melody.'

'Rosa.'

Ned had found them on EliteCompanions.de. The text on their pages made them seem intelligent. In her photographs, Rosa looked rather like a younger Julianne Moore, Ned thought; Melody advertised herself as a BBW escort, and had a set of photographs taken in a luxury hotel, in which she drank champagne in her bathrobe and sat among a sea of bubbles in the bath; Natalya looked stylish and artful, with tattoos winding up her arms, back and one side of her neck, and a shaved-in undercut. Her page had said that she was educated to graduate level, spoke fluent English, French, German and Russian, and was an artist, financing her work by doing escort work for a small number of clients each week. In the last photo in her gallery, the camera looked over her shoulder across her arched back, to where her heart-shaped bottom emerged from a black negligee. It was an arrangement that Ned found almost painfully attractive.

He had a hunch that Natalya would be helpful. She would have firm ideas on what she wanted from an escorting platform, and would see the topic from angles that Ned and his team hadn't anticipated. When he emailed her to ask if she would be willing to come in for a focus group, at her normal outcall rate of €150 per hour, she seemed sceptical, insisting that they speak on Skype in advance, and that she be paid for one hour upfront. When she arrived, she was dressed smartly, in jeans, a white shirt and a grey blazer, topped off with a pork-pie hat.

'Thanks,' Ned said. 'The reason we've brought you in today is to help us develop a new product that we're working on just now, which is an app targeted at sex workers and their clients. The headline that we're going for is that it will be a sort of Uber for escorts – it will be a platform that essentially connects service providers and people seeking services in the most efficient way, with the smallest overheads.'

'I am interested in what you say,' said Natalya, 'but I must say at the start that I am not such a big admirer of this particular brand because, you know, everyone in Berlin hates Uber.'

'Umm, right, of course.'

'And Airbnb as well. You know? It is these platforms that are moving taxi drivers into becoming workless, and making rents become impossible for normal people who have been for many years living here, and causing the – how do you say it? – the *Gentrifizierung*—'

'Gentrification,' Jaki said softly.

'And from my background, which is in anarchist politics and the squatting movement, it is really an evil thing to be saying you are a new Uber. So I am recommending that you do not use this comparison if you want your app to find success here.'

'Right, yes,' said Ned, feeling somewhat thrown. 'I suppose what we meant is just that this app is seeking to disrupt the existing relation of how service providers and clients interact. But unlike Uber, our intention is to improve conditions for people who do sex work – to make it easier for them to manage their own business and keep a record of their clients and vet potential clients by sharing information with other service providers, and that sort of thing.'

Natalya looked unimpressed.

Folasade said, 'What we want, Natalya, is really to build a product that works for you and your colleagues.'

'Sure. As well as making profit from our labour, yes? It sounds like this is the typical attempt at rescuing sex workers, but that is exactly what we do not need. We do not need outsiders to save us, we just need rights and respect and legal and social protections.'

Ned was starting to think this would be a long two hours. He hadn't expected the first escorts they brought in to include a hostile anti-capitalist. Still, he found that it made Natalya more attractive to him. There was something about the punkness, brattishness, of those moments when she leaned back in her chair and said, 'Sure,' that really did it for him.

'Look,' he said, 'it's true that we want to run this as a profit-making venture, but at the commission rates that we have in mind, we're confident that using the app will be a better financial option for escorts than selling their services through a brothel or a super-club. It will give them autonomy.'

'But already we are all independent. We run our own businesses and we pay only a small fee to the website where you found us.'

'Okay, but in that case, our app would give you a centralised platform, with the functionality of your website, your email account, your appointments calendar, your texts, your video messaging service, your PayPal, your gift wishlist site – all of these things brought together in one place, which will also be the first place the potential clients go to when they want an escort. All in one, ready to go. We're even thinking that if phase one is a success, then phase two could involve expanding to a function that helps escorts rent apartments for their work, either as individuals or in co-operatives, so that the whole problem of navigating landlords and the property market would be solved too. And what we have in mind, in return for saving escorts all that time and hassle and organisational effort, is a low-percentage commission on the transactions that go through the site. And of course people could still arrange meetings where the client pays in cash in the traditional way, and we won't see a penny of that. A cent, I mean.'

Rosa had leaned forward in her seat.

'Does that sound like something that would make a contribution?' Ned said.

'I would certainly be interested,' said Rosa. Melody nodded agreement. Natalya was tilting her head from side to side, as if weighing up the proposition, and Ned knew that he was going to win her around. They were in business.

Ned stood next to Folasade as she watched over the designer's shoulder and told him to rotate the logo in the top left corner anti-clockwise through a few more degrees. In the bottom right went the addresses and QR codes for the app and desktop versions, along with the code for the introductory offer, and after some debate, they decided to leave the card blank of any other descriptive information. It was better to leave a sense of discretion, they thought. The only other mark was a small gold keyhole, to hint at a concealed promise of sensuality.

It was Folasade's idea to print business cards instead of flyers, and it was Ned's idea to lure people to the site with a freebie: each new member who entered the code on the card would be credited with five euros to spend on webcam minutes or subscription gallery content. Folasade oversaw the design. The cards needed to look different from traditional sex-worker or strip-club flyers, Ned told her; they should be restrained, luxurious, gold-embossed, printed on good-quality card stock. They should look professional and discreet, the way he imagined the membership cards for a private members' club.

Together with Folasade, Ned had surveyed the competition and the structure of the market – insofar as that was possible in an industry so shady – come up with a short-term and medium-term strategy, and sketched in a plan for achieving scale by expanding the app's reach into further services and territories.

The Thing Factory had expanded so much in the last few weeks, with the launch of brand content on social and the development of the sex-work app, that Ned and Alice decided to extend into the empty office space next door to theirs. They knocked an arch through the internal wall so that you could move between the two. In the new space, they installed a Japanese-style zen garden, a dedicated gaming corner with beanbags and a huge screen bolted to the wall, and a bank of twelve work spaces for hot-desking. Much of the development and build work took place in the annexe.

Once Folasade had written the project brief, drawing on what they had learned from the focus groups, Ned and the developers got on with the build. It went quickly, and in a week it was ready to be beta-tested.

Richard was keen that they give the app a woman's name. In the same way that Siri and Alexa had women's names, he thought it would be cool to call the app Stella or Candi or Brandi or Suzi Q; he thought it would make it seem user-friendly and non-threatening, like the app was just a female friend helping to set you up with someone for a hook-up.

Others thought this too cutesy. No, the app should have an impersonal name, perhaps something lightly suggestive, but not overtly sexual: Salt 'n' Pepper, someone said, or Cherrypie, or Peaches. Ned didn't like any of these suggestions, nor the suggestions Honeypot, Honigtopf, Sugarbowl or Matchbox. Folasade suggested they call it Meetcute, and this gained considerable support, but Ned had never heard the expression before and didn't think enough people would know what it meant; maybe then it could be Meetmate, someone said, but another voice said that both these suggestions sounded too much like dating websites, and were too idiomatic for a German market.

One of the interns asked why they didn't just call it Sexarbeit, but Ned knew they could do better than that. He sent a sub-team away with a thesaurus and the company credit card to The Mint Gun Club to generate more ideas. He wanted them to come back with a name that had a less distinct sense, but the correct feel, and one that worked across different languages. That evening the sub-team leader brought forward the result of the session, in the project chat on Cubicle: names on their shortlist included Cucumber, U-cumber, Instanter, Heiß and Genau, but their number one suggestion was the name Gliss.

Ned liked it. Gliss, Gliss: he tried it out for size, let it linger and reverberate in his voice. Folasade was first to respond on Cubicle, to ask what it actually meant, and the sub-team leader explained that in music a glissando is when you glide from one note to another, so it implied smoothness and elegance and ease. But the sub-team also liked the fact that it sounded – though they couldn't say why – rather sexy. Maybe because it sounded a bit like kiss, and bliss, and, more remotely, clit. Richard suggested that it sounded like a brand of lubricant, pervy and chemical at once, like Astroglide. Yes, it was just what Ned wanted.

IN THE FIRST TWO days after Gliss went live, the twenty escorts Ned had paid to sign up were joined by thirty service providers who signed up on their own initiative, and more than four hundred users seeking services. For on-the-ground promotional work, they hired ten glamour models to give out the cards Folasade had designed, and targeted the red light districts – Kurfürstenstraße, Gleisdreieck, Oranienstraße – the streets near the megabrothels, and the men coming out of busy bars and clubs. In the course of five nights they gave out 30,000 cards. Ned kept the download and site-visit counters in the control panel open on his laptop and saw the numbers flying up, with a decent conversion rate of visits to sign-ups. By the end of the weekend, there were more than 3,000 users seeking services, and the number of escorts offering services had grown ten-fold.

The first escort to sign up went under the name *Mia*. Like the first twenty others, she was paid seventy-five euros for setting up a profile, with a further commission on each new service provider (up to twenty) who joined on her referral. Ned knew that Mia would be an influential adopter:

on her own website she had excellent feedback from punters; she ran a professional operation, replying to messages fast and courteously; and she had print-quality, model-grade photos to go in her gallery. Ned wasn't surprised when she quickly got a further eight top-rate escorts to sign up.

Soon the app's front page displayed a grid of beautiful women, and the occasional man, all with the green light lit up to signal their availability today. Ned looked at it with satisfaction. There was *AngelMaria*, pouting in a selfie in front of the view from a skyscraper window; next to her was *Rosebella*, shot from behind and below so that her impressive backside dominated the foreground of the picture; and next to her was *AlexaKonnikova*, lying on a hotel bed in red bra and knickers. Clicking on *AlexaKonnikova*'s thumbnail took Ned to a profile page where heart emojis studded the text, and where her preferences and capabilities, her hourly rates and her extras, were laid out with unfussy clarity. Clients could come in her mouth, at her discretion, for a surcharge of thirty euros.

Spring was emerging in little hints and previews. Some afternoons, the sun came out; people sat at tables outside restaurants in the evenings; Ned tentatively put his winter coat in the suitcase he kept in the top of his wardrobe. In Gliss's second week, his efforts at attracting media attention started to pay off. He had sent out a press release about how

Gliss was transforming sex work in Berlin and improving conditions for escorts, which gave some inflated figures for the number of active profiles on the site. The first person to get in touch in response was Yulia from the *Berliner Zeitung*, who emailed one morning, and conducted a Skype interview with Ned that afternoon. They spoke for forty-five minutes, and it seemed to Ned that they established a rapport, but when they published her story online the next day ('"Uber for Escorts" Launches in Berlin'), she quoted barely twenty words from Ned, in which he said that sex work was 'a really interesting part of contemporary life' and that his business philosophy was 'if it's not broken, break it'. Okay, he *had* said those words to Yulia, but he'd thought they were clearly being spoken in quotation marks; Yulia had been laughing along, he thought, at his sarcastic parroting of the clichés of start-up culture. But here it was, in the cold light of print, or at least of digital pixels. Fuck it, he thought, it was probably true enough. It probably was his business philosophy.

On the day of publication, Yulia's article was shared 118,000 times. In the next few hours, writers from five more newspapers and magazines were in touch.

A T THE PLENARY THAT week, Ned was only half-
listening to the reports from the social team on how
their campaigns were going. They had a new social media
manager now, Heather, a Scottish woman in her early twenties with a pixie cut who had been chosen by Alice and
Tristan, and who seemed really good; they were working
with three clients and seemed to be in a state of high excitement at how fast things were developing. They'd had big
success with a video they'd made with some freerunners,
to advertise a clothing company. It didn't seem very interesting to Ned.

When the meeting moved on to Gliss, he kicked into
gear. He gave a quick account of how the user-base was
growing, and the media coverage Gliss had gained. The
social team seemed impressed. Someone asked how much
revenue Gliss had actually generated so far, and Ned said,
'Not so much, to be honest, but in the expansion phase we're
not alarmed by that. It's not profitable yet, but when it is,
you'll be the first to know. Right, Daniel?'

Daniel put two thumbs up.

'What I want to do now,' Ned said, 'is take a moment to think about what the next step will be, and the step after that, if we want to grow this thing.'

'If it's not broken, break it,' Folasade said with a grin.

'Exactly. Could we start by talking about expansion?'

'Well,' said Daniel, 'word of mouth is so strong now that we could set up the app for Frankfurt, for München, and so on, with almost no effort. It was in the medium-term plan but we actually could do it right now. I think at this stage we wouldn't need so much marketing, because everyone has heard of us online and people would sign up spontaneously. All we are needing to do is increase the area that the mapping function covers.'

'And the maps just come from Google, right?'

'Exactly.'

Alice spoke up after a pause. 'If it's so easy to widen the market domestically, why couldn't you go internationally now too?'

'There's the legal situation,' Ned said.

'Yeah,' said Folasade, 'but if we just tweak it so that profiles registered in the UK have a disclaimer about how all people are paying for is the time and companionship, blah blah blah, anything that occurs during the meeting is the choice of two consenting adults. I mean, AdultWork has never been taken down in the UK, right? So why would we get shut down? And our app is so much better than theirs.'

'Why not?' said Ned. 'There's nothing to lose really, is there? We'd just need a few people to pay attention to the situation on the ground in the new territories, a few more moderators for each country. That would be it. I think we should do it as quickly as we can. How quickly is that?'

'Other German cities, early next week, and other countries maybe the week after,' said Folasade.

B Y THE END OF April, Gliss had over 5,000 service providers signed up. Ned liked to refresh the front page and see which new profiles appeared. *Geil für dich* advertised himself as a bisexual escort happy to work with couples or groups as well as singles, and had a gallery of photos showing himself oiled up, sunbathing, posing for a headshot and masturbating while lying on the floor of a shower stall, his thickly haired chest, armpits and groin slick with sudsy water. *Milf Ingeborg* was a sharp-featured redhead with a thoughtful cast to her expression, who spoke fluent English and Italian as well as German (she had studied in Pisa, she said, and loved to be taken out for Italian food). In many of her photos she was pictured alongside her tortoiseshell-furred cat, Giovanni; she mentioned that she couldn't accept incallers who were allergic to cat fur. Her preferred bookings were overnights in hotels with mature gentlemen with whom she could establish an ongoing bond as regular clients; she didn't like to do short encounters because they seemed too impersonal. She had set her rate for one-hour bookings at an eye-watering €300 accordingly. She didn't accept thirty-minute bookings at all.

Transfrau Bonnie was a trans woman with the slender limbs of a catwalk model. In the final shot in her subscription gallery, she lay on her side on a sofa, t-shirt pulled up above her breasts, having recently ejaculated on to her belly, and looking flushed and slightly stoned. Her profile described her as shy and quiet but tigerish in bed; she was happiest when the talking stopped and she had a hard cock in her mouth, she said.

By early May, Gliss had 50,000 users seeking services in Berlin. For a city of just over three million people, Ned considered this rather good going, and in the meantime, the apps for other German cities and for the Netherlands, France and the UK had been soft-launched. They were picking up new users spontaneously without any marketing.

The escort on the UK app who had caught Ned's eye was *FLORA_ROCKS*, a young-looking British-Chinese woman. Her advertised age was nineteen, but Ned thought early twenties was more likely. She had two full sleeves of tattoos, floral designs woven in with dragons and sea creatures, and her profile text was written in the voice of a bratty teenager, ending:

If you get off on the thought of a tiny Chinese girl fisting your arse, punishing your pathetic dick and telling you what a lying cheating scumbag you are, my humiliation services are available for an extra £50. Me love you long time.

She had also started a loyalty card system. It was designed to look like a coffee-shop card ('in case wifey goes snooping through your wallet'), and her clients got one stamp for a half-hour booking and two for an hour. When a client had filled their card with ten stamps, she said, they would be entitled to 'a free half-hour of fucking my pussy and arse, choking me, making me gag on your cock, etc.'

When Ned came across her profile he was amused, and showed it to Folasade with a smirk. 'Oh my days,' Folasade said. 'That's certainly very enterprising of her.'

To FOSTER A COMMUNITY of Gliss users, Ned had set up an unofficial discussion forum, with all the early posts written by him or one of the interns under different usernames. Within a few weeks, a network of relationships seemed to be forming among the real forum members. The UK forum soon reached the point where it needed moderation. Too many irrelevant, troll-like posts were appearing, and too many that were obviously drumming up fake kudos for escorts, probably written by the same group of people. One of them had such a distinctive style, his posts jumpy with uppercase letters and abrupt shifts of tone ('Passionate-Lilly is a PERFECT COMPANION for the sophisticated gentleman and a TRUE CUM SLUT'), that Folasade nick-named him the Caps-Lock Pimp. Ned asked two of the earliest forum members, *Moschino Man* and *Claude Littner*, who both seemed to spend all day long on there, if they'd like to be volunteer moderators, with full administrative privileges to delete posts by service-seeking members or to block particular IP addresses. That seemed to help.

Ned checked into the discussion forums periodically. His

ambition to build a community in which users could talk freely and share experiences was being realised. He knew too that the forums held a greater, more lurid personal fascination for him. His own attention to detail, his ability to concentrate on a large field of information, to order and systematise it, found an echo in the way the keenest users on the forums discussed their hobby.

A user called *WYSIWYG* had started a thread that now had many replies, with the title 'What's your PTK (Punting Travel Kit)?' Ned laughed at the abbreviation. 'For me,' *WYSIWYG* wrote,

> punting tends to be a daylong affair (I live in a remote place) so I wanted to share with you the details of my PTK (Punting Travel Kit, I call it the PTK for short) and to ask your tips on how I might pair it back. Any feedback would be appreciated. I need it to be as light and compact as possible while containing everything I need for a day trip. Contents:
>
> 1. Punting phone. Essential for contacting Working Girls w/o being caught by the O/H. I use a cheap prepaid top-up phone, if I buy £10 credit it tends to last for a few months since I only text with WGs (too shy to speak on phone!)

2. Charger. One of the bulkier items in the PTK and I would appreciate advice on how to upgrade it, maybe a portable battery? But my pay as you go phone doesn't accept USB power plug-in thing which most of them seem to have.

3. Cash. I carry enough for the punt plus £20–40 extra in case extras e.g. anal or facial are on offer. Plus enough for a post-punt meal and sundries.

4. Lightweight Hygiene Kit. Contains foldable travel tooth-brush with cover (taken from hotel), toothpaste, floss, gum, breath mints, interdental brush, chapstick, anti-bacterial hand gel, wet wipes (travel size), deodorant/antiperspirant, moisturiser (taken from hotel) and travel-sized cocoa butter in case post-punt shower is unavailable and I need to mask smell of e.g. perfume, pussy, before returning home. To reduce bulk I am considering changing to dental wipes but do they really work? Obviously I only carry three of four lengths of floss, not the whole roll!

5. Pill box. For Viagra/Cialis (at my age, essential) and vitamins to replenish when I eat post-punt (usually a hearty steak and chips if I can find it). I am considering decanting the pills into a Pez dispenser to be less conspicuous when I take them, usually on public transport on the way to the punt.

6. Arginine and Citrulline powder sachets.

7. Water bottle. Essential for swallowing pills, powders, etc., and maintaining hydration, but unfortunately very bulky. I use a hiker's bottle made from lightweight metal but the liquid is still very heavy and the bottle bulky.

8. Headphones. For distraction and self-improvement (podcasts etc.) while on route.

The first reply came from *teddy ruxpin*, and said simply, 'You are insane.' Next, *Bucks_Outcaller* had written:

> Oh boy, I bet you're a nightmare packing for a holiday. Me I carry cash, wallet, breath mints, and that's it. Don't have a punting phone – just use your regular smartphone and clear your history afterwards and ensure your social media privacy is tight enough that no one can find you by the phone number alone. So really the only extra thing I need to carry, that I don't normally carry around day to day, is breath mints.

To this, *Bavon Arksdale* replied:

> Sounds about right to me. WYSIWYG, you're forgetting your ballistic plate, body armour, main sidearm (.45 HK), back-up Glock, and compass. Also suncream?

More helpfully, *Jeremy Punt* had written, 'Get a small power-bank with low charge capacity – v. portable.' The majority of replies, however, were written with the intention of teasing the original poster. 'Some people take this waaaaaaaaaaay too seriously,' *6 Puttonyos* had written, while *Harrison Marks Presents* wrote:

> Just travel light with no ID in case she's nosey while you shower, and nothing valuable in case she's a thief. Da fuck is a PTK anyway?

Ned put down his tablet, switched to the laptop where he was logged in as *BeastMode84* and wrote:

> Thank god you remembered your headphone for self-improving podcasts, WYSIWYG. Tell me, do you take them off during the punt or do you fuck while listening to Serial?

In the next few minutes, Ned's comment was liked by twelve users.

N ED SAT ON A beanbag in the annexe drinking a flat white and looking at Gliss on his phone. The caffeine jostled with his hangover, the bottle of Club-Mate he had drunk on waking and the 200 milligrams of Modafinil that took the edge off his tiredness. On his mind were the events of yesterday evening. A Sunday. Ned, Folasade and Daniel had been the last in the office at seven thirty, and had gone for a drink in The Mint Gun Club, before Daniel had peeled off after an hour to go home and cook dinner.

'What do you fancy?' Ned said. 'We could do another one here, or we could go somewhere more exciting. Or we could call it a day.'

Folasade looked at her watch, at her empty glass, and said, 'Let's get out of here. I want to go somewhere fancy and get some champagne.'

Ned drained his beer. 'We could go to that brasserie at Gendarmenmarkt. The old art-deco one. It's pretty cool.'

They were seated in a booth at the brasserie within twenty minutes; within twenty-five, a white-coated waiter had brought them a sixty-five-euro bottle of champagne;

they finished it and ordered a second within an hour, and when the volume rose as diners filled the place, Ned left his chair and came to sit next to Folasade on the banquette. Their shoulders were touching. They had to turn their heads to talk to each other, leaning in. They spoke about the election that had happened in the UK two weeks ago. There had been a party in the office where people watched the coverage, but Ned had left as soon as the exit poll came in. They were discussing the comparative merits of the original and US versions of *The Office*, and whether *Parks and Recreation* was as good, when Folasade rested her hand on Ned's leg. He lifted her hand up and placed it in his own.

'This is nice,' she said.

'Yeah.'

They grinned at each other.

'Do you remember that time we snogged at the Mint?' she said.

'Of course.'

'What did you think about that?'

After a pause, Ned said, 'It was nice.'

'I thought it was nice too. I mean, I wondered if it was a bit disloyal to Alice, because, you know . . .'

'Oh, no, that's fine. We've been just friends for ages.'

Folasade smiled and sipped her champagne with her left

hand, her right hand still holding Ned's. 'Do you want to know a secret?'

Ned met her eyes, and she leaned towards him and said, 'After that time we snogged, I went home and made myself come like five times.'

And then Ned moved their linked hands on to Folasade's thigh, and they kissed for a few minutes, before Ned leaned back against the banquette, sipped his champagne, and said, 'Now. Right.' He drummed his fingers on the table, took a breath, ignored how hard his cock was and the patch of pre-come in his jeans, and said, 'I don't think we should do this tonight. I mean, you know I really like you, right? But I think we should leave this for now. We've both drunk a whole bottle of wine.'

'Plus the ones in the Mint.'

'Exactly. Plus, you know, I *am* your boss.'

'Yes,' Folasade said, 'let's be sensible,' and did a smart little mime of pulling her shoulders and back straight up, crossing her hands primly in her lap.

'But I do want to,' said Ned.

'Me too,' she said, then giggled and placed her hand thrillingly high up on Ned's thigh, almost touching the tip of his cock where it lay squeezed flat by his jeans.

'Let's do it one day,' Ned said.

'Let's.'

Then they endured a deliciously exciting ten minutes of conversation, holding hands under the table, before they left and went their separate ways. At home, Ned ate a shish kebab he had bought on the way back, drank a Club-Mate, and masturbated sitting on his sofa.

Now it was the next morning. Ned's hangover didn't feel too bad. When he woke up, he had forced himself into an early jog along the bank of the canal and a set of press-ups, planks and chin-ups before his shower. Folasade hadn't come into work yet, and Ned had spent most of his morning on the beanbags, getting on top of emails and planning tasks for Gliss.

He wasn't sure what to think about last night. The truth was, he really did like Folasade. He enjoyed her company, felt good when he spent time with her, found himself thinking of silly things to make her laugh or impress her. And he also thought she was sexy. So what was the problem? Something else in him stopped it adding up to the obvious conclusion – that they should try being together – and when he thought about it, he suspected Folasade was probably right. It must be Alice. That must be the source of his reticence. He knew he didn't really care about the professional situation. That would be fine. But he thought of the previous time he and Folasade had been out together, when they went to that ridiculous bone-broth place, and how even though nothing had happened that night, he had found himself telling a pointless lie to Alice the next day about how late they had stayed out. The fact that he felt like he had to hide it from Alice, when there was no reason to – that must tell him something, right? Otherwise why would he have felt any reservations last night about someone he was already close to, someone he found attractive and who was basically asking him to fuck her? This realisation, however, didn't help him much as to how he should proceed.

The ways things had gone with Rachel back in January had made him cautious as well. He couldn't think about it without feeling a physical unease, almost a sick feeling. They had gone to bed together on their first date, having had so much fun at the restaurant, and had done so four more times in the next three weeks. Even though she had said at the outset that she was down for having some fun and keeping things relaxed, when he told her he wanted to cool things off, it was clear that she felt terribly hurt. Used, was her word. And Ned wanted to say, well, we used each other, we both got what we said we wanted at the beginning of things, but he held his tongue. He was willing to be the bad guy, even though he knew that Rachel had herself held all sorts of reservations about him. She'd told him about them. So why was it so hurtful to be told that he didn't want to be her boyfriend?

She was a really good person though, and didn't deserve to have her self-esteem injured just because his needs didn't co-incide with hers. But now that he was being cautious, holding back from further entanglements, it felt like a hole in his life.

'Ned?' It was Richard, leaning into the arch that led into the annexe.

'Yeah?'

'There's a call for you on the landline. She says it's your mum.'

'I didn't know we had a landline.'

'Apparently we do. It started ringing and we all looked round like, what the fuck? – but then we found it down behind some old stuff on the bottom shelf in that corner.'

'Weird. Okay, give it here.'

Richard handed over the portable handset, a piece of chunky white plastic that seemed comical to Ned, and backed out of the room.

'Mum, hi.'

'Hello, Edmund, it's your mother.'

'I know. How are you?'

'I couldn't get hold of you on your mobile—'

'Oh, yeah, sorry about that, I changed number—'

'– and you never gave us your home landline number.'

'I don't have a landline, Mum. No one has a landline.'

'Well, we have a landline. Anyway, I found your office

number in Google. Was that one of your, um, employees, who answered?'

'Yeah, that was Richard.'

'It's very impressive how you're doing all these things in Germany. Running a business and whatnot. I wouldn't even know how to order a cup of tea in German.'

'You can get by with speaking English out here, to be honest. My German's just okay. But I'm a bit busy, Mum. Was there something in particular? Otherwise I could Face-Time you and Dad when I'm home tonight.'

'That was what I wanted to talk to you about actually. It's your dad—'

'Just a sec,' Ned said. Folasade had put her head into the annexe. So she had made it into work. Ned placed his hand over the receiver and said, 'What is it?'

'No problem if you're busy, but there's something slightly time-sensitive that needs your attention.'

'How sensitive? From one to ten.'

'Six?'

'Cool, I'll be there soon. Hi, sorry, Mum – you were saying.'

'It's your dad, Edmund. Dad's had a bit of a turn, and he had to go to a hospital last night. They think he might have had a stroke.'

'Jesus. Oh god. How – how bad is it?'

109

'We don't know yet. He's asleep at the moment. I was in the hospital with him last night, but they said he's stable so they let me go home. I was hoping to get some sleep, but I don't know if I'll be able to.'

'Oh, Mum. I don't know what to say. This is so terrible. Were you with him when it happened?'

'I was indoors but he was out in the garden doing some weeding, and he called out and said he felt unwell, and I didn't really think anything of it at first – you know what he's like for worrying about his health. But then he seemed to get very tired and confused, and he wasn't speaking clearly, and I was going to drive him to the hospital but then he couldn't move at all down his left side, so I called the ambulance people.'

'My god. That must have been so scary.'

When he had hung up, Ned remembered that his father had been having some fainting spells a while ago, but he had downplayed them when they spoke on FaceTime and said it was just the blood-pressure medication making him feel odd. Reassured, and distracted by work, Ned hadn't given it any further thought. He wondered whether the stroke had been developing already, and no one had done anything about it. His dad hadn't even been to see a doctor. Ned felt sick in his stomach.

He rose from the beanbag and stepped into the main

office. Folasade had her gaze fixed on her tablet as she scrolled down the front page of the web version of Gliss for the UK, very slowly. When she noticed Ned, she beckoned him over.

'Sorry to interrupt,' she said. 'It's just, there's been a really weird message on the support email.'

'Which one?'

'German.'

'Anything juicy?'

'Well, it . . . I think you should just read it, to be honest. In fact, it's not the first one. There were, like, two last week and we just ignored them because they looked so mad.'

'Okay. Give us a look. It's in German?'

'Yeah, here it is.'

Folasade handed Ned her tablet. It was certainly a strange message, in what looked like broken German. The grammar was weird, and each sentence was studded with crackly phonetic twists on standard spelling; some words Ned couldn't make out at all. But the message seemed to be a threat. Shut the app down, it seemed to be saying, cease now, call things off, and we'll leave you alone, but if not, there will be consequences. 'Diese Stadt gehört uns', the last sentence said. Ned didn't need to consult a dictionary to know that it meant 'this city belongs to us'.

He stared at the message for a few more seconds but

found that he couldn't focus on it; he felt hollowed out, slightly outside of his own body, and possibly as if he were going to faint.

'Oh, Ned, are you okay?' Folasade said. She had her hand on his arm. 'Here, you're crying, Ned.'

Ned just about managed to get out the words, 'It's my dad.'

N ED's FATHER LAY WITH his head raised. A bandage cap covered the upper part of his head, he had tubes coming from his mouth and nostrils, and there were wires connecting his wrists and chest to machines that softly beeped and flashed next to the bed. The ward was sunk in a dim peacefulness. Grey lighting and the quiet whispers of the attendants, nothing else.

On landing at City Airport, planning to head out for his parents' town on the train, Ned had found a sequence of texts and voicemails from his mother that, pieced together, showed the situation getting rapidly worse in the time Ned had been in the air. When she got back to the hospital, she was told that the CT scan had discovered a large bleed on the right side of Ned's father's brain, and that he was being transferred to a specialist hospital in London for immediate neurosurgery. Philip was sitting up and talking when she got to him, but within minutes his face began to droop down one side and his speech became slurred. He complained of a headache and nausea and was given painkillers and an injection to stop him vomiting, then began to lose consciousness. His eyes were twitching and he was calling for a doctor. Ned's mother asked him to give her a sign that he could hear her; the first time, he gave her hand a limp squeeze, but each time after that, nothing. Very quickly he had been hurried away to the resuscitation room, to the ambulance, to the London hospital and into surgery, while Ned's mother had taken a taxi to London, and hadn't seen her husband again until he was in the same place and condition in which Ned was about to encounter him.

Ned replanned his route to head to the hospital and felt the familiar estrangement of returning to London. The traffic coming down the wrong side of the road as he stepped out into it; the button on the tube carriage doors not needing pressing, so that he stood there pressing it like a fool; the button on the traffic lights needing pressing, so that he stood there not having pressed it like a fool while the cars sailed past. The awkwardness when he automatically said '*Danke schön*' in the coffee shop.

When he arrived at the hospital and found his father, he didn't at first want to look at him. He was unrecognisable under the bandage and the tubes; it struck Ned how few times he had seen him without his glasses on. Without them his face looked naked.

'You don't have any cash on you, do you?' his mother asked. 'I left my handbag at the other hospital in all the confusion and they're going to bring it along, but I wouldn't mind a bun from the shop.'

'My wallet's on the side there, I've only got euros, but you can take my card. Take the Amex one.'

Ned's mother leaned across to take Ned's wallet from the table, looked in it, and looked up at him: 'Oh, but Edmund, you shouldn't carry this much cash with you. How much have you got here? It must be thousands of euros.'

'Not many places in Berlin take cards. In restaurants and bars you mainly need cash. I don't know, there's maybe a thousand euros in there?'

'But that's just silly. What if you lost your wallet?'

'I've made it to thirty-three without losing a wallet, so I'll probably take the risk.'

'But what if you got mugged?'

'I live in Berlin, Mum, not Damascus. It's very safe. Anyway, I'm pretty rich these days, you know.'

Ned's mother looked worried. 'Well, I never.'

'Here, take the Amex card and get some food. If it doesn't do contactless then it's two, zero, six, zero.'

'Let me just write that down.'

Ned rolled his eyes. 'Think of it as 2060. The year when we all move to Mars.'

She departed, and Ned was left alone with his father, wondering how to act towards somebody who lay there silent and still, with his eyes closed.

B Y DAY THREE OF the bedside vigil, Ned was growing restless. He had opened Cubicle on his tablet and was keeping an eye on the project chats. Alice had arranged a party to celebrate the first quarter of brand content on social, and everyone was talking about it excitedly. It was the first Ned had heard of it. In fact, Ned realised, Alice hadn't been in touch with him at all since he came to London. He looked at the chats for the international versions of Gliss. Even with very little promotional effort, the app was growing and adding users quickly in the UK and the Netherlands, though not yet many in France. Ned contributed occasional comments to the chat being led by Folasade on the reasons for the slow uptake there. Never mind though: in the UK there were thousands of service providers and a huge number of users seeking services signed up already, and apparently there had been some coverage in the newspapers.

Ned knew they needed to increase revenue. He was pretty sure that pornography companies, or companies selling Cialis, could be persuaded to buy advertising space, and maybe, if they made the adverts pop up in annoying enough ways, further down the line they could introduce a premium membership without ads for a fee. Ned mentioned this on the project chat, outlined his train of thought, and asked for a volunteer to draw up a proposal for how it might be implemented.

There was a new thread on the Gliss chat headed MESSAGES OF CONCERN. Folasade had started it, posting translations made by Jaki of the odd messages that had come through the help account. There were three more since the message she had shown to Ned on Monday, and the most recent, received last night, read:

> You don't seem to be listening. This is the final time we will ask this politely. The business named Gliss must cease to operate in Berlin by the end of this week or there will be very serious consequences. This is no joke. Sex in Kreuzberg and Neukölln belongs to us, and sex in other districts belongs to friends of ours. You are badly mistaken if you think you can become involved in this trade without our permission. We know who you are and where you are based. Last warning. Be sensible and STOP immediately.

Following that message, Folasade wrote, was another from the same address that contained nothing but a link to a newspaper story. Ned clicked the link and found himself reading about the funeral of a Palestinian, born in Lebanon, who was a notorious member of the Berlin underworld and had been shot in front of his family in Hasenheide Park earlier that summer. Two thousand people turned out for his funeral, it said, in the Islamic section of the cemetery. Police believed he had fallen out with another of the Lebanese crime clans over a territorial issue.

The first reply came from Daniel, who said that these were almost certainly prank messages. His friend ran a bar-café in a Neukölln neighbourhood controlled by the clans, he said, and this friend had told him that they would never email anybody rather than coming round in person, and that they were primarily businessmen these days; it was more likely that they would try to negotiate a deal than begin with veiled threats like these. Jaki, however, wasn't so sure. He wrote in reply that the language of the emails was authentic Berlin-Middle Eastern, and he'd been googling the Miri and Al-Zein clans, and the details of the messages checked out. The link about the funeral was a clear threat: they were saying they could have people killed and get away with it, if their interests were encroached on. He posted a few links about the clans. Ned opened them in new tabs for later.

'I don't understand how you can work in these circumstances,' Ned's mother said, with an edge of accusation in her neutral tone that Ned recognised very well.

'You're reading your magazine, aren't you? It doesn't take much more concentration than that to cast an eye over a few messages.'

'I just wonder if we should be making the most of this time. Because, you know, there might not be many more chances to spend time with Dad. You could read a book to him, for example.'

'Do you think he can hear us?'

'I don't know. Nobody knows; the brain's still a great mystery really, as the consultant was saying. But some people do think that hearing is the last sense to go in this sort of scenario. It can't do any harm anyway.'

'I don't have any books.'

'Me neither. Maybe you could pop to Smith's? Or you could look at the books in the family room – there's a little library there of books people have donated.'

After gathering his things and putting on his jacket, Ned gave his father's warm hand a squeeze, placed it gently back down on the bed and headed for the lift. A few minutes later he was picking through the two shelves of discarded books. Thrillers, romances, Harry Potters, Margaret Drabbles: somehow none of these seemed the thing, though Ned found himself at a loss to say what sort of novel his father would like. He read books about history, railways, and model railways, and there were none of those here.

He decided to walk to WHSmith's. It would do him good to get out of the hospital, and away from his mother, for a few minutes. By the time he was at the hospital's front entrance, his hand was sliding his phone out of his pocket. He opened Gliss, confirmed that he wanted the UK version, and searched by proximity. Twenty-one results were returned within a distance of two miles. He switched to the map view and saw the tiny thumbnail pictures displayed in an orderly array, radiating outwards from those only a few hundred metres from the hospital to those on the edge of the circle.

'COULD YOU COME BACK to the hospital?' the text from Ned's mother said two hours later.

Ned knew at once what it would be. He ordered an Uber to pick him up from the coffee shop and was immediately stuck in rush-hour traffic. A bland eurodance track wormed its way into his head from the radio; the driver seemed to sense his irritation, asked if he wanted a different station, and Ned told him flatly no. He wondered what he ought to be doing in preparation for what was about to happen. He made an effort to recall happy scenes from his childhood. That holiday in Holland – it must have been 1992, Ned remembered watching the Barcelona Olympics on TV in the chalet. His dad had taken them to an amusement park full of scale models of everything in the country, and had been more enthused by it than any of them. Ned wondered if it still existed, googled 'netherlands scale model park' on his phone, and there it was. Yes, the model of the PSV Eindhoven football stadium, that was the one he had liked. There was a famous family photograph in one of the old albums showing Ned, ten years old, standing over it and squinting into the sun. And it was on that holiday – was it maybe even that same day? – that his mother had an allergic reaction to the prawn crackers in a Thai restaurant, an incident that she brought up frequently to this day. Christ, his dad must only have been forty that year. Only seven years older than Ned was now.

What was the last thing he had said to his father? Ned couldn't for the life of him remember. They had spoken on FaceTime two weeks ago – Ned remembered because it was just as he was finishing some tasks off before the general election party. He'd been in a rush and hadn't bothered to fill in the conversational gaps when his parents' news had run dry after a few minutes. He told them about the long johns he had bought from Uniqlo in preparation for next winter, and his plan to buy one of those jackets worn by construction workers that had battery-powered heating units sewn into them. His dad thought that was a good idea. Just don't wear it when you go through airport security or they'll think it's a suicide vest! Ned had laughed. He had surely said goodbye, and that they would speak soon. He hadn't told his father that he loved him.

The car was moving again. Ned wondered why he hadn't gone through with contacting an escort just now. He'd had the app all ready, he had thought about it, he had been excited by the idea, and then he had just sat in a coffee shop, not contacting any of the service providers in the area. Why not? He found the location map on Gliss richly exciting: the sense that all around the familiar city there were anonymous apartments and hotel rooms where normal social relations were suspended and a riotous intimacy was immediately allowed. It seemed like it could be an elegant solution to the problem of sex: he could simply top up his sense of sexual gratification every so often, and keep it apart from the rest of his life.

Ned had learned from his experience with Rachel, and with Tinder dating in general, that at his age, even when the woman said she was down for fooling around and keeping things casual, if you actually fooled around and kept things casual – went for drinks and fucked every so often, and that was the end of it – you were in fact treating her affections much too lightly. In almost every case, you were actually hurting somebody if you wanted to have sex with them without it developing into a more enmeshed relationship. Visiting escorts seemed like a clean, hygienic solution to the problem of hurting other people's feelings. Yet Ned knew on some level that it would be crossing a line. If he did it, he could never go back; he could never again be someone who hadn't paid for sex.

When Ned returned to the ward, the consultant explained to him and his mother that autonomic brain function might appear to improve after a longer time on the machines, and that this might cause some involuntary movement of the limbs and neck, but that it would be a mistake to conclude that there was any chance of Ned's father regaining consciousness. It was common, he said, for families to grow attached to the figure sleeping peacefully next to them, but they needed to understand that while this situation could be sustained indefinitely, it would not change. Ned's father was effectively brain-dead, had been ever since the moment he lost consciousness. Ned tried to remember what he had been doing at the last moment when his father was conscious, when his fingers had last twitched against Ned's mother's hand. It was probably while Ned was watching an episode of *Girls* on the plane.

Ned's mother was weeping, unable to speak. Ned knew she had heard all this an hour ago, and the consultant was going over it again for his benefit. He held her hand while the consultant said that in his view they needed to prepare to let Philip go tomorrow.

NED'S FATHER'S HEART RATE slowed and became irregular as the sedation was increased. From time to time the steady beeping of the monitor became a shockingly continuous note, the sound Ned associated from TV shows with people flatlining, but the nurse said this was normal. It had been agreed that the ventilator tubes would be removed that evening.

Ned left the room and sat in the hallway while his mother washed his father's body and a nurse shaved his face and put him into a new gown. When Ned came back in, the bandage cap had been removed and he saw his father's shaven head for the first time. A huge wound, sewn up with a rail track of black stitches, ran in a half-moon curve from the right ear to the back of the skull, and Ned grasped for the first time the reality of the surgery: sawing through the skull, removing a large section of it, delving in soft parts of the brain with knives and scalpels and god knows what – lasers, was that what they used these days? – and then piecing it back together. He thought of trying to piece a chocolate Easter egg back together once the side of it has been stoved in, and consciously turned away from the thought.

'What do you think, shall we put a clean cap on him?' Ned's mother said.

'That scar is pretty x-rated.'

The nurse fetched a new bandage cap and placed it over the shaven head. Ned asked if they could put his dad's glasses back on him, and the nurse said yes; Ned took the glasses from their case, found them smudged with fingerprints, took them to the sink, cleaned them with a little soap and warm water, dried them off and placed them on his father's face. He looked more like himself now.

Ned, his mother and the nurse sat in silence for some time, before Ned's mother spoke: 'Hi Philip, I wanted to have a talk with you about what's going to happen now.'

She was better than Ned at talking to the unresponsive figure on the bed. At one point Ned had returned from a coffee break to overhear her nattering away about something in her magazine about a soap actor, then becoming self-conscious when she noticed that Ned had returned. Now she spoke with a clarity and decisiveness Ned was unused to.

'What we're going to do now is turn your ventilator off, and it's very likely that you won't be able to breathe on your own after that, and that you'll die within the next few minutes. I don't know if you can really hear me or not, but I want you to know that you don't need to be—'

She stopped abruptly, emitted a powerful sob, looked down at the floor for a few seconds and resumed in a voice on the edge of breaking – 'that you don't need to be scared, that I'll be holding your hand throughout it all, and I want you to know that you've been a wonderful husband and a father to Edmund, and that you've given me a lot of happiness in the last forty years. I know we didn't quite make it to our fortieth, but we got very close, and I want you to know as well that I'll always love you. So that's all I've got to say, apart from goodbye, Philip, good night, and I love you.'

After Ned had spoken some words of his own, with great care the nurse removed the breathing tubes. A gargling sound came from Ned's father as the tube emerged from his throat, and within seconds his skin turned bluish. Ned had two fingers on the inside of his father's wrist, while his mother had her hand laid on his chest, and together they felt the beating of his heart. It continued for what felt like a long time, and then it stopped. His skin colour changed quickly from blue to pink. Ned's mother was weeping, but he felt oddly calm.

O N HIS FIRST MORNING back at work, Ned woke early and took a longer route into the office, winding into Neukölln and pausing to look in the windows of vintage shops, a bookshop, and a Turkish bakery. A beautiful day in early June. Sparrows gathered in dozens around the scrappy grass under the trees and picked at the gravel. They seemed smaller than sparrows in London, intricate and delicate, their brown-grey breasts fading into caramel at the edge of their red-brown hoods, all the colours shifting in the light.

As he looped back in the direction of Kottbusser Tor, Ned saw Folasade twenty metres ahead, and had the sensation of seeing her as a stranger would. She looked glamorous, dressed all in black with gold-framed sunglasses. When Ned quickened his pace and moved closer, Folasade seemed to sense his presence; she looked up from her phone, turned around, and gave him a wave. As he walked he held his gaze on her, smiling gently, and was surprised when she did likewise rather than looking away, or looking at her phone. It didn't seem awkward.

'Good morning,' he said.

Folasade moved to Ned, looked him meaningfully in the eyes, and hugged him. 'How are you?'

'I'm okay,' he said. 'More or less. I got back last night.'

They walked on side by side, and Folasade said, 'Quite a lot has happened since you left. I expect you saw it all on Cubicle.'

Ned had been away almost a full two weeks. 'Some of it,' he said.

'Social has gone cray-cray. At the last plenary it was, like, wow, we're all going to be billionaires. And obviously there's the big party on Thursday to celebrate the first quarter. Alice says she's really close to sealing this huge deal she's been mentioning. She was away for half of last week with Tristan, having meetings about it.'

'Where did they go?'

'They didn't say, but Heather booked the flights for them and she said it was Salzburg.'

'Weird. She went to Salzburg once already this summer, but she said that was just for a holiday. Maybe they're doing a secret deal to promote Mozart on Instagram. Or that chocolate cake, what's it called?'

'*Sachertorte.*'

'Well, if they make enough money from it, I can sell up and retire,' Ned said. 'God, it's really boiling, isn't it? Has it been this hot since I left?'

'Pretty much. It's good to have you back though. How was the funeral?'

They walked on five or sixes paces before Ned answered. The funeral was the previous Thursday. 'It was tough, to be honest. Because he died so unexpectedly he'd never said anything about what he wanted for a ceremony, and Mum was in too much of a state to make any decisions, so she let the local vicar plan it, and it was all just off-the-peg Christian stuff. Bible readings and hymns that wouldn't have meant anything to Dad. He was a quantity surveyor, you know? He liked engineering and science and machines and stuff. I can't remember him ever going to church in my life.'

'Were there eulogies?'

'I'd written this thing but when I got up there, I got into the first paragraph and I was too choked to do it. And then I was pinching the skin on the back of my hand to keep from breaking up again, but I still cut it short in the end because I knew I wouldn't get through it. That felt good though, just to have a bit of a cry. And then there was a reception at the local pub with lots of food.'

'Did lots of people come?'

'Yeah, I was relieved about that – all his old colleagues came, and some old clients, and his people from the model-train things, and then my aunts and uncles and cousins.'

'How's your mum doing?'

They had crossed the bridge on to Kottbusser Straße.

'I'm a bit worried about her. I'm not sure she's really got any friends. I might get her to come out here actually.'

'Do you think she'd like it?'

'I wonder. She always says she doesn't like the food abroad, but when she gets there she's fine with it. And all the sausages and potatoes would be up her street.'

'And the *Spätzle*. I love that stuff.'

'Yeah. And I think it would just be good to get her out of the house for a while. And for us to be closer. If she's here I could just see her for lunch and stuff. Though I guess she wouldn't know anyone else.'

'You could give her a job at the office. Get her to run some social accounts for Tristan.'

'Ha, I could get her to be a moderator on the Gliss forums.'

'Lol.'

'But that's not a bad idea actually, to keep her busy. I could get her a place on a language course, and then for a month she'd have something to do and people to see every day.'

'Would she stay with you?'

'God, no, that would be a nightmare. I'd have to get her an apartment.'

'Well, you should ask her,' Folasade said. 'And just to

say, I'm really happy that you're back, and I hope that we can—' but before she could finish the sentence, she and Ned reached the corner of the street and almost bumped into Richard and Daniel heading the same way from the other direction.

N ED REALISED HE WAS being followed on his way to the office the next day when the man in the orange tracksuit reappeared behind him after Ned had ducked into a convenience store to buy a bottle of sparkling water: there the guy was, with a look about him at once shifty and cocky. Before, Ned had thought he was being paranoid, but no, it really was happening. The orange tracksuit had been there that morning outside Karstadt when Ned was grocery shopping, and had been there again when Ned waited at the crossing on the Damm. When Ned headed towards the U-Bahn, there was the orange tracksuit looming into his peripheral vision as he bent down, and he had spent at least ninety seconds in the shop buying his water, so that there was no reason for the man not to have passed by if he wasn't following him.

Ned turned around, stock-still in the middle of the pavement, and looked directly at him; the man pretended to flick through the postcards on the rotating rack outside the shop with a fatuous smirk on his face.

Well, fuck him. Ned walked towards him before he had decided what to do, and when he reached him he asked what time it was and held the man in a long stare. The man slowly took his phone from his pocket and held its screen up to Ned's gaze. 09:37.

Now he was closer up he appreciated how large and heavy-looking the guy was: slow-moving, a bit out of shape perhaps, but so broad-backed and thick-armed that he could definitely handle himself, or at least scare off anybody who might have been tempted to try anything. Could Ned take him, if it came to it? It was touch and go – the man might have weighed fifteen, sixteen stone, and would be seriously hard to throw over. Ned turned from him contemptuously, started to walk away, and was infuriated to hear the man snickering to himself. No, leave it, he told himself, leave it. Fuck that guy.

The incident played on Ned's mind as he carried on to the office, and gave a sour note to his thoughts. He found himself eyeing every rough-looking man with suspicion, daring them with a scowl to try and follow him. And he recalled the weird guy who'd been in The Mint Gun Club last night after work. Was it the same guy who was following him this morning? Ned had been walking to the toilet from his corner table and seen the man move from his position under the coat hooks and walk towards the door. He had paused at the toilet door, glanced at the man again and found him looking at him; after they had made eye contact, the man lowered his gaze and left the bar. Ned couldn't remember what he looked like now.

'I'M JUST UNEASY ABOUT the way we're assuming that they're Lebanese,' said Richard. A new message from the same email address had arrived that morning.

'If it is an organised crime group, they might just as easily be Albanians, or Turks, or Hell's Angels,' said Ned.

'My point is that it seems a bit orientalist to position them as this threatening other that we define in opposition to ourselves.'

'But Richard, they literally are threatening us,' said Folasade.

'I just think we shouldn't be centring that or calling them "the Lebanese" as if they represent a whole ethnic group.'

'Then what should we call them?'

'At the moment all we know is that someone is sending us strange emails. Nothing more than that.'

'We could call them the Emailers,' said Folasade.

'That would be preferable.'

'I was joking, Richard. Anyway, if they're sending us threatening links insinuating that they've killed people, basically telling us that they're from one of the Lebanese crime clans, it's not exactly racist to assume that they're Lebanese.'

'I said orientalist, not racist.'

'You may not have noticed,' said Jaki, 'but Fola is black, so she can't be racist, can she?'

Ned frowned. 'I don't think that's quite how it works.'

Two people spoke up at once ('No—' 'Well—'), but Ned raised a palm to cut them off: 'Guys, guys, this isn't getting us anywhere. All we need to do at the moment is decide whether we want to make a police report or not.'

Ned didn't know when exactly he had decided that he wouldn't tell the team that he was being followed. He hadn't reasoned it out. All he knew was that he didn't want to scare people. He was the boss, the co-founder; he was in charge of Gliss, and if anybody wanted to come after him, he'd have to handle it himself.

Alice hadn't spoken since the social team had finished their part of the meeting. Now she said, 'I think it would be an overreaction to go to the police at this stage. I think Daniel is probably right that these are just prank messages being done by some bored kid, or some minor pimp you've annoyed. And if these clans are already in charge of organised crime and black markets and that sort of thing, it's not like the police could do anything about some rather ambiguous emails.'

'They don't seem ambiguous to me,' said Jaki. 'They directly threaten us.'

'I agree with Alice,' said Ned. 'These aren't real threats. Let's just keep logging and translating the messages so we have a record of them, push on with the work cycle as usual, and be vigilant for anything out of the ordinary.'

'Aren't you worried?'

'Nah. Fuck the haters, I say.'

Everyone laughed.

'On that note,' said Alice, 'I think we're probably done for today. Remember that we've got Tristan's stand-up gig tonight in Wedding, and it would be really nice if everyone could come. And then we've got the big party for social tomorrow night, at the observation deck of Panoramapunkt at Potsdamer Platz, so if you're going straight from work, bring something a bit smart to change into tomorrow. If that's your style.'

She looked pointedly at Jaki, who was wearing a badly faded Iron Maiden t-shirt with a hole in the armpit, and he mouthed back at her, 'What?!'

The meeting broke up. Ned had half-forgotten about the party tomorrow. He wasn't looking forward to it. There was just too much in his head at the moment to make space for it. His dad, and Folasade and Alice, and Gliss and the man following him . . . He felt like he was running at top speed, unable to stop for long enough to be really present in any one moment, let alone to enjoy a fancy party with all the clients and contacts. At the top of some silly tourist attraction, with champagne and waiters and hors d'oeuvres. It was the last thing he needed.

Alice tapped him on the shoulder as he was picking up a final vegan brownie, and said, 'Ned, could we find time to talk in private today?'

Mouth full, Ned said, 'Now works for me.'

She closed the door of the meeting room. 'Okay.'

'What is it?'

'I think at some point we need to make a decision about the structure of the company.'

'Oh yes?'

'Yeah. Social is on the verge of going really huge, is the thing. I don't know how much you've been keeping an eye on it.'

Ned confessed that in the last few weeks he hadn't really, what with Gliss and his dad and everything. He knew of course that it was going well, and he could see how excited everyone was about it, but he couldn't have said precisely what had been happening.

'The thing is,' Alice said, 'we're getting serious investor approaches. Not just for equity shares but for a potential buy-out.'

'How serious is serious?'

'Let's say it doesn't seem wild to think about eight figures. And not the lowest eight figures either.'

'Fuck. Euros, you mean?'

'Well, I don't mean lire, do I? I don't mean Vietnamese dong.'

Ned laughed, and said, 'As the actress said to Ho Chi Minh.'

'Very good. Look, we don't want to get complacent, but if we do this right, we could soon be unbelievably wealthy.'

'So what's the problem with the structure?'

'It's Gliss. It's to do with reputation really. These investment firms and groups, they're crazy about start-ups but they still scare easily. They don't want to go near anything that looks dodgy. So having a sex-work app in the same company is looking a bit unwise right now.'

'But Gliss is legit. We went through it, it's all legal and ethical. You were the one who made all the arguments for that. Why it was morally good.'

'I know. I mean, I still believe that, but it's the optics at this stage. For most people, sex work still means exploitation, trafficking . . . It's toxic. And now we have this weird thing with the messages. It doesn't seem worth the risk.'

'Hmm,' Ned said.

'I mean, is it even going to make any real money?'

'It will. It is already, a bit. The on-demand content's going okay. And we might start running ads soon.'

'Okay. But social is on course to make millions. Literally millions, in year one. And all we need to do is hive Gliss off into its own separate company. It would be easy. It can still run out of the office, still be staffed by you and Fola and everyone, but it needs to be off the books, legally and officially. We need a firewall between Gliss and social.'

Ned paused for a long time, trying to work out why he felt defensive on this point. As if he felt attacked, or shamed. But surely Alice was right, and it would be as simple as she said. They could just incorporate Gliss as a separate company. And if what she said about the eight figures was true . . . 'I'll think about it,' he said. 'It sounds pretty reasonable to me.'

'Thanks, Ned,' said Alice, and gave his arm a squeeze. 'It needs to be decided quickly though. We're growing at an insane rate.'

WHEN HE GOT INSIDE the venue for Tristan's stand-up gig in Wedding, Ned was surprised by the size of the place: there were maybe thirty round tables with chairs set out, and a large standing area over by the bar. It must have been able to hold 300 people, and it looked about half full already. Almost everyone from the office had come, arriving in a fleet of Ubers booked on the company account, after three rounds of drinks at The Mint Gun Club.

Ned and Folasade sat at the back of the room talking through most of the first two acts, then moved forward to the tables Alice had reserved. Ned had no idea until now that there was such a large English-language stand-up scene in Berlin. It was Tristan's turn. Before he left the bar to make his way over, he'd been saying he felt nervous. It was his first set in six months, he'd been so busy. The compère wound up to saying, 'He's zany, he's goofy, he's wacky, you're going to love him . . . give it up for . . . Tristan . . . Rodgers!'

Whoops came from The Thing Factory tables; applause smattered from elsewhere in the room. Tristan walked, very slowly, on to the stage, his arms rigid at his side and his face impassive. He stood before the microphone for a moment, two seconds, three, and said in a muted voice, 'Good evening. *Guten Abend.*'

He held the pause while someone sniggered nervously. 'Actually, I'm not feeling very goofy today. I want to talk about an issue that's very important to me right now, and I think it says a lot about the moment we're in, the whole climate of politics and social morals.'

He turned his head to the right, coming out of range of the microphone, looked out at someone on the front table and sadly mouthed the word 'goofy'. The room cracked up, and Tristan held a perfectly straight face while the laughter died down. In spite of himself, Ned had to admit that Tristan's command of the audience was impressive. Much more so than the first two acts. The room was with him.

'Obviously this has been a difficult year for lots of us,' Tristan said. 'There's the Greek crisis, we've had the refugee crisis. We've had a general election in the UK. Depressing. But the thing that's really pushed me over the edge is this.'

A long pause, broken by giggles.

'They've changed – sorry—'

He paused, in a convincing impression of someone too moved to speak, drew back from the microphone, composed himself, stepped forward and said in a whisper, 'They've changed the recipe for Club-Mate.'

The room broke into a storm of laughter.

'I don't know if it's everywhere. I haven't sampled every batch, obviously. Just the ones from my local shop. But it's really hit me hard. I wrote a poem about it actually. Just a short poem.'

Tristan took a small piece of white paper from his breast pocket, unfolded it, and held it close to his nose.

'Here's the poem. It's called "Poem". Here it is:'

Oh Club-Mate,

Oh Club-Mate,

How entirely have you stolen my heart-eh?

I wouldn't even know where to start-eh.

Oh Club-Mate,

Oh Club-Mate.

'Thank you,' Tristan said. The poem had earned a round of applause, punctured at points by laughter.

'The crazy thing is though, my girlfriend doesn't like Club-Mate. Can you believe it? She'll have a sip of mine – to be honest I make her have a sip of mine, she's got to learn, doesn't she? – anyway, she'll have a sip of mine and she'll be like . . .' (Tristan pouted into a high-pitched, posh English voice), *'Gosh, it tastes like stale cigarettes.'*

Laughs hovered around the room. Folasade flashed Ned

a look, and Ned looked at Alice, who was smiling. It was one of her lines. Tristan sighed, slumped into a dejected posture, flashed Alice a look from the stage, and mouthed, 'Sorry, baby.' Ned saw her smile crack into a laugh, and he felt a tension, a tightness, taking over his face and whole body. It was exactly what he had dreaded. Surely not? Tristan? Tristan and Alice? And he was the last to know about it?

Ned rose from his chair, headed to the bar, swerved towards the toilets at the back of the room, and swerved again for the exit while Tristan segued into his next bit. When Ned emerged from the venue, he had no precise sense of the neighbourhood he was in. He must be near Schillerpark, he thought. He decided not to look at Citymapper but to walk until he came across something he recognised, or an U-Bahn station. His phone came to life, and he found a text from Folasade: 'u ok? xx'

He didn't know if he was okay or not. Of course, now that he thought about it, it had been coming. He had seen the evidence of Tristan and Alice's closeness for months. The way she looked at him, laughed at his jokes. But it was another thing to have it announced on stage like that. For it to be real. He tried to think it through dispassionately. It was none of his business, they were both friends of his, it didn't change anything, he and Alice had finished years ago. But still . . .

He had gone thirty yards down an unpromising-looking street, changed his mind, and turned back on himself, when he saw the man who'd been following him yesterday, walking towards him and staring. For a moment Ned considered approaching him, telling him he would report him to the *Polizei*. But the man hadn't exactly done anything. Ned hesitated; the man was looking down now; had crossed the street; was about to pass Ned on the other side; had passed him. Ned turned to look at his departing back but the man carried on away, head bowed.

Ned walked back down the way he had come, annoyed. Who was that guy? Could he be an undercover cop? Had they caught up with him about one of the scam sites? Surely not. If they had any evidence it would come from breaking the Tor encryption or tracking his Bitcoins or the parcels he was sending. And if they'd done that, they could simply come and arrest him. They knew where he lived.

No, it must be connected to the weird messages the Gliss account had been receiving. But those messages, and this guy, who wasn't taking any care to conceal the fact that he was following Ned, seemed pretty amateurish. Clearly, if they were being this obvious about it, they wanted Ned to know that he was being followed. Ned would have to be vigilant; he decided not to feel scared.

His heart was running slightly faster than usual now.

Each footfall he heard behind him caused him to turn around sharply. He was on the verge of calling an Uber when he reached the end of the block, found himself on Müllerstraße under bright street lighting, saw the U-Bahn station, and knew what his route home would be.

N ED WAS WOKEN BY his phone. Half awake, he had a brief confusion over where exactly the sound was coming from, then remembered it was charging in the front room, where it sat on the low windowsill. He groped his way through the dark apartment, almost tripping headlong over his loose bedsocks in the process. It was Folasade ringing. 03:42.

Several thoughts went through Ned's mind at once. Probably Folasade was high and waking him up for no reason, and he felt annoyed by that already, even while his annoyance was tempered by affection for her enthusiasm. She must be out at a club, and wanted to say hello. But then again it might be something serious, for her to call him so late.

'Fola, what the fuck?'

Silence and the noise of traffic. Her voice, when it came on, sounded scared. 'Oh, Ned. This is so fucked up.'

'Sweetie, calm down. What is it?'

'It's my apartment, Ned, it's gone, it's . . . I might have lost everything.'

'Hang on, what do you mean?'

'I could have died in there. In my own bed.'

'Fola, Fola, slow down. What happened?'

'I'm really scared, Ned. The police asked if I knew anyone who'd target me and I didn't even know what to say, I was so shocked. I think I'm actually in shock. It looked like they were targeting me.'

'Fola, you still haven't told me what's happened yet.'

'My apartment's burned down. It looks like the whole block might go down or be gutted or something. If the bang hadn't woken me up I would have died in there. They're not saying what it was yet, but it looks like it was a firework or something through the window in my kitchen. I mean, the smoke was coming under my bedroom door already and I hardly made it out of the flat, the heat was so intense. Oh, Ned—' and her speech became incoherent as tears overtook her.

'Sweetie, it's okay. I'll look after you. Where are you now? You must be freezing. Do you want to come round here?'

'Could I?'

'Of course, of course. I'll make up the spare room. Send me a location pin and I'll get you an Uber on my account, yeah?'

'Thank you so much, Ned. I think I need to ask the police if I'm allowed to leave yet. But I'll tell you when I'm ready.'

After Ned had got dressed and sorted out the car, he reflected on what he'd just heard. He knew at once, with a sickening feeling, that it was the people who'd been following him. Had to be. This was their way of escalating.

Wide awake now, Ned sat on the sofa and pieced it all together in his mind. They must have traced Folasade's home address or followed her home one day. The last thing he needed was for her to quit the company. She'd be irreplaceable. From now on, anyway, he had to make sure security was watertight. That was just for starters. He had to get some muscle on his side, in case they came back for more. But where would he go to hire some protection? He knew he had two choices: he could either stand up to them or he could back down now. The second was the safer option. The sound of Folasade's terrified voice, the thought of her being woken up in the middle of night to find her apartment blazing and smoking – it made Ned sick with dread. But he knew at once that he wouldn't be able to back down.

By the time Folasade arrived, fifty minutes later, Ned had put clean sheets on the spare bed, and devised a plan. He would ask Folasade not to tell anyone at work for now, so that Alice and Tristan could have the party for social tomorrow night, and he could take steps before everyone panicked. In the morning, he would find a private investigator to get to the bottom of who these people were, and a security firm to give The Thing Factory round-the-clock protection. He would sort out an interim apartment for Folasade. And he would strategise.

Folasade buzzed herself up, and Ned heard her coming up the stairs. Here she was. She was wearing a scruffy Captain Haddock t-shirt, pink tracksuit bottoms and a pair of espadrilles – either what she wore in bed, or the easiest thing she could pull on in a rush. It reminded Ned of his student days, how the smoke alarm would go off early in his halls when some sporty type burned their toast, and everyone would pile out into the morning sheepishly. Ned hugged her and said, 'You made it.'

She gestured to her outfit. 'I'm sorry for this.'

'It's a strong look. Would you like a cup of tea or water or anything? Or some different clothes?'

'Peppermint? And maybe a hoodie or something?'

Ned went and busied himself. When he came through, she had her feet up on the sofa, and was flicking through a book from Ned's coffee table on cabinets of curiosities. He put the tea down in front of her and she lifted her feet to indicate that he should sit down. Ned did, and she put her feet up on his legs.

'These corals are crazy.' She turned the book towards him. It showed a tiny figurine of a woman that had been carved from a piece of red coral, its two prongs forming her arms, upraised in a gesture of priestly exclamation.

'It's a really cool book,' Ned said.

Folasade flicked for a few more pages, sipped her tea, and said, 'Fucking hell though. Tonight.'

'What have the police said?'

'They just took a statement. They don't know anything because it was still too hot to go in the apartment. They said it looked like kids throwing a firecracker through the window.'

'Shit. Are you okay?'

'Yeah. Bit shocked though. I'm feeling that sort of adrenaline feeling of being totally buzzed still.'

'How big was the fire when you got out?'

'It was just in the kitchen and the front room. Luckily the path was clear to the front door. But it spread quickly after that.'

'You can stay here as long as you like. And when you're ready, I'll sort you out a new place.'

'It's nice to be here.'

She jiggled her foot affectionately against his leg, and Ned realised that the contact of her legs on his had given him an erection.

'I was thinking,' he said, 'since the police are on it already, maybe it would be best not to tell the rest of the team about it just yet. Just so Alice and Tristan can have their big party.'

'Oh yeah, I was thinking that too. It's such a big moment for them. I think I'll just need to sleep tomorrow anyway.'

'Take the day off, definitely,' Ned said.

They sat in silence for a moment, before Folasade said, 'Fucking hell, I'd forgotten about the Alice thing. From tonight. Or last night.'

'It seems like ages ago.'

'That was some way to announce to your colleagues that you're dating your boss.'

'Oof,' said Ned. 'Did no one else know about it?'

'I certainly didn't. Are you okay about it?'

'It's fine. They're probably quite good for each other.'

It was almost five thirty. In the kitchen Ned swallowed a 200-milligram Modafinil to help him feel sharp in the morning, and offered one to Folasade. She declined. He said he ought to be getting to bed. She too, she said. Ned found a clean towel and laid it out on the spare bed for her. But after they had brushed their teeth together in the bathroom, she took Ned's hand and followed him into his room.

NED STEPPED BRISKLY INTO the bar-café. It was empty except for the woman behind the counter. '*Hallo,*' she said, trying for the German word, but sounding English.

'Hi,' said Ned.

'Can I get you anything?'

'Just a Club-Mate. Ooh, maybe the *Weißwurst* too, actually.'

'Cool. Take a seat and I'll bring them over.'

Ned moved to the windows and looked back out along the street. The guy who'd followed him last night was loitering across the road, facing the window of a gift shop and, Ned suspected, using the plate-glass reflection to look back over his own shoulder towards the door of the bar-café.

Ned glanced at his watch. It had been a long day. When he had woken ten hours ago, it had been a lovely surprise to find the warmth of another body in his bed. It seemed right that they had shared a bed but not slept together last night. He carefully got out of bed, had a piss, and put the kettle on for some coffee. He tried to be quiet but while he was in the kitchen he heard, over the kettle's roar, the toilet flushing again. When he carried two coffees back into the bedroom, Folasade had sat up.

Ned handed her the coffee, got back into bed, and placed his own mug on his bedside table. When he turned back she lifted the duvet and pulled him in towards her, meeting his tentative mouth with her own. She tasted of coffee.

'Are you sure about this?' Ned said.

'Don't worry. I need this.'

Half an hour later, she was back asleep and Ned had showered and dressed, feeling fully alert from the caffeine and Modafinil. Hopping between laptop, tablet and phone he made shortlists of five suitable Airbnbs for Folasade, three private investigation firms and two security companies. He found a scrap of paper, wrote a note to say that he'd be out all day, gently opened the bedroom door, and propped the message on the empty pillow next to her, then took it back up again to add two kisses.

Next he had sat in Zitrone on the corner of his street over a Club-Mate, emailed the choice of apartments to Folasade, and made phone calls to the PI and security firms. Only one of each could see him today. He headed first to Friedrichshain to meet with Olympus security. The intercom buzzed. *'Hallo?'*

'Hallo, guten Morgen, ich heiße Ned, von der Thing Factory.'

He heard the latch click and shouldered the heavy door open. Up a narrow flight of stairs, to a small office on the third floor, with the door open to show a surprisingly slight and dapper middle-aged man sat behind a desk. He beckoned Ned in, gestured towards the coat hooks on the wall, and invited him to take a seat, all without rising from his own chair, then said in English, 'My name is Melczyk. So tell me, what is your situation?'

Ned immediately had a sense of the man's quiet competence. He seemed somehow authoritative – someone who was aware of his power and was choosing to hold it in reserve. He agreed to provide a twenty-four-hour guard for the office and two additional guards on round-the-clock call for any of the staff, and to accompany them to and from work if they wanted. It would cost thousands of euros, and Ned suspected the guys would probably be no better than nightclub bouncers. But it would reassure people. And Melczyk said that most of his men had service experience, even if they wouldn't be armed.

By the time Ned had left the meeting and checked his messages, Folasade had replied, choosing the Airbnb nearest to his own place in Kreuzberg, so Ned booked that for her. He realised he was late for the PI meeting.

He arrived sweaty and unready at the office in the east of Kreuzberg, and after he had given Nocerino, the head of the PI company, all the information, he could tell that the man thought he was a fantasist. It would just be kids with a firecracker, Nocerino said; it happened all the time. Not the style of the Miri or the Al-Zein clan. He shook his head when Ned said he needed the report early next week. When Ned took out his wallet and handed him two thousand euros in cash, his attitude changed. Of course, he said. He would personally oversee the job. 'And we will meet us on Monday afternoon, yes?'

When Ned left Nocerino's office it had been 04:40. He hadn't checked in with work all day. The party at Panoramapunkt started at seven. He needed to take stock of things, shower, change his clothes, catch up on messages. He walked in the direction of a café he remembered going to with Alice a year ago, in the planning stage for The Thing Factory, and checked Cubicle on his phone while he walked. Then he noticed that the guy was following him again.

'Expecting someone?' said the waitress. She placed a bottle of Club-Mate, a glass of ice, and the plate of *Weißwurst* on Ned's table. The sausages were floating in a bowl of hot water, and came with a salty pretzel, a pot of sweet mustard and some straggly salad leaves.

Ned grinned at her. 'You see that man across the street? With his back to us?'

The woman's eyes widened as she looked.

'I'm pretty sure that man's following me. He's been doing it for a few days. I popped in here to see if I could lose him, but he saw me. So now he's hovering there, pretending to look at that shop while he waits for me to come out.'

Ned tore off a chunk of pretzel, cut a slice of sausage, dipped both into the mustard and placed them on his tongue.

'How do you know he's pretending? He looks like he's just looking in the shop window.'

'Well, he *is* looking in the shop window, but only to look like he's doing something. What would you look at anyway – what does that shop sell?'

'Like, fancy wooden toys and ornaments and stuff. Dead expensive.'

'Exactly. Why would he have spent five minutes looking at their window display?'

'He must just like that kind of bougie stuff. Maybe he's looking for a gift. Oh shit, no, you're right. He just peeked round at our door. Are you scared?'

'Not particularly.'

'What does he want with you? Are you in trouble? Are you, like, a spy or something?'

'Ha, not exactly. What makes you think that?'

'Just the way you seem so calm about it. He looks like a big guy.'

'I don't think he wants to hurt me. At least not today.

He's just trying to send a message. That's why he's been so obvious about following me.'

The woman continued looking out the window for a moment, then turned back to Ned. 'I think you should walk right out and go up to him,' she said. 'Let him know you're not afraid.'

'I did that already the other day. Went right up to him and asked him the time, and he just gave me this dumb stare.'

A group of three customers entered the bar-café. The woman mouthed 'excuse me' to Ned and went to serve them.

Ned decided to stick it out. There was a pile of newspapers in the corner of the room; he took up a copy of *Kicker* and tried to read the football transfer gossip in German, pleased to find that he knew most of the words. Let the guy wait. Ned looked at his back again. He had his right arm raised in front of him, smoking a cigarette, perhaps.

Who was he? It was frustrating not to know. Ned decided to give him a name. That would help. Abdel, he would call him, after a boy he'd gone to school with. Let's see how long Abdel could stand there like an idiot, pretending to look at handmade wooden toys. It was a battle Ned knew he could win.

N OW THAT HE HAD lost Abdel, who had eventually wandered off from his station when Ned didn't emerge from the bar-café, Ned's thoughts turned back to Alice. He didn't want her to worry about his absence from the office today, so he sent her a text saying, 'Was WFH today. Brain-storming in a caff going well so will stay here a bit.' He kept his eyes on his phone, saw the double tick that meant she had opened and read his message. It said that Alice was typing a reply – '. . .' – then after some seconds the dots disappeared. She must have given up or been distracted.

Yes, she was definitely upset with him. Well, worried about him – that was a better way of putting it. And maybe she was right to worry. At times he could look objectively at his own behaviour, and it worried him too. But he knew why the threat from Abdel was so interesting to him. It had changed his routine; it had challenged him, made him feel more alive – literally more awake – than he had in ages. It had forced him to take control of his circumstances.

On a whim, Ned went into the shop on the corner that sold liquorice. It had always been one of his things, in the family mythology, that he loved liquorice, and he still some-times received packets of Allsorts at Christmas. Inside, the shop was like a fashion boutique, all clean white surfaces and polished glass. Ned tried a few samples and departed, feeling vaguely embarrassed, with a pot of fifty grams of salty-tasting liquorice he had paid almost five euros for.

He walked past the pavement tables outside a restaurant and gave a start when he saw Abdel emerging from the swing doors. His t-shirt gave him the air of a boxer in training. Ned held back, slowing his pace almost to a stand-still, and kept close in to the wall of the building, afraid that Abdel would turn around and see him. Abdel crossed the street, walking away from Ned, and turned right on to the bridge across the canal. Ned followed him at twenty feet's remove.

When he was across the bridge, Abdel turned left, crossed the street and went into a bar-café. Ned waited for him to emerge, started following him again, and saw him enter another, fifty feet down the street, and a third ten minutes after that. In the third bar-café, the windows gave a clear view to the back of the room. Ned grew emboldened, stood by the door, and turned to look in from time to time. After chatting to the owner, Abdel went to the two slot machines – the *Automaten* – and used a key to open and empty their change drawers. That must have been what he was doing in the last places too, the thing Ned hadn't been able to make out through the darkened panes. At the next bar-café the same routine was repeated. The staff looked tense, smiling in an overly polite way, offering him a free espresso or a fresh mint tea, and he would sit for a minute at the bar before emptying the machine. It was a protection racket, presumably: the owner of the bar-café can run his establishment in the neighbourhood unthreatened, on condition that he let Abdel's people install their own machines in there.

When he finally left the last bar-café, Abdel turned back on himself and made for the bus stop, joining a line of a dozen people, waiting. Ned followed him, lowering his gaze while he crossed the street in case Abdel turned around, then faced in the other direction pretending to look at his phone while he waited for the bus. He wanted to see Abdel's face. Now he had turned away, Ned wondered whether he hadn't in fact been mistaken in thinking it was Abdel. He hadn't had a good clear sight of him, after all. But he knew that if he turned around, he might be spotted. He waited.

The 171 arrived; Ned sensed the bustle of people boarding it, then turned and got on too. He flashed his *Monatskarte* to the driver, started down the aisle, saw Abdel standing to his right looking out the window, made it past him unseen, and took up a position near the back of the bus. It was crowded. Abdel pulled his headphones from his pocket. He looked like he was settling in for a long journey.

After a few minutes there was a moment of tension, when an old woman barked something at Abdel that Ned couldn't catch. It seemed like she wanted to put her wheelie trolley in the space where Abdel stood, and at one point she pushed the trolley hard into his shins, at which he merely turned impassively and gave her a blank look, keeping his headphones in. Outside the window, greenery and the blue-brown canal scrolled past. The bus was headed south-east into Neukölln. The old woman looked towards the other people on the bus for support in her disapproval towards Abdel, but they blanked her. Ned realised as she muttered to herself that she was speaking Russian, not German; that was why he couldn't understand her.

The bus cruised towards Hertzbergplatz and Abdel moved towards the exit door in the middle of the vehicle. He was facing Ned now; he would only need to focus on the face to his left and he would have Ned directly in his sights. He left the bus the moment the doors opened, and Ned scrambled behind the three other people alighting to make it off before the doors closed. Abdel was twenty feet in front of him now on the pavement. It was a quiet area. No need to follow him too closely.

Ned had never been to this neighbourhood before. On

the main street, it seemed that every second establishment was an internet café or a shop devoted to mobile phones, international phone cards, and phone unlocking; many of them doubled as shisha joints, with clouds of honeyish smoke leaking from their front doors. The food outlets – bakeries, patisseries, kebab shops and the occasional restaurant – were all Turkish. Loud Turkish pop came from a hole in the wall outlet, next to which more than a dozen people sat on benches eating *Döner*.

An elderly passer-by stopped to engage with Abdel. Ned thought he was asking directions, until Abdel embraced him, laughing fondly and slapping his back. So they must know each other; this must be Abdel's neighbourhood. Ned turned to look at the information on the bus stop, trying to keep one eye on Abdel but ultimately missing the moment when he moved on, so that when Ned got going again, Abdel was forty feet away. Abdel crossed the wide street, turned left on the pavement and pushed through the doors of a casino, its windows blocked out by pictures of poker chips against a bright green and red background.

Ned weighed up his options. He walked past the casino, managed to see through the tinted glass of the swing doors and identified Abdel's back, sitting on a bar stool chatting to the man behind the bar. Ned moved on. Looking back across the street, he saw a convenience store with a bench outside, where he'd be able to sit and keep an eye on the casino's door. Yes, he would give it an hour. If Abdel hadn't come out after that, he would give up.

Settled down with a bottle of Bitburger and a copy of *GQ*, Ned began his vigil. Ten minutes passed. Abdel didn't seem to have been looking for him with much ardour, Ned thought, to have wandered off to do his rounds of the *Automaten* and get the bus home just a few minutes after being given the slip. Ned felt almost let down – hurt, neglected – by Abdel's casualness. Wasn't Ned supposed to be his top priority? And there he was, wandering around town, listening to music, playing with his phone, and going into casinos. Ned was doing a better job of tailing him than he had done of tailing Ned.

Five men were going into the casino. Ned's attention was caught by them. They looked like old friends, casual in their relation to each other's space, and relaxed, perhaps after a long lunch. They seemed to be laughing. When they entered the casino they performed a charade of elaborate courteousness around who entered first and who held the door for whom, before breaking off into play-fighting. Through the open door Ned perceived Abdel greeting them warmly. It looked like he had been waiting for them.

Ned knew he was going to enter the casino for a closer look. He knew too how unwise this was, and how, if he debated the pros and cons in his mind, he would talk himself out of it, so he banished all doubt from his mind and rose from the bench. Next to the convenience store was a cheap shop selling suitcases, cleaning products, household goods and clothing. Ned impulsively chose a fluorescent green hoodie and a red baseball cap, paying in cash and asking the man behind the counter to remove the tags. When he had put both of them on, he felt bolstered against the risk — disguised and thereby protected. He guessed that Abdel would be the only one among the six men capable of recognising his face, but when Abdel had last seen him Ned had been wearing the blue polo shirt that was now hidden beneath the hoodie. Yes, surely the change wrought on him by his new outfit would be enough to keep him from being recognised.

Ned left the shop and was briefly struck by how strange his life had become. His father had been dead two weeks, and here he was, walking into a confrontation with the men who last night had probably tried to kill the woman he had fucked this morning. He crossed the street and entered the casino.

ALL SIX WERE SITTING around a table in the corner, talking and smoking, when Ned entered. One of them stood up and walked slowly behind the bar. Ned disguised his voice behind an American tourist accent, and said, 'Hi! *Ich habe ein Bier?* And fruit machines *spielen*?'

The man silently served him a bottle of Warsteiner, nodded towards the *Automaten* by the back wall, returned to his table, and told his friends that it was okay, the guy could hardly speak a word of German. Another voice at the table said something about Americans that Ned didn't quite catch, followed by laughter from the group.

Ned sat on a stool in front of the bank of slot machines, his back to the table. In the reflection on the glass panel at eye level he could see most of the men. The oldest-looking guy, thickly bearded, with passages of grey hair above his ears, spoke the most, in a voice that seemed decisive and commanding. Abdel said very little, but seemed agitated when he did speak. A shaven-headed guy in a grey sweater was more talkative, and his contributions were short, aggressive-sounding, and often greeted with laughs.

As he loaded coins into the slot and hit the twist and hold buttons almost at random, Ned found that he could follow very little of the conversation, or could follow it only at a distance. They spoke fast and slangily, in heavy accents. The bearded guy – who was, Ned had decided, the head of the clan – was saying something about a building he either wanted to buy or to sell, or maybe a building he was trying to get built, and his point was either a complaint about how slowly either solicitors or people in the construction industry worked, or that he wished the deal or job was going more slowly. While all these possible meanings jostled for room in Ned's understanding, someone whose face Ned couldn't see said something, in a tone of annoyance, about a union – Ned guessed it was the union for construction workers – and how they were all useless, and then the drift was lost to Ned completely, until he remembered that Union was the football team in the south-east of the city, not the word for a trade union at all. Yes, they were talking about football. Ned was more or less back on track with the conversation now. He held a row of two lemons; the third came up as a bunch of purple grapes.

The hanging smell of cigarette smoke mixed queasily with the smell of cleaning products. Ned guessed he was the first customer of the day. The carpet was immaculate. It didn't seem like a thriving business. They had even looked surprised when he came in, until they learned that he was a clueless American. The casino was a front, Ned assumed, for cleaning their money. He had heard about such things. And presumably the costs of running it were very low. Someone had explained to Ned the laws here about rent controls for existing businesses, and he still felt vaguely resentful that places like this were paying a rate that had hardly risen in decades, when The Thing Factory had to pay through the nose for their office. What were these fuckers doing to deserve such a cushy ride?

Ned checked his phone: still no reply from Alice. She must be at the venue for the party now. Ned span again, and wondered what his plan should be. Alice would think he was crazy, walking in here, if she knew the whole story. Folasade too. That thought led to the memory, rising unbidden, of Folasade's body this morning, how tenderly she had beckoned him into the bed, how soft her skin was, how powerfully she had come when she sat on top of him and leaned forward, grinding her clit against his pubic hair. It was lovely that she could come from fucking like that . . . Ned realised he hadn't been paying attention to his row. A lemon came up, and he was bust.

He fed in another three euros, span again, and realised that Abdel was talking about Folasade. *Die Afrikanische*, he called her, the African girl: he was saying that he must have scared her, or perhaps that he was scared he had killed her, or scared that he hadn't killed her. Then Ned heard his own name. Abdel was laughing to himself; he seemed to be saying that Ned had spent all day wandering around town, hanging out in bars, and then he said something Ned didn't understand. The others laughed. This must be Abdel reporting back to the boss, because the bearded man said in reply something neutral-sounding about *die Situation*, which Ned took to mean that they would carry on monitoring things. It didn't sound like they were planning anything drastic, anyway. Ned reflected with satisfaction on the steps he had taken today. The PI, the security firm, tracking them down to their base. These guys didn't realise that he was now at least one step ahead of them.

Ned had finished his beer and used up all his change, and the conversation had moved on to territory he couldn't get any bearings on at all. He stood up from his stool, called out *Ciao* without looking back, and made for the door.

N ED FELT A RUSH of freedom as he walked away from the casino. The situation was going to be okay. He didn't quite know how it would work out, but he knew it would. His investigator would get the low-down on them, his security guys would keep everyone safe. He could tell the team about the arrangements tomorrow, after the party, at the same time that they learned about the fire at Folasade's place. Anyway, no one but him knew for sure that the fire was anything to do with the Gliss situation. They might not even suspect it. The police didn't seem to think so, from what Folasade had said. It would all be fine. If people were worried, the security arrangements would head off their concerns.

Ned took off the cap, which was by now making his hair sweaty, and left it on a windowsill. Just down the street from the casino, he stopped to look at a construction site that covered a whole city block. Hoardings around the edge said it was going to be a block of luxury apartments, starting at 225,000 euros. The complex was being built using a crane that stood in the middle of the structure itself, and was gradually being swallowed up, as the higher storeys rose around it, by the very thing it had made. Ned wondered how they would eventually remove the crane from the middle. His dad would have been able to explain it to him, he knew. He took his phone out and was trying to get a good photo of it – the sun was coming from behind the building, making it difficult – when he heard a voice, close behind him: *'Mister Gliss, jah?'*

Ned started to turn, and then was made to spin around by Abdel's heavy hands on his shoulders. Before he knew it, he had been bundled down a quiet side street, and into an empty lot being used as a car park. He had fallen on his backside, pushed two-handed in the chest by Abdel. *'Bleib,'* Abdel said, in the voice you would use to tell a dog to stay.

Ned leaned back and propped himself up on his hands. He had scuffed up the knuckles on his right hand as he fell across the gravelly concrete. He felt oddly calm, almost as if this moment had been inevitable, the point towards which he and Abdel had been inexorably converging all week as they followed each other and were followed back across the city.

'You've got my trousers dirty,' Ned said.

'Was?'

'Du hast meine Hose schmutzig gemacht.'

Abdel laughed to himself, took out a packet of Camel

Blues, offered one to Ned, lit his own, and tossed Ned the lighter. They smoked in silence for a moment, before Abdel said, *'Bist du ins Casino gekommen?'*

Yes, Ned nodded, he had been in the casino.

Abdel grinned. *'Du bist total verrückt.'*

Totally crazy: he said it as if it were a term of praise. Ned shrugged. Yes, it probably was a mad thing he had done, and it had landed him here, sat on his arse being towered over by someone unafraid to kill people. Almost certainly he *had* killed people. Maybe it was Abdel who had done the job in Hasenheide, the one in the newspaper story. Ned asked him if he was part of the Miri clan, and he spat on the floor and said no, Al-Zein. Then, in English, 'Miri-clan, sons of bitches.' But he said it with a smirk, aware of playing a role. Ned felt as if he liked the guy. He seemed smart and funny. His gifts seemed underemployed, if he was just the muscle for the clan.

Ned finished his cigarette, pondered his options, and began a speech in halting German. The Thing Factory wouldn't stop running Gliss in Berlin, he said. It was a success. It was clear that the sex industry would be changed by digital at some point, and his organisation had been the ones to do it right. In the long run, there was nothing Al-Zein could do. If Gliss went away, someone else would come up with a copy of the idea, or an improvement on it, and the clan would have the same problem. So they needed to act like adults. They needed to act like businessmen. In fact, Ned said, his company were looking for new investors right now. So why didn't they work together? Al-Zein could buy into Gliss, and get their slice of the profit.

Ned paused. The mental effort of such a long speech in German was exhausting, and he wasn't sure how much of what he'd said was correct enough to be understood. He made a smoking gesture. Abdel took out his pack, lit another cigarette for himself, and flicked one down to Ned, who caught it cleanly in his hand.

As Abdel smoked he paced from side to side, thinking. He had an alternative proposition, he finally said. Al-Zein would allow Gliss to continue, at their standard rate of a forty per cent cut, and they would pay nothing. Al-Zein didn't pay.

So what did he get from the deal, asked Ned.

'*Der Schutz,*' Abdel said.

Protection. Of course.

Did you see what we did to the African girl? Abdel said. Then he made the noise of an explosion with his mouth, like a child playing at war movies.

Ned told him that she was a Londoner, not African.

Abdel stood smiling at him inanely, said that they could do the same to Ned, no problem, and pulled up his t-shirt to show Ned the black handgun tucked into his belt, riding just behind his hip.

The smoke from his cigarette felt good in Ned's lungs, heavy and harsh. He took a long draw on it, held it in for a second, breathed out in a long plume, and said, *'Wie heißt du?'*

'Abdel,' said Abdel, and looked perplexed when Ned let out a mad laugh.

'Und wie heißt der Boss? Mit dem großen Bart?'

'Abbas.'

'Abdel und Abbas,' Ned said. *'Brüder?'*

'Jah.'

Ned asked Abdel if he could give Abbas a message from him. Abdel shrugged. Ned waited until he asked what the message was, then said, *'Fick dich, Arschloch.'*

Keeping his stare fixed on Ned, Abdel reached under his t-shirt, removed the gun from his waistband, and pointed it at Ned's head.

3

FOUR MONTHS EARLIER, AFTER Tristan had told her that he thought social was ready to start publishing brand content, Alice moved quickly. She went to her three strongest contacts with potential clients – a clothing company called Rubric; the spiritual tourism company who ran the One-Month Monk programme that Daniel had told them about; and ACT!V!SMUS, a charity promoting environmental activism among the under-twenty-fives – and to each of them she presented a specially curated pitch, drawn up in collaboration with Tristan, Richard and Heather, the new social media manager. It showed a storyboard explaining The Thing Factory's method, a profile of the influencers they would use to promote the brand message, and projections for the scale of meaningful engagement the organisations could expect to generate in return for different levels of investment. Within a week, all three had agreed to come in at the highest level Alice had suggested.

There was a mood of excited anticipation at the first plenary since social went live. An intern was despatched with the company credit card and brought back a huge box of coffees, flapjacks and muffins. Alice felt a little nervous, but in control. She knew that she and Tristan were doing something special.

'Alice, Tristan,' Ned said, carefully peeling back the paper case from his triple-chocolate muffin, 'shall we start with social?'

'Sure,' Tristan said. 'There's a lot of stuff to report, but to keep it brief, we want to give you the big picture of major clients and where we're at with the deliverables, then drill down into one particular case study. We're currently working with three clients, the ones we mentioned last week. There's also a relationship that Alice has been working on with a really huge company, one that would really be a game changer for us. But we'll keep that under our hats for now.'

Alice watched Tristan as he carried on. It had made for a great few weeks, working so closely together. She knew they made a good team: the way they could bounce ideas off each other, energise each other, take up the slack from one another when needed, and often reached the same breakthrough at the same moment. The way they could make each other laugh, even when they were busier than they'd ever been. It made the pressure feel invigorating rather than stressful.

'So we've hit all our deadlines,' Tristan was saying, 'and we're getting to a place now where our client reports to them are able to communicate some significant wins. The impressions and likes and engagements we've got for the content have really wowed them, so everyone's super-impressed, and I think all three clients are keen to ramp it up and work in a bigger way with us. I don't want to jinx things, but we're potentially looking at six-figure commitments from at least two of the clients. But to put some meat on the bones of all this, I'm going to hand over to Alice to talk about the specificities of the client relationship with Rubric.'

'Thanks, Tris. So, Rubric, obviously you all know who they are. We're talking about a very forward-looking, youthful brand whose products are fashion-oriented but wearable and sporty, and who sell high-volume at high-street prices. They've been going two years, and something like Superdry would be a comparison of where they want to be in another few years. With them we focussed on eight of our influencers who all have a highly engaged following, some of them in the fashion vertical but others more broadly lifestyle and sport-oriented. From that, starting last Sunday evening, we managed to get eighteen million impressions, just over a million video views, and two million engagements for this really cool video that we made with them over at Teufelsberg, where you have the ruins of the old cold-war listening station with the big domes. I hope you've all watched the video by now, obviously it's a couple of freerunners doing their thing all over the site, which is a really edgy, spooky place, while wearing Rubric's jackets. And on the back of that we got the hashtag *guerrillagear* trending for a lot of Monday through Wednesday. Credit for that hashtag goes to Heather, who's done really great work on this campaign since she started, and it fits perfectly with the brand and the video — which was shot guerrilla-style, since I don't think anyone has permission legally to go up on Teufelsberg, let alone make a film there. There was a little bit of pushback from people commenting on how dangerous the video was, and it's true you could basically fall to your death at any moment up on the towers, but that didn't get much traction. And obviously the freerunners are from that urbex background where they'll do any daredevil thing you suggest to them.'

'I should add,' said Daniel, 'that they all signed non-liability agreements before the shooting, so they couldn't sue us if anything happened.'

'Indeed,' said Alice. Tristan sniggered, and Alice smiled to herself before carrying on. 'So Rubric seem really thrilled with what we've done, and we're now assessing how all this top-of-funnel activity, the impressions and engagements, is going to convert into mailing list sign-ups and actual sales. We don't want to rely on the vanity metrics. We're waiting for numbers from Rubric, and as we've said before, the relationship between top-of-funnel and sales is sometimes unpredictable, but when we get those numbers they'll inform how we think about our social campaigns going forward.'

'Brilliant, thanks,' said Ned vaguely. 'Any questions about any of that?'

A pause, before an intern said, 'Do we get any free clothes from them? I could do with a new jacket for the summer.'

'Ha, we did, actually,' said Tristan. 'I'm afraid all the samples were snaffled by the social team but if members of the Gliss team want some, maybe we could barter. I'll swap my bomber jacket for a freebie from one of your glamour models.'

'Naughty naughty,' Ned said. 'They're not glamour models; they're escorts. Although some of them are also glamour models.'

'Are there any upcoming events, any seasonal moments we should be thinking about for the next cycle?' Richard said.

'I'm not decided about this yet,' said Alice, 'but we're wondering about May Day, since there's such strong branding potential around that whole Kreuzberg, anti-capitalist vibe. We're looking into doing something to tie in with that for one of our edgier clients. Maybe Rubric, actually.'

In the next few weeks, clients started coming direct to

The Thing Factory wanting their services. Already it was more than they could take on. Alice and Tristan could choose their own clients, making sure to work only with companies for whom they knew they could get results. By the end of month one, they had brought in revenue equal to their total costs since starting up. The Thing Factory was becoming profitable.

Alice decided to reinvest the profits in expansion. They funded the development costs for Gliss, the expansion of the office into the annexe, and the hiring of four new colleagues to work in-house on client strategies and liaise with their content creators. This meant that The Thing Factory could take on more clients: by month three, they were working with nine companies.

When word got around in the industry about the results they were getting, the possibility of a huge deal emerged. Alice had been negotiating via an advertising broker with Fox Pop, the energy drink company, and when she went to Salzburg in early May to pitch to them, they came back and told her that they wanted more than she was offering. They were considering using The Thing Factory as their exclusive agency for social in Europe, and increasing their marketing split in that direction so that a third of their online advertising budget would go towards influencer marketing. When Alice finished her fourth call with the Fox Pop executive, Rolf, she called Tristan into the meeting room to tell him what Rolf had just told her. 'It looks like shit just got real,' Tristan said.

On the day after Alice's first meeting with Fox Pop, there was a general election in the UK. Everyone in the office had sent in their postal votes, and Alice organised an all-night election party in the annexe, with extra beanbags, crates of beer, wine and spirits, and dozens of pizzas ordered in. By eight o'clock, everyone was enjoying themselves, slightly drunk already. Buoyed by their own unstoppable success, they seemed sure that it would carry forward into a decisive victory for Ed Miliband. As they got more drunk, they produced more content on their personal channels, building up to a series of tweets in which Tristan re-enacted moments from the Miliband campaign: in one photo, he ate a sloppy bacon sandwich as it spewed brown sauce across his lips and chin; in another, he posed with a goofy grin and double thumbs up next to a cardboard imitation of the stone tablet on which Miliband's election pledges were chis-elled, modified in Tristan's version so that pledge five read 'Free bacon sarnies for all', and pledge six, 'State subsidies for having it large and being an absolute legend'. The tweets soon had tens of thousands of engagements.

Ned seemed subdued, to Alice. He wasn't drinking as freely as everyone else, or laughing at Tristan's jokes, and Alice reflected, not for the first time, on how awkward he was around Tristan. Really, it was good that he had diverted his attentions on to Gliss; she knew that social wouldn't have grown so fast, been executed so boldly, or been so much fun to work on, if she'd had to run the project with Ned. She congratulated herself on such a neat solution; it was with her encouragement that Ned had allowed the thought of diversifying to grow, and when he had arrived at the idea for a sex-work app he had thrown himself into it with new vigour, not seeming to realise that in removing himself from social he was carrying out something Alice had been manoeuvring him towards. Was that bad of her? No, surely not. Growth was growth, and the profits social was bringing in were transforming the value of Ned's fifty per cent share in the company as much as hers. It was good for him that social was a success, even if it necessitated him not working on it. Alice knew that they had diversified too early with Gliss. They'd effectively launched a new business within the existing one before it had established itself. It was crazy. But it also had its advantages, now she thought about it.

Actually, her reservations about Gliss itself were growing too. She'd been supportive of it in the early planning stages; in principle she thought it was good, it was in tune with her beliefs about supporting sex workers, all the things that her friend Rebecca had convinced her of years ago. But the reality of seeing the app developed and run from the office she worked in — that was something else. It meant that her working day involved constant encounters with pornography. Fair enough, people doing sex work needed to advertise their services to potential clients in the way that would be most attractive to them, but it meant that while Alice sat at a hot-desking spot working on a client's weekly report, there would be a grim discussion going on next to her about whether they should allow facial cum-shot pictures in the free galleries or restrict them to subscription content, whether they should allow bareback to be advertised on the app . . . She would wonder how this had become her life. At moments she even doubted her principles: yes, it was good to improve the autonomy, the safety, the knowledge-sharing capabilities of sex workers, but it was clear that lots of the profiles on the app were for Polish and Romanian escorts who almost certainly didn't have control of their own accounts or appointments. Lots of the profile texts were clearly written by the same people. What if The Thing Factory was making it easier for profiteers to exploit these women? What if the increased efficiency just meant that these women were compelled to see more clients a day, with most of the money still going to the men who managed the operation? Was that a price worth paying for improving conditions for the escorts who were truly independent? And what proportion of the industry did they make up? Alice really didn't know. When all those escorts had come in for the focus groups, it had seemed easy to accept the image of escorting as an autonomous choice taken by relatively empowered, well-educated women. But when she looked at the app, it seemed much less clear. And all the pornography in the office made her uneasy. What would Rolf from Fox Pop think when he came in for a meeting with his new agency partner and found people in the office flicking through galleries of gang-bang photographs to make sure they weren't being pirated from commercial online content? Well, that was something to deal with another day, but Alice knew the day would come soon. Gliss had to be separated from social. But she would let Ned get it up and running first.

When the exit poll was about to be revealed, the room fell silent. Big Ben rang. 'And here it is, ten o'clock,' David Dimbleby said, 'and we are saying that the Conservatives are the largest party.' The chimes carried on, and David Cameron's gormless face loomed on the left of a graphic dominated by a thick stripe of blue. 'And here are the figures which we have – quite remarkable, this exit poll – the Conservatives on 316, that's up nine since the last election in 2010. Ed Miliband for Labour, seventy-seven behind him at 239, down nineteen from the last election . . .'

The bells were still chiming but the mood in the room

had changed. Folasade had tears in her eyes, as an absurd graphic showed Cameron standing like a suited mannequin in a blue ring with 316 written on it, a miniature Miliband some way behind in his red ring. 'So that's the remarkable scene that our exit poll is revealing. We shall discover, when the first results start coming in, how accurate it is, but if that is the story, it is a quite sensational story.'

Everyone was silent until Tristan said, 'That's unbelievable. That's an actual majority, isn't it?'

'I think it's enough to form a government.'

'Hang on, they're explaining it.'

A computer mock-up of the Houses of Parliament had appeared on screen, the benches populated by video-game MPs who occasionally twitched or moved their hands to show they were alive.

'Right, I'm going to bed,' Ned said blankly, and stood up to leave.

It felt as if all the air had been sucked out of the room. They watched the coverage in captivated flatness, moving from a defiant optimism that they knew to be false when the early results from northern constituencies came in, to an appalled fascination as it became clear that the scale of the defeat for the Labour party was in fact larger, even worse, than the exit poll had predicted. A drinking game started, in which they drank a shot of Sambuca each time the Conservatives took another ten seats, and when the Sambuca ran out, they moved on to Pfeffi, the peppermint spirit that Alice found completely foul. She choked it back with a wince as each seat fell.

By three o'clock, the crowd was starting to thin. Everyone had been given the next morning off but for most of the staff, an all-nighter after a long day's work was unappealing. Soon Alice and Tristan were the last two remaining, lying back next to each other on beanbags in the darkened annexe with the large screen casting ghoulish light effects across their faces. They decided they might as well stay up for the speeches.

Alice had grown bored of the election coverage. The steady trickle of seats had become an implacable tide of Conservative victories, the map filling itself out in near-unbroken blue all across England, with only London standing out, a red island stranded in the sea. With the constant, repetitive attempts by the presenters to keep the conversation going, rotating between any pundits and politicians they could get their hands on, all of them saying the same stunned and yet cautious things . . . Tristan and Alice shifted into talking about work; about client strategies; about the Fox Pop deal, and whether they should tell more people in the team about it, or share it with Ned; about the future. Tristan said that they should throw a party, a proper party, to celebrate the first quarter of their work with clients. Alice liked the idea, and they spoke about venues. Tristan favoured the top of the TV Tower.

'Once Gliss is bedded in and financing itself,' Alice said, 'what role do you see Ned having on social?'

'Hmm,' said Tristan. 'It's tricky.'

'Say more.'

'I mean, I don't want to be disloyal. He gave me my job, right? And social was his idea initially.'

'We developed it together,' Alice said. 'And we put in the founder capital equally. I agree, though, that it's hard to see a role for him going forward.'

'I didn't say that.'

'I'm saying it. It's tricky, is what I mean. Social's running perfectly at the moment, and I can't see a way of bringing him back in that doesn't derail that.'

'But he does own half the company.'

'He does.'

Pause.

'So what are you thinking about it?'

Alice took a deep breath and sipped her wine. 'I'm thinking I'll puke if I keep on mixing my drinks.'

'Lol.'

'What I'm really thinking is this – but you can't tell this to anyone.'

'Cub's honour.'

'We need to change the management structure. Well, we need to do several things. And we need to do them soon. First, we need to disaggregate Gliss. It fucks up the brand, and I don't think it'll even make serious money. So that should be a separate company, and Ned can have it. I don't like it.'

'I agree. I know we're all pro-sex workers and all that, but it's actually kind of . . . weird, isn't it?'

'It's toxic. So if we can move that aside . . . I think we actually need to do something bolder with the management structure as well. And the ownership structure. Gosh, it sounds big when I say it aloud. Basically – you can't tell anyone this – but basically I've been talking to this M&A advisor—'

'Mixed Martial Arts?'

'Mergers and Acquisitions, doofus. With our growth and our uniqueness, he's pretty confident we could find investors for, like, crazy amounts. Millions and millions. And millions.'

'What, you're looking to sell the business?'

Alice paused for a long time, and a smile played across her face. 'Not exactly. I'm looking to have Ned sell his half. He'll sell his fifty per cent to a venture capital firm, we'd get a massive injection of capital, and we could take on dozens and dozens of clients. We could open offices in the UK and the US. It would explode. If we can get a foothold now in the US, in the UK, while our idea is still unique and people are scrambling to catch up with us, that's much more important than the bottom line. We can deliver the geography, so we'll be generating value and not just income. Then I'd be sole CEO, I'd get a proper management board with some really experienced people on it, a supervisory board, and you could be COO—'

'Wow.'

'— then below you, we'd have a structure of directors — like a finance director, creative, campaigns, legal. Some of them could be filled in-house by Fola or Daniel or whoever, but we'd hire in the best people as well.'

'Ned doesn't know about any of this?'

Alice tilted on to her side on the beanbag to face Tristan, her body almost touching his now. 'You can't tell him. I need to present it to him as a *fait accompli*.'

'Why would he want to sell though?'

'If I present it to him the right way, I don't think he'll have a choice.'

'Sounds a bit Machiavellian.'

Alice laughed. 'Let's just say there are things I know about Ned that put me in a strong position to give him no choice.'

'I'm gonna make you an offer you can't refuse,' said Tristan in a strangulated voice.

'That's a really lame impression.'

'What is it you've got on him? Is Ned a paedo or something?'

Alice threw her head back on the beanbag and silently laughed. 'No, not that. You realise that's my ex you're talking about?'

'Sorry, lol.'

Alice wondered whether she should tell Tristan how Ned had raised his half of the seed money for the company. Would it make sense to Tristan? It seemed like a lot of effort, to explain the different scams Ned had been running in the time she'd known him. She decided not to. Not yet.

'No, but there are things about his past that could get him in serious trouble, or at least force him to resign. I'll present it to him as, either you accept this buy-out or I make these things known. And it'll be simple: either he can be totally disgraced, and maybe face some serious legal difficulties, or he can take five million quid for his fifty per cent.'

'Not a bad dilemma to have,' said Tristan. 'I won't ask for the dirt on him.'

'Best not. But anyway, what do you think: would you like to be COO?'

'Coo, coo,' said Tristan, flapping his hands.

'Is that a dove?'

'Wood pigeon. Same diff. Yeah, I think I could handle that. But we'd have to talk about my package.'

They were both giggling now, and couldn't stop; it was infectious, and their excitement built up rather manically, and Tristan was tickling Alice around her ribs and hips, and she was squealing and play-fighting back, and she shifted her weight on to him, laying her arms across his chest, and they were kissing.

Soon they both had their t-shirts off. Tristan had taken Alice's bra off and was kissing her breasts while she sat on top of him and rocked slowly back and forth against the hard-on she could feel in his jeans. He lay his head back down, looked up at her with a smile, and said, 'Babes?'

'Yeah?'

'I think we should leave this for now.'

Alice pouted with pretended disappointment and said, 'What's the matter, don't you like my boobies?' looking down at them appraisingly.

'I love your boobies, I want to marry your boobies. But I think we should wait for a time when we're not completely pissed. And it's not five in the morning. And the Tories haven't just won an election.'

'It does seem like a bad omen.'

'Big time. Although in fairness, it could work out okay for top-rate taxpayers.'

She scooted her weight further down his legs so she could lean in and kiss him, and twisted round to lie on her back next to him on the beanbag. 'You're probably right though,' she said. She found her phone on the carpet, scrolled through her alerts, scanning some desolate texts from friends in the UK and a goading one from her jubilant father – god, he was such a wanker – then opened the camera app and extended her arm above them. Their image appeared on the screen. The TV's light flattered them. 'For posterity,' she said. Tristan stared broodingly down the lens for the first picture, and leaned across to nuzzle at her breast with a deranged expression on his face for the second.

'We look naked. You cropped out the fact that we kept our jeans on.'

'Our little secret,' Alice said.

Around seven in the morning, when they had their shirts back on and were drinking strong coffees, David Cameron spoke at his constituency, more or less declaring his victory.

'This is pretty fucked,' Tristan said after a silence. 'Do you think he'll really call a referendum on the EU?'

'That was just to appease all those weird back benchers.

Osborne would never let it actually happen. It's made so much money for everyone, and things like this' – she gestured vaguely outwards with her right hand to indicate the office, Berlin, the whole life they were living – 'nobody would vote to give up being able to come and live out here. Or to retire to the Costa del Sol or wherever.'

ALICE HAD HAD TWO meetings already with her M&A advisor, David Singh from Bishop & Morley. He knew her father, and had given her his card when they met socially at a family party last year, and she decided to arrange a lunch with him when the Fox Pop deal first arose as a possibility. Late April. The restaurant at the Ritz-Carlton. *Flammkuchen* with bacon from apple-fed pigs, followed by suckling pig in the Baden style. Wine from glasses with six-inch stems. She could get used to this, she thought. When she told David about the Fox Pop interest, he puffed out his cheeks and said, 'What you're describing here is truly explosive early growth. I've only ever seen it in a handful of businesses in my career. It's exactly what VC firms go nuts for. But there are things you need to sort out in order to be ready for that. Some of them might be tough.'

'Such as?'

'You need to have the right management team in place. The right structure. And if need be, you sideline the current team. You need to be ruthless. You need the structure to be clear and effective, but most importantly you need it to be made up of the very best people for the roles. It's tough to do, but if your team can't take the business to the next level, they need to be changed. Bought out, paid off, sacked, whatever.'

'And what if they're the co-founder?'

'Tricky. But do-able. You can make them non-executive, make them a sleeping partner. You can buy them out. Or you do a part-sale. Some of the VC cash goes to your partner to buy him out, and the rest goes into the business for expansion.'

'Hmm,' said Alice.

She had hardly spoken to Ned that week: Gliss was about to launch internationally, and he was running around the place dealing with that. She wondered how she would tell him she wanted him to sell up his half of the company.

'And as well as getting the management sorted, you need to get your data in place,' David said. 'Finances, track record, projections. Everything needs to be clear, to present it to investors. Do you have confidence in your finance director?'

'We have a finance and legal officer, Daniel. But he's not a director.'

'Is he good?'

'I think so.'

'Okay, step one, get him in the loop. Tell him he's in line to be finance director in the new structure. Then get him to gather it all together. It's a big job. I could bring in someone to help with it, if you like.'

'Maybe, yeah,' Alice said. She would have to get Daniel to prepare the information without letting Ned know he was doing it.

'And I can bring in a professional plan writer to work with you on the IM.'

'What's IM again?'

'Information Memorandum. The document that goes to investors. I've got this fantastic woman I use who's done hundreds of them. Once we've got the IM ready, I can take it to market, and I'd say venture capital is where you want to look first. VC lives for this kind of thing: explosive growth, untested, high-risk, but also high potential reward. And they can go big. In fact, for a serious VC firm, it's as much effort to invest two million as it is to do ten million, with the legal stuff, the due diligence, so they prefer to go big. Lot of them won't do anything under two mill. If you want a fast, bold injection of cash, they're your guys.'

'I actually have a contact there already,' Alice said. 'Yuri Martin and Aytan Khlebnikov.'

She had met them in the spring at a networking event, and ended up staying out for too many Old Fashioneds with them at Scotch & Sofa in Prenzlauer Berg afterwards, by the end of which they seemed to be trying to recruit her to come and work for them.

'Oh, Yuri and Aytan from Eccola? Fantastic. They're serious.'

When his brown eyes fixed on her, she saw an amusement in them, an appetite, and a challenge thrown down that she was determined to meet. She wanted to live in David's world, a world where deals worth tens of millions could be spoken of with playful, calm composure. He spoke about the task of finding a buyer for Ned's share as if it were a game he would barely need to exert himself over.

'This all sounds great. But can I ask how much it's all going to cost? From your end, I mean.'

'Now we're talking. I charge a success fee, which is based on the eventual sale price, and also a retainer. That would kick in immediately, if we go ahead.'

He took a fountain pen from his pocket, scribbled on the back of the credit card receipt, and passed it across the table to Alice, hidden under his fingers. She took it from him and slid it into her jacket pocket. 'I'll read that later.'

'Okey-dokey. Well, let me know. I can bring all the advisors in. The people I've mentioned but also the account-ants, the lawyers. The whole team. And then I would go out and fight to get the best deal for you. I'll be the gladiator you send into the ring. I'll be your nomad—'

'My what?'

'Ha, your nominated advisor.'

'Nomad. Very good. The thing I still don't understand though is why you're so confident that investors would be interested. We've only been in profit for two months.'

'What makes this high reward is the quality of the proposition. That's what you're selling. You're doing something no one else is doing exactly, because you've understood something about social media that the bigger agencies haven't grasped yet.'

'What's that?'

'The key point is the first thing you said to me: the importance of micro. You've understood how marketing today is about the micro-scale, micro-influencers who can target consumers in very precise ways. That's where you and Tristan make the other agencies look like dinosaurs.'

Alice glowed in the flattering light of David's redescription of what she had said to him. Yes, that was right, wasn't it? She hadn't put it to herself quite as plainly as that before, but David made it seem perfectly clear. She liked the open-collared eloquence with which he assessed the situation, equally in command of the big picture and the details. Over the next month, she worked hard at putting her plans into place. The more dealings she had with David, the more impressive she found him. She liked his way of shifting from polite small talk into decisive shop talk with perfect timing, then shifting back out again once two or three key questions had been addressed. Alice felt like she was learning from him, and she had taken on his manner of using snatches of jargon with a dry awareness of their silliness: SWOT analysis and sweat equity, EBITDAs and BIMBOs. When David knew that an important detail had been worked out, he would say briskly, 'Nice one, Cyril,' and immediately turn to some remark about the restaurant or the menu or what Alice thought he should do with his afternoon in Berlin, though she knew full well that he was flying straight back to London after the meeting.

David began sounding out potential investors in mid-May after their third meeting, getting each of them to sign Non-Disclosure Agreements before discussions began. Alice was paying his retainer already; he had brought in his plan writer to help Alice with the information memorandum. There was no turning back from this now, she knew. Within a month, David said, he could have found the best buyer and negotiated the sale, leaving only the due diligence to be completed. But due diligence could take months and months, he warned.

Alice was considering how to handle the moment when she would present the proposition to Ned. What she would do, she thought, was to tell Ned they needed to have a lunch meeting, and in the car on the way to the restaurant she would ask him if he ever worried about anyone connecting the fake steroids, the fake diet pills, or the rainforest scam to him. He would be surprised by the question, she thought – they hadn't mentioned any of that in months. He might be defensive, but more likely jokily dismissive of the idea. He seemed to have totally compartmentalised these things, made himself forget they had even happened. He had convinced himself he was just a regular entrepreneur. In the car, she would then say something like, maybe they should make an exit plan from the business, think about selling up, in case there were ever any comeback – just to plant the seed of the idea. No doubt Ned would laugh it off. But then they would arrive at the restaurant and David would be there with one of his lawyers, ready to present Ned with a fully worked-out offer for his half of the company and the plan for the management restructure. The implication of the talk in the car would be clear, without Alice needing to make any explicit threat.

She was thinking about all this and texting with David – good progress was being made on the buyer front – on the day that Ned's dad was taken into hospital. This changed things. When Ned flew back to London and told her that his father was in a coma, that he was likely to die, that he had died, Alice doubted whether she was doing the right thing. On the one hand, they'd known each other for years now, they had a history and a closeness, and The Thing Factory had been Ned's idea in the first place. It was his idea too to put in all the start-up capital themselves rather than bringing in third-party equity, so that they owned all of the business. She owed him a lot for that. It would be a clear betrayal, to cut him out now, and when his father had just died as well.

On the other hand, she wasn't fully convinced that Ned would actually experience grief for his father at all. He seemed able to insulate himself from his own feelings, as if he could simply decide not to feel them. And he was a liability for the company in so many other ways. He said that no one could possibly trace the scams back to him, that it was all safely encrypted, that the money had been cleaned – but how could Alice be sure of this? The more successful the company became, the more their images appeared in the media, the greater the risk became. What's more, the way that Ned had thrown himself into Gliss was a red light in itself. It diverted resources away from the core activities of the business, it barely added to the bottom line, and it posed the danger of serious reputational damage.

And it wasn't as if she were planning to turn him out on the streets, or in to the police. He would be paid for his fifty per cent, he deserved it, and it would make him a very wealthy man by any standard. Yes, she had to go through with it. Now might even be a more opportune moment to act, if Ned was going to be doubly distracted, by Gliss and by his father's death. She and Tristan were going to Salzburg again next week; it was possible the Fox Pop deal could be sealed that soon.

In the weeks since they had started sleeping together, Alice and Tristan's relationship had become deeper and more intimate, and Alice felt she had seen a different side of him, not jokey at all but in fact rather earnest, moral and old-fashioned. She liked it. She liked his surprising capacity for taking his own life seriously, making reasoned decisions about how to spend his time in ways that would increase his happiness. On the morning after the first night they spent together, she had come into the kitchen to find him sitting over his iPad with an intent look on his face, and when she asked him what he was up to, he said that since he had a busy few weeks ahead, with work and a stand-up gig he was doing – his first in months – he was planning some fun things: a hike out to Teufelsberg; a day at a lake with friends from the stand-up scene; a round of crazy golf with his ex; and did Alice want to go to the opera next weekend? Yes, she would love to. Tristan started telling her about Handel's *Jephtha* – in fact it was an oratorio, not an opera, he'd never seen it before but there was one particular aria he loved – and Alice found herself staring at him in delighted amusement. 'What's so funny?' he said.

'It's just a long way from what you normally listen to. What was that song you were playing the other day – "Barbie Girl"?'

'By Aqua. A flawless masterpiece. But yes, I like Handel too. Feel free to be touched that I'm showing you my unexpected depths.'

Alice came to stand behind him, putting her hands on his shoulders and leaning her torso into his back as he pressed back against her. 'I like being shown them.'

It pleased her to see how straightforwardly he was able to plan pleasures for himself; to think about what he wanted, what would make him happy, and to do it. Like with the idea for the party to celebrate the first quarter of social. That had been arranged for the first week in June. The TV Tower was unavailable so they had gone for the observation deck at the top of the Panoramapunkt. Everyone was excited about it. 'I'm a fan of organised fun,' Alice said. Tristan tilted his head back and Alice leaned in for an upside-down kiss.

Three weeks later, Alice was going over the pros and cons of the Ned situation on a page from a yellow legal pad which she had divided into two columns, sitting in the bar-café on the street where she lived, when Tristan arrived to meet her. They were both working from home this morning. Since the night of the election party, they had seen each other every day, and were in constant message contact. When Alice went to work in the bar-café, Tristan crossed town from Wedding to Prenzlauer Berg to meet her so they could head into work together after lunch. He messaged her stop by stop updates on the progress of his journey – 'At Prinzenallee', 'Just pulling out of Prinzenallee', 'Approaching Schönhauser, arriving in T minus 10 mins', 'Knaackstr: T minus 5' – then when he walked in the door, he said, 'Surprise!'

'What a coincidence.'

'Yeah, I was in the hood, so . . .' Tristan sat, took his denim jacket off, lowered it over the back of his chair, and pointed to Alice's glass. 'Is that fizzy rhubarb?'

'Watermelon and mint. It's nice.'

Tristan leaned in, slurped from Alice's straw, and nodded. 'I'll pass.'

'I'm going to have a mushroom omelette.'

'A very good choice,' Tristan said in the voice of a waiter.

They ordered and ate. Tristan told Alice about the thoughts he'd had that morning on the Fox Pop strategy, and she told him about her latest discussions with David

Singh. Tristan said he'd heard that Ned was coming back to Berlin that weekend.

'I've been thinking about that,' Alice said. 'My plan is to talk to him next Wednesday after the plenary about disaggregating Gliss. I can present that as simply a sensible thing to do, I think, and he won't guess that it's part of a larger move. I think they'll actually have some profits to report from Gliss on Wednesday. The international uptake has increased. So if they announce that, I can explain the need to hive Gliss off in a way that plays into the positive momentum around it.'

'How close is David to finding a buyer?'

'Close. It could be a matter of weeks. He's marketed it pretty widely and he says there's four interested parties who are serious. I know one of them actually, it's the VC group run by these guys Aytan and Yuri who I met with in the spring.'

'So is it going to be an auction-type scenario?'

'Potentially. But David doesn't just want the people who'll pay the most money. He's looking for who's going to bring the most excellence to the business too.'

'Very wise. How's your omelette?'

'A bit rubbery.'

'Have some of mine if you like. The brunch portions are insane.'

After lunch, Alice and Tristan made their way into the office, where they spent the afternoon overseeing three new client strategies. Ned returned to Berlin that weekend, and on Monday Alice thought that he seemed distant at work. He didn't want to talk about his father's death or the funeral, though Folasade told Alice that he'd opened up to her a bit about it, when they walked into work together that morning. He seemed evasive on work details as well; he hardly seemed to be listening when Alice updated him on social. It was understandable, she supposed. But she felt like he was cutting himself off from her in a way that went beyond what one might expect from a grieving or a depressed person. It seemed like he was absenting himself, somehow holding reality at bay, even while he was standing there in front of you.

The next day Alice met with David again and they spoke more about the management structure. 'You'll want some non-executive directors,' David said. 'NEDs, for short. Ironically. Guys with proven experience and expertise.'

'Or girls.'

'Quite. But some grown-ups who've been there and done it all, basically. So your board might be made up of, for example, the CEO, the COO, the FD, the MD, and several NEDs. The chairman could even be a NED. In some ways it's better to have a non-exec chairman, because he can bring outside perspective to things. Plus, with experienced non-exec board members, you get the benefit of their little black books. That's a huge thing. You get their contacts, their squash partners, their pals from the college rowing team, the boys who had to warm their beds at Eton who are now cabinet ministers. When you have that network, you're in business.'

He briefed her on the progress of the sale. When Alice questioned him on the asking price he had in mind, he said, 'We don't ask. We wait for their offer. Last time I did this, the client wanted twenty million and I advised him not to say a word. Don't give it away. He held his nerve, the first offer was thirty-seven million, and we settled for forty-two. Essentially it's all about the multiple. The value is calculated as a multiple of your profits, and you could potentially achieve a big multiple because of the speed of your growth and having the Fox Pop deal in the works.'

'What's a big multiple?'

'Practically no limit, in this scenario. Ten. Twenty. Thirty isn't unheard of.'

'Thirty times the monthly profit?'

'That's adorable. No, thirty times the projected *annual* profit.'

Alice attempted a quick calculation in her head but

couldn't tell, after two glasses of wine, if she had the right number of zeroes.

After the lunch, Alice stopped in a bar-café to gather her thoughts. Things were moving quickly. She ordered a fresh ginger tea and took out the notebook in which she had been writing things from her meetings with David. *NEDs, multiple based on annual profit.* She felt a moment of doubt as to whether she could do this, and decided with a flourish that she could. David made her feel as if she could. The waiter was approaching with her tea; Roxy Music were playing on the speakers, 'In Every Dream Home a Heartache'; in the other corner of the room a couple were deep in conversation – and Alice started with a panicking sense of recognition. She snuck a second look. Christ, yes, it was him, that dreadful guy she had slept with back in January. He was sitting with a woman. Denim jackets, healthy smiles, laughing at each other across the menu. It was definitely him. Alice angled her body away, buried her face in her phone while groping in her jacket pocket for a note. She came up with a ten, twisted between her fingers. It was a lot to pay for a tea she hadn't even sipped, but better than hanging around for change. She slipped it under the edge of the saucer, stood up and walked out, without looking back. The waiter called out *'Ciao'* and then 'Thank you!' in an amused voice – clearly he had found the three hundred per cent tip – but Alice was gone already. She walked fast to the corner, turned, walked on another block, and took the next right, only stopping to look back when she was three streets away.

She felt queasy. Of course, the city was large, but the ex-pat world was much smaller; she was always going to bump into him sooner or later. It felt like a reminder of something, a dark, self-thwarting version of herself that she preferred to think of as far in the past. She didn't know why she had done it. He had been awful over dinner, talking over her about his guns and his record label, obnoxious and boring; she had been longing to get away from him; and then she had gone back to his flat in Mitte and fucked him, and done it twice more in the next fortnight. Christ, imagine if he had been there in the restaurant while she was meeting with David – if he had come over and said hello, and she'd had to make a polite, awkward introduction between them. Her mind blanked at the prospect.

At the weekly plenary two days later, the Gliss team became wrapped up in a bizarre discussion of some prank emails they had been receiving. Alice had no patience with the whole thing, it was ridiculous. Of course, she thought, if you start messing around in online sex work you'll start receiving messages from weirdos. The notion that they should go to the police with them was ridiculous. And anyway, the last thing she needed while David was negotiating the sale was for the police to start paying attention to them. What if they looked into how Ned's start-up money was raised, or pressed the question of Gliss's legality. It might be fine in Germany and the Netherlands, but surely running an escort app in France and the UK was pretty dubious, even with the fig leaf of the disclaimer saying that people were only paying for the escorts' time. Alice stepped into the conversation and told them firmly that they ought not to go to the police. That seemed to settle things.

As everyone was leaving the meeting room, she took Ned aside. She wanted to speak to him in private, she said. Now was a good time for him. He was stuffing his face with a muffin or something, and wasn't even looking at her when she said, 'I think at some point we need to make a decision about the structure of the company.'

That got his attention. She explained to him the need to disincorporate Gliss from The Thing Factory. He seemed to take it pretty well, but it was hard to judge. When she mentioned the amount of money potentially at stake, he said 'fuck' softly under his breath. Alice wasn't sure he had properly taken it in, but he said he would think about it. That was a start. As he left the room, Alice thought: you don't know the half of it.

Tristan came into the meeting room and took a brownie from the tray bake. 'How was it?'

'I'm not sure,' said Alice. 'I think he'll be persuadable about hiving off Gliss. He didn't seem to be strongly against the idea. Just a bit surprised.'

'He doesn't seem very with it.'

'No.'

'I guess his dad has just died.'

Alice gently pushed Tristan into the space behind the door, hidden from the view of the main office, and put her hands around his waist. 'How are you feeling about tonight?'

It was the night of his gig at a comedy club in Wedding.

'Got a few flutterbys. There's some new bits in the set tonight that I'm not sure about.'

Four hours later, Alice sat watching Tristan doing his bit about Club-Mate. In truth, she didn't find it especially funny. The delivery was good, Tristan himself was funny, though the material seemed over-rehearsed to her. But she always thought this about stand-up. She liked comedians, but not stand-up comedy; she liked them on podcasts, talking, riffing, and bouncing off other people. She liked it when associations would spontaneously gather and chime with each other in moments of rightness that came from nowhere and lasted a second. Whereas stand-up felt un-realised, to her: it wasn't written and refined enough to be good in the way that writing or drama were good, and it was too stilted to have the energy of talk.

The acts who had come on before Tristan were dismal. That first guy, an uncharismatic Londoner doing observational stuff on the differences between German and English. Bits that weren't even true. Germans, he said, didn't make jokes in the same way British people did. He acted out an English person jokily, nervously apologising for a mistake, saying, 'Ooh, sorry, why did I do that? I'm must be going mad!' and then a stern-faced German looking back at him and saying, 'I am sorry to hear that you are experiencing mental health problems.' The guy was dying on his feet, and he didn't even seem to realise it. His own friends were barely laughing. At least Tristan had presence, in comparison. Even if some of his material was just okay, he had star quality. Alice was asking herself whether she would still have thought this if she wasn't sleeping with him, when he said, 'My girlfriend doesn't like Club-Mate.' That got her attention. Then Tristan was saying, 'Gosh, it tastes like stale cigarettes,' in the voice he used when he was teasing her for being so posh. He was staring straight at her.

It wasn't cool, to do that in front of the whole team. But

Alice couldn't help smiling. To her right, she could sense Ned's agitation. She realised without looking at him that he was getting up and leaving. Well, it was out now. Alice found that she couldn't be annoyed with Tristan, even though she had wanted to break the news of their relationship to the team herself. The moment when his eyes had found hers from the stage, and he'd said, 'Sorry, baby' with a sparkle in his eye, sent a shiver through her. She admired the cockiness of the gesture, the deliberate fuck-you to Ned that it represented, and she liked the thought of her lover ('girlfriend' had been his word, not a word they had used to each other yet but, yes, okay) – she liked the thought of her boyfriend causing her ex to cringe away into the darkness at the back of the room. Fuck it, let him cringe, and let the rest of the team know that they were together. They could be a power couple. Tristan had used that phrase ironically when they were talking in bed yesterday, but Alice liked the idea.

Folasade had leaned over to her and brought her mouth up to Alice's ear. 'Three words: Oh. Em. Gee!'

Alice turned to her and raised an eyebrow.

Tristan had moved into his next bit now. Alice knew this was the last part of his set. From his discovery of Club-Mate, he had segued into things he found strange about the city. 'So when I get here, I'm looking for an apartment, right?

And I find this terrific place in Wedding – really nice, high ceilings, two balconies, courtyard, all the good stuff – and it's only seven hundred a month. And the landlord says to me,' (he slid into a thick German accent), 'he said, *Jah, you know, this is not such an expensive price, but we are deciding it because it will be* unmöbliert, *jah?*'

This drew laughs from the crowd. Alice knew that Tristan considered accents and impressions to be cheap ways of getting laughs, but here it worked pretty well. The room was with him. He asked the audience, '*Unmöbliert auf Englisch?*' and someone obligingly called out, 'Unfurnished!'

'*Genau,*' Tristan said. '*Unmöbliert,* unfurnished. So I thought: *Kein Problem.* KP. It's a great apartment, great place, I'll just get a van, whizz round IKEA, bed, mattress, futon, cheap table, folding chairs, five hundred euros. KP. And the day to move in arrives. Get up bright and early. Feeling all excited. Off to get the keys. Doing my Instagram story about moving-in day, my Snapchats, all excited. Lovely stuff . . . And I open the door and there's nothing. It's all gone. "Unfurnished", he called it. Right. They've taken the oven out, and left a bare gas pipe poking out of the wall. They've taken the fridge. They've taken the sink out. The curtains, the lampshades. The kitchen cabinets. Get this: they've unscrewed the fucking *light bulbs.* How much is a light bulb – one euro fifty? Oh no, sir, we couldn't possibly let you keep those. And I'm wandering around, genuinely unsure whether I've been totally ripped off, or whether there's been some sort of very localised apocalypse. Because the whole place is wiped out. Everything gone. A bare landscape. But what you've got to imagine is an apocalypse that's also remarkably clean. Because the place is spotless. The apocalypse has scrubbed the floors, hoovered, dusted along the picture rail.'

(There was a constant rolling wave of laughter from the crowd.)

'Anyway, I've now got a one-year rental contract, 700 a month, six weeks' deposit, and not only do I have to buy everything, I've got to get the kitchen fitted and the pipes plumbed in. I've basically got to do a new-build. And what am I going to do in a year's time when I move out? Rip it all out again? Sell it? And then I thought . . . I know! I'll open a fucking reclamation yard. I'll rival IKEA!'

People were laughing hard now. Tristan looked at the person who had shouted out earlier and said to her, 'There's one for your vocab: *Wie sagt man "reclamation yard" auf Deutsch?*'

After a pause, an answer that Alice couldn't make out over the laughter came back from the darkness behind her.

'And on that note, I've been Tristan Rodgers, thank you very much, and goodnight!'

As he walked off stage, he blew kisses to the crowd and mimed picking long-stemmed roses out from a bouquet and throwing them out. The audience gave him a barrage of claps and whoops, held up by continuing laughter.

After the gig, everyone went for more drinks. Tristan seemed happy but drained. In the hubbub of the bar, he and Alice found a quieter corner where they could talk. She stroked his back. 'I remember that feeling. Tired but wired. My approach was always just to take loads of coke after a performance.'

'Yeah. I could go for a bit of coke and a bit of heroin at the same time.'

'Might be tricky to source. I could probably get you a Modafinil and a Valium.'

'Ha, yes, please. The low-fat alternatives.'

Alice kissed him. It felt good, it felt liberating, to do that without worrying who saw them. Across the table, Folasade had her phone out and pretended to take a photo of them. 'You've been papped. I'll sell that straight to the *Daily Star*. Start-Up Boss in Staff Snog Shock.'

'Nice to CEO You,' said Richard.

Tristan feigned throwing a scrunched-up napkin at them. The conversation passed on to other matters. People were excited about the Panoramapunkt party tomorrow, and discussed what to wear; the performances of the four comics on the bill tonight were discussed, with a general agreement that Tristan had been the best; the question of why Ned had left early was raised, and then tactfully let drop. Tristan and Alice kept quiet on that one. Folasade said she was going to head home. Richard tried to convince people to head on to somewhere they could dance, but it was clear that the tide had turned. Within twenty minutes, everyone had gone their separate ways.

ALICE WOKE FEELING SURPRISINGLY fresh the next morning. She was first into the office, and on the way she made a list of her tasks for the day on her phone. There was a lot to do. They had to send off five client reports today and have Skype meetings with a further three clients. She had to give a written warning to a content creator who had failed to meet the deadline for his deliverables, causing Tristan to scramble to do the work himself last week. She had to liaise with the people at Panoramapunkt about the party tonight; to check that all the client, partner and sector guests were still coming, and happy with their arrangements; and to prepare for the party herself. And she needed something to wear.

By mid-morning, neither Ned nor Folasade had shown their faces. A message came from Folasade on Cubicle saying that she was taking a personal day. This was annoying, frankly, if it meant she wasn't coming to the party, and Alice was unimpressed. She sighed heavily. And where was Ned? Was he in a sulk with her about Tristan? It was childish.

Alice worked through her tasks steadily. Everyone had

completed their draft reports on time, and she had only a few improvements to suggest before signing them off. One of the interns worked her way down the list of key guests for tonight, confirming with their assistants that they were all set to arrive in Berlin on time, and Alice phoned David Singh to check he was still coming, and to tell him that she had broached the idea of disaggregating Gliss with Ned, but hadn't told him anything more. It would be odd, having David there without being able to acknowledge to anyone except Tristan how far advanced the deal was. She liked the idea of introducing David to Ned as simply a valuable contact she had made, with Ned having no idea that they had met five times over the last few weeks, and been in constant contact. Why was that so pleasing to her? She puzzled at it. Maybe it was because she knew how highly Ned valued having secrets of his own.

At lunchtime Alice had her hair styled at a salon, dealing with messages throughout the process, then took a car to the Mall of Berlin, put a black dress and a new pair of shoes from Armani on her credit card, and headed back to the office. It amused her how everyone drank bottles of beer on the U-Bahn, right in front of signs saying that it was forbidden to drink alcohol on the transport network – signs undermined by the fact that alcoholic drinks were sold from kiosks on the station platforms. Like how everyone smoked in bars in the evening, right in front of the no-smoking signs. It seemed very Berlin, making so many rules in order that everybody could break them.

When she got back to the office it was half past three. Leroi at Panoramapunkt had been in touch to confirm final details on the party, and Alice phoned him back. The client reports had all been sent. There was a new development: Rolf Warsheimer, the Fox Pop executive she had been dealing with, was coming to the party. This was a good sign. Maybe the deal would be ready to confirm. Alice almost couldn't allow herself to think it, it seemed to be tempting fate. At around half past four a hitch arose, when Leroi phoned to say that the singer from the band they had booked had a sore throat, but within thirty minutes an understudy had been lined up, and ten minutes after that, the original singer confirmed that he'd be okay to perform.

Anyway, where the fuck was Ned? Around five o'clock Alice had a message from him: he'd been working from home, he said, and was now 'brainstorming in a caff'. Alice typed 'WTF', deleted it, wrote, 'You know the party starts in two hours?' and found herself so angry at him that she deleted that too. Fuck it, let him hang. This was her night. If he came, he would probably only say something weird to an important guest, or start talking about sex work.

Soon it was time to leave for the venue. She was meeting

Leroi there at 06:15 to check the set-up. When she arrived in the car with Heather, the place looked splendid. They paused in the foyer, looking up at acres of highly polished marble, and Heather said, 'This is a bit of glitz and glamour, isn't it?'

'Get used to it. Apparently they have the fastest lift in Europe.'

Upstairs, Alice found Leroi. The lift up twenty-four storeys had been very fast. The caterers, waiters, and technicians for the band were busy at work. Everything seemed to be in place. She changed into her dress and shoes and re-did her make-up in the bathroom upstairs from the venue. By the time she emerged, half of The Thing Factory team had arrived. They looked good, dressed up in shirts and jackets, or dresses. A long table had been populated with champagne flutes that glinted in the light from the windows. The bottles were on ice; the smell of the canapés came faintly from the kitchen downstairs. Outside the windows that wrapped around the room, the sun was starting to sink over Berlin.

When the first guests arrived at seven, the waiters circulated with champagne and, ten minutes later, canapés. As they swooped and dipped around in their white jackets, the scene struck Alice as possibly wrong: too formal, too grand, not what she had in mind for the party at all. She found that she needed to pee again, and upstairs in the bathroom mirror she had doubts about her dress: the flowing body and ruffled sleeves had seemed just the thing in the shop, but now she thought it looked a bit shapeless. Did it make her look pregnant? She should have bought a little belt to cinch it in. She tried different postures. No, she definitely shouldn't put her hands in her pockets. She grinned at herself in the mirror, checking her teeth for any strands of spinach. All good. It was too late now to change anything. She had to enjoy the party.

When she came back down to the venue, four or five small groups had formed already, drinking champagne and chatting companionably. Tristan was talking to someone she recognised but couldn't place, with other members of the team listening in. Alice observed him holding court, tried to guess what he was saying. He looked in control, applying his charm in a restrained way, now asking questions of somebody with an interested expression on his face. Ah, yes, it was Jerome, the finance director at Rubric. He looked different to when Alice had last seen him, earlier in the summer: slimmer, suntanned, and glowing in the filtered early-evening light. Alice took a flute of champagne from the waiter and hovered towards the group that contained Daniel, Richard and, she now saw, David Singh. The semicircle opened to admit her, and she smiled at David. He was looking handsome in his exquisite blue suit, a sprig of grey chest hair emerging from his undone second shirt button. He smiled back at her. 'We've been discussing politics. Never wise at a party.'

'Indeed.'

'Who was it,' Daniel said, 'who said that politics is just show business for ugly people?'

'I thought that was the definition of business,' David said, fixing his gaze on Alice, clearly pleased at his own mischievousness.

She stared back. 'I prefer the definition by Albert Camus, that business is a combination of sport and war.'

David sipped from his flute. 'I must write that down.'

Daniel enquired about David's flight to Berlin, and his hotel. He was staying at the Grand Hyatt round the corner – 'So I can stumble back in the small hours.'

'Very convenient.'

Daniel asked whether that was the hotel he normally stayed at. David smiled politely at his boringness, and in that moment a waiter popped up to offer him a refill. David watched him with a courteous passivity while he poured the wine, twisting the bottle to catch the drip, then he thanked him. 'I get my PA to book hotels,' he said, in a tone that meant that the topic was dealt with. 'But I mustn't detain you, Alice. Isn't that Rolf from you-know-where?'

He mouthed the word *mingle* at her, and she turned to see Rolf from Fox Pop across the room. The crowd had doubled now; glancing across it, she was struck by the strangeness of seeing her team, all these people she had appointed, mixing so easily with the very rich, perhaps feeling their way into being at home in that company. She stepped away from the circle. As she did so, Heather breezed across her path towards a waiter and whispered in her ear, 'He is so fucking fit.'

'David? He's certainly a very capable man. And also old enough to be your father.'

'Oh my god, I would let him absolutely *ruin* me if he wanted to.'

'I think someone's getting overexcited.' Alice moved away, sensing that David's eyes had been on them, as if he knew he was being talked about. Rolf was talking to Leroi, and when she stepped towards him he offered her his hand.

'Are you enjoying celebrating your success?'

'I am. I'm so glad you could make it.'

'And I am glad for having also the opportunity to meet your team, since it was such a pleasure meeting you and Tristan.'

Leroi excused himself, and they were alone among the bustle of the assembling crowd. Rolf was congratulating Alice on the wisdom of holding this party ('It is so important to enjoy the journey'), and explaining to her the benefits of making occasions to celebrate your success in terms of company spirit and staff retention. Just as the feeling of being patronised was rising in her, he said, 'But of course you understand this already.'

'Well, it's always good to get advice from more experienced colleagues in the industry.'

'Experienced . . . that is a very diplomatic way of putting it. This party was making me feel a little antique.'

'Oh, not at all.'

'But luckily I like to be around young, energetic people.' He raised his flute minutely and touched it to Alice's. 'To The Thing Factory. I trust you will be delivering a speech this evening?'

'Yes. I thought at seven forty, once everyone has arrived.'

'And your co-founder also is here?'

Alice hadn't thought about Ned once since she arrived at the venue. It was ridiculous that he wasn't here. She smiled and said, 'He's running a little late, I'm afraid. Actually, his father died recently, so he's been dealing with that.'

'I am very sorry to hear that. And I will hope later to meet him. Alice, I wonder if you could permit me to make a small announcement of my own, after you have made your speech?'

'That would be lovely. I'll introduce you.'

A pulse of excitement passed through Alice, and it was all she could do not to skip on the spot, or squeal, or hug this funny little Austrian, with his awful goatee. If he wanted to speak, it could only mean that Fox Pop had decided on the deal.

Across the room, David Singh was talking to Yuri and Aytan from the venture capital firm. Alice watched them through the jumble of heads, enjoying the discretion with which they seemed to be behaving, as if they had never met before. Perhaps it meant that they were the favoured buyers. To the right of them, Tristan was coming to the end of a story, his hand gestures growing more dramatic, and Alice saw the group that was closed tightly around him break into laughter as he reached his punchline. A high-net-worth individual in a shimmering azure dress rocked back on her stilettos, tottering slightly, and Tristan sipped his wine with a look of contained triumph. The golden lighting in the venue contrasted now with the darkening evening outside, the gloom punctured by millions of lights coming on. Everyone was here, everyone was talking and enjoying themselves. An atmosphere of noisy anticipation was building. Alice looked at her watch and saw that it was 07:42.

She found Leroi. He confirmed that the canapés were all finished now, and instructed the waiters to make sure everyone's glasses were filled; they buzzed around the room with accelerated efficiency. Alice moved to the north-west side of the room and positioned herself in front of the window, with the Deutsche Bank building looming behind her, and Leroi tapped a fork against a flute five times, cutting through the roar. As the silence mounted, a lone German voice, now shockingly loud, was still saying, 'No, the carrier was KLM', and stopped dead in surprise at being overheard.

'Ladies and gentlemen,' said Leroi. 'A word from Alice Williams, co-founder and joint CEO of The Thing Factory.'

The applause came hard and died down fast; Alice felt a shimmer of excitement at finding each eye in the room turned towards her.

'Good evening, colleagues, associates, clients and friends. It's wonderful to be here with you, and I'd like to thank Leroi and his team for putting on such a splendid party, and also to encourage you all to take in the magnificent views here at the Panoramapunkt, if you haven't already done so. I think you can even see our office building from that side of the observation deck, though I wouldn't say it's an architectural highlight exactly.'

(Laughs rebounded across the room.)

'It was the philosopher Albert Camus who said that business is a combination of sport and war. Well, it's an improvement on the remark made by my friend David Singh from Bishop & Morley this evening, who said that business is just show business for ugly people.'

(More laughs, and a nod of canny acknowledgement from David.)

'But I think that Camus was missing something as well. It seems to me that the business of The Thing Factory is more like a combination of friendship and play. Play, in the sense that we come in every day and we're creative, we make things, we try things out, we experiment when inspiration hits us. And friendship in the sense that we all have each other's backs when the experiments don't come off. I'd like to keep that spirit going as we grow and expand, and as we start working with a larger staff and a larger group of clients. And I'm delighted to be celebrating a fantastically successful first quarter on our social marketing and brand advocacy programme, and delighted to be making so many new friends tonight. So, ladies and gentlemen, I'd like you to join me in a toast: to The Thing Factory, and to friendships new and old.'

Alice's final words echoed back to her amid a sea of raised glasses and camera-phone flashes. She held her flute high in front of her for a second, slowly brought it back towards her, and took a sip. The groundswell of noise resumed, and Tristan was at her side, pecking her discreetly on the cheek. 'Did you just make that up off the cuff? You should be Prime Minister.'

She gave his hand a squeeze, half feeling as if she were

about to cry, and hurrying the impulse away. Not a good look, to be moved to tears by your own speech.

'One thing though,' Tristan said. 'I googled that quote. I thought it didn't sound like something Camus would say, and it's not, it's someone called André Maurois.'

'Who's he?'

'Dunno. Some other French guy.'

Alice giggled, and the giggles passed on to Tristan at precisely the moment that Rolf Warsheimer cut through the din again, tapping on his glass with his car keys. Alice had forgotten to introduce him.

'Ladies and gentlemen, not many of you will know me, but I hope I am being counted as one of the new friends that Alice is mentioning. My name is Rolf Warsheimer and I am an executive director at Fox Pop GmbH. I hope that some of you may have tried our products, our energy drinks, and perhaps one or two of you might support one of our very successful sports teams. No booing, please.'

Obliging chuckles, and one good-natured parody of a boo came from the back of the room.

'Very well. Now, I am not so much of a philosophical speaker as Alice, so I want only to make a short talk to you now. First I want to congratulate you on your very excellent work you have been doing. My only reservation is around your name. Unfortunately, we do not have this *th* sound in the German language, and I have experimented with calling you The Ding Factory, but I think that is not so stylish. My American colleagues tell me it sounds like a company for the manufacture of bells! But more importantly, I want to announce another partnership, or I perhaps should say a friendship, which is between The Thing Factory and Fox Pop. Because all the ideas and innovation you have been making have not gone unnoticed at the headquarters of Fox Pop, just outside Salzburg – which is a very lovely city, even if it is not quite so hip and happening as Berlin. It is rather more *bürgerlich*, as we say in German, but sometimes an old bourgeois like me can even recognise an exciting proposition. So I want to announce tonight that Fox Pop has decided to move all of its social media marketing into the hands of The Thing Factory, and to make that area one of the major focuses of its overall budget for advertising.'

Around the room, Alice could see eyebrows raising, eyes literally widening.

'So you will be seeing very much more of me and my colleagues in the future, and I am sure that this can be a very happy and profitable friendship for all of us. So let us now make another toast, to the friendship between Fox Pop and The Thing Factory.'

As the toast blended with the noise of excited voices,

music came from the speakers. Rolf strode towards Alice, kissed her on both cheeks, and held his handshake with her for the benefit of a photographer who had popped up from somewhere.

Under the thick, collective roar of music and voices, the band was almost ready to begin. People instinctively cleared a space, and a brisk waiter picked up the flutes and napkins that had been dropped or placed down on what was now the dance floor. The Rich Richards Orchestra: Alice wasn't sure how they would go down, but now that her speech and Rolf's announcement had come off so perfectly, she didn't care. The night was a triumph, whatever happened now. She had delegated to Tristan the task of choosing a band from the shortlist that Leroi had supplied, and Tristan thought these guys were the best – a covers band who actually had some style of their own. Alice had passed on Tristan's instruction that the set should be danceable.

They started with a strangely moving version of Meatloaf's 'Bat Out of Hell', re-cast as a melancholy torch song before exploding into heavy-driving rock for its final two minutes. A blur of jangling limbs formed from the crowd who had been tentatively swaying their shoulders so far. Alice joined them, and was found by Tristan. He was a good dancer, his precise movements set off by a certain wit, with dramatic pouts and frowns throwing his performance of sexiness into ironic relief. Alice was glad to discover this about him.

At the end of the song, Alice shimmied away towards the stairs up to the bathroom. She splashed a little water on her face in the mirror while she waited for a stall to be free. Her cheeks were slightly flushed. She'd hardly eaten anything this evening – not very sensible – but her flute had only been refilled twice, she thought, and she had sipped sparingly. Maybe three times, she forgot. In the stall, she took her phone from her bag and found a message from David Singh, sent thirty minutes ago: 'Smoking on deck. A+ speech! Rolf keen to meet Ned, is he coming?'

In reply, she typed 'idk, stall him pls'. Back on the dance floor, Alice found herself being embraced and drawn into clusters of dancing by excitable members of her team. She felt good, and smiled at Yuri and Aytan, who were dancing dorkily apart from the rest. They suddenly looked like boys at a school disco, fearful of the girls and of themselves. Strange to think they were the richest people in the room by some distance. Alice saw Richard, not far from them, snogging a woman she didn't recognise. She put her arm around Heather and said in her ear, 'Looks like someone's networking is going well' – and when Heather's gaze followed Alice's eyeline she screamed in excitement. The band were playing 'MacArthur Park'. When the singer came to the crescendo, he howled the lines with such intensity that the ludicrousness of the song – was it really about a lost cake recipe? – transformed into something sublime. Even Jaki, standing alone at the edge of the group, was nodding profoundly. At the end of the song, visibly beaded in sweat and with his hair ruffled from the exertion, the singer spoke into the microphone. 'Good evening, *guten Abend*. We are the Rich Richards Orchestra, I'm Rich Richards, and this is "Watching the Detectives".'

A jangling reggae beat started. Tristan caught Alice's eye with a cigarette gesture, nodded towards the observation deck, and walked in that direction. She started to follow him but was diverted by Rolf Warsheimer, who told her he was leaving, congratulated her on such a splendid party, and expressed his regret at not meeting Ned, and then by Heather, who clasped Alice's shoulders unsteadily and mentioned how drunk she was. Pushing through the doors into the fresh air, it suddenly struck her how hot the room had become since the dancing started. Tristan was talking to David Singh; when David saw her, he mimed hiding his smoking hand behind his back. 'You mustn't tell Asmita. Tristan made me do it anyway.'

Alice smiled at the pretence that she knew David's wife. 'Your secret's safe with me. I thought I'd join you for my annual cigarette, actually.'

'That's very restrained of you.'

'Alice has transcended worldly desires,' Tristan said, 'ever since she found nirvana.'

'Ah,' said David intelligently. 'You'll have to send me a location pin. How are you feeling anyway, Alice?'

'Terrific.' As she heard herself say it, she wondered if it were true.

'It's been a great party. I'm so glad Rolf could be here, and Yuri and Aytan. I was just telling our new COO about the latest developments.'

Tristan winked at Alice. She was glad to see the two of them getting along. 'Excellent. It's like everything's converging. Actually, David, since we're here, I wanted to ask you something else. I've been thinking more about the make-up of the new board, and increasingly I agree with you about getting a non-exec chairman. And I was thinking, maybe we've got the best candidate already. How would you feel about being the chairman of the board?'

She felt like this had come out wrongly, like she had struck an off note, but David looked pleased. 'We'd have to see what Yuri and Aytan say, of course. Or – excuse me – whoever the buyer turns out to be. But that sounds like a very interesting proposition. I'd certainly enjoy spending more time in Berlin.'

Tristan flicked the butt of his cigarette in a high arc out

through the railings. 'Gentlemen, it's been a pleasure but I'm going to leave you.'

Alice watched him walk back towards the low bass rumble of the music coming through the thick glass doors, and exchanged a satisfied look with David. Then she saw Ned walking towards her. She almost jumped in surprise. He looked terrible, and what was he wearing – a fucking hoodie? David said 'Jesus' under his breath and walked behind Alice towards the door. Ned was at her side.

'Great party,' Ned said.

'Are you drunk?'

'So are you.'

'I've been at the party. Where have you been?'

'I'll explain tomorrow. I had a lot of things to sort out.'

'What were you sorting out while wearing a tourist hoodie and drinking whisky?'

'Spiced rum, actually. That was after the sorting out. To get me in the mood for the party.'

'You missed the party.'

'I'm here, aren't I?'

'You missed everything important. I'm surprised they let you in, looking like that.'

'It helps that I own the company.'

'Half the company.'

'Fair point. So what did I miss?'

'Ned, do you understand that this was an important evening for me?'

'Yeah, of course.'

'Then why didn't you come?'

'I have come.'

'It's eleven o'clock or something!'

'I'm on Berlin time.'

'Fuck off, I'm being serious. This was a really important night. It's really upsetting that you didn't think it was worth coming. Everyone else was here. Except Fola – have you been with her?'

'I saw her this morning.'

He seemed shifty on this point; Alice didn't pursue it. She looked out over the city and sighed. 'You missed the chance to develop our contacts with a lot of valuable people. You missed my speech, which was brilliant, of course. And you missed a really important announcement.'

'Oh yes?'

'You know I said we had a really huge deal in the works for social? I was telling you just before your dad got sick. The exec was here and he announced today that they're going for it.'

'Who is it?'

'Fox Pop. I didn't tell everyone before because I didn't want them to freak when it wasn't confirmed yet.'

'Fuck. That's big.'

'It's huge, Ned. It's millions and millions. We're going to be doing all their social for them, which will be a big chunk of their online budget.'

'That's wonderful. We'll have to start drinking Fox Pop instead of Club-Mate.'

Alice smiled. 'That's just for starters. It's going to entail a lot of changes. Big things. And they need to be done straight away.'

'But then, you did always say that Club-Mate tastes like stale cigarettes.'

Alice left a respectful pause. 'I'm sorry that you found out that way, that was tactless of Tristan. I was going to tell you.'

Ned turned to her. 'That's okay. He's a good guy.'

'He is.'

'And to be honest, it looks like me and Fola might get together.'

Alice couldn't tell how she felt about this. 'I wondered if that would happen. That sounds nice.'

Ned had moved closer to her now, standing under a halogen light that showed how dreadful he looked. Bags under his eyes, his cheeks and nose flushed red, unshaven, grimy, and with a crazy look in his eye. He seemed very drunk. Alice turned from him back to the view. Lights were coming on and going off. They glinted across the tall buildings to the north and glinted over in the east, each one like a little spark of meaningful engagement. 'It's a wonderful view,' Ned said.

Alice nodded.

Ned was looking for something out to the south-east. 'I was in a building over there this afternoon,' he said. 'In Neukölln.'

'Why?'

'Oh, just visiting a friend,' he said vaguely.

He turned back, and together they looked out over the Reichstag, the Holocaust Memorial that looked like a huge empty car park from this angle, the TV Tower striding high and silvery alone above the east. 'It makes me think of that poem,' Ned said. 'How does it go? We did it in school. I listen to money singing, and it is like looking down, on something something. On an old French town? It is intensely sad.'

Alice turned to him. 'I haven't got the faintest idea what you're talking about. Ned, fucking hell, are those blood spots on your top? Your cuff, look. You're covered in it.'

4

IN THE THREE HOURS before he arrived at Panorama-punkt, Ned had sat outside the bar attached to a mini-golf course on the bank of the canal in Kreuzberg, drinking neat rum and considering his situation. He knew he had crossed a line now. He had made it to thirty-three without ever seeing a seriously wounded person before, even from a distance. Now the unbroken plain of crimson on Abdel's skin, the mess or mush that had become of his face, the pink and the grey – these were things he wouldn't forget. They still seemed somehow unreal. Ned didn't feel real about them. He felt like this was television. When the waiter came around he ordered another rum, his fourth in a row, and observed the larking stag-do groups, the families with whining children, the married couples sitting glumly over their lack of things to say to each other, and he enjoyed a vain sense of self-dramatisation, acting out his own desperation.

When he had told Abdel to tell Abbas to fuck himself, and Abdel had taken out his gun and pointed it at Ned's head, Ned had smiled. '*Entschuldigung,*' he said. '*Meine Deutsch ist sehr klein. Ich wollte sagen, dass ich gerne verhandeln würde.*'

I meant to say that I'd be happy to negotiate.

Abdel laughed, lowered the gun for a moment, and turned away from Ned to flick his cigarette butt towards the corner of the car park. Ned moved quickly: in an instant he was on his feet and had launched himself at Abdel, knocking him to the ground on his front and pinning him down with both knees on his shoulder blades. Abdel tried to jerk his upper body back and throw Ned off but Ned managed to keep his shoulders down, and when Abdel strained his neck back, reaching for Ned with a headbutt, Ned put both hands on the back of his skull, smashed his face down into the concrete, heard Abdel groan, pulled his head back up and smashed his face down into the ground again, three times, as hard as he could.

There was no resistance now. Ned shifted his weight off Abdel's shoulders and crouched over him. He was clearly unconscious. Ned jogged out of the car park on to the street, turned left and broke into a brisk walk when he reached the main road. His pulse was sounding in his neck, and he felt a minor tremor coming through his hands. If he could only think, think, then surely he would know what to do. He had at least knocked Abdel unconscious, maybe fractured his skull. What were the consequences of that?

He was three minutes down the street when the answer came to him with a sickening force. If he had only injured

Abdel, he would have a seriously angry enemy on his hands. An enemy whom he knew to be unafraid of violence, an enemy who had probably killed people. When Abdel woke up, he would come after Ned with renewed ferocity. Even if Abdel didn't wake up, the other men from the casino might do that anyway. But there was always the chance that Abdel had pursued him from the casino on his own initiative, rather than under instructions from the others. There had been no sign from their conversation that they knew who Ned was. Abdel might not even have recognised him in the casino; he might have chanced upon him in the street. And if that was the case, then Abdel was the only one who knew about their encounter in the car park. And that meant that the situation would be significantly better if Ned were sure that Abdel could never report back to his friends from the casino as to what Ned had done to him. It meant that Ned had to go back and make sure he had finished the job.

When Ned turned back into the car park, Abdel still lay face down, exactly where he had left him. It seemed rather comical. Whoops-a-daisy, someone's fallen over. Ned grinned. He knelt down, prised the gun from Abdel's grip, and picked it up. He hadn't held a gun since shooting an air-rifle on the school camping trip in year eight. It was warm in his hand from Abdel's body heat. It had a complicated arrangement of knobs and catches, characters and numbers engraved into the metal.

Ned tried holding it in a firing grip, jiggling it in his hand to grow used to it. He hid his hand behind his back, walked to the front of the car park and looked up and down the street. No one around. He walked back to Abdel, laid the gun down on the ground, bent from the knees to flip him over – trying not to look at the sudden terrible flash of his mangled face – and dragged him by the legs to the side of the car park, behind a large wheelie bin. Then he picked up the gun, walked back to Abdel, stood over him with a stable stance, feet apart and knees slightly bent, and slid the top part of the barrel back as he had seen people in films do. Something inside it clicked into place. He gripped the gun in both hands, and with great care shot Abdel in the forehead from point-black range.

Ned caught the attention of the waiter and ordered his fifth rum. In the immediate aftermath of the shooting, he had taken two steps he was glad of now. First he had trundled the wheelie bin over so that it covered Abdel's body entirely, its clearance from the ground just high enough to make it over the broken bridge of his nose. Then he had tucked the gun into his belt in the way that Abdel had carried it. After catching the bus back to Kreuzberg, he waited until he was out of anyone's sight, quickly wiped the gun on the sleeve of his hoodie, and dropped it in the canal from the middle of Admiralbrücke. It made a forceful splash, but Ned was fairly certain he was the only person who noticed it.

When his rum came, he held his hand up before his face, fingers extended, and saw that it was still trembling slightly. He concentrated on it, tried to master the situation, and the trembling reduced. He slid twenty-five euros from his wallet for the drinks, took his phone out and checked the route. If he caught the M41, it would take fifteen minutes to reach Potsdamer Platz. He had a party to get to.

FOLASADE WAS STILL IN the apartment when Ned got back from the party. He hurried into the shower before she could see what a mess he was and buried his bloodstained hoodie at the bottom of the laundry basket. By the time he came to bed, cleaned up and exhausted, she only rolled over lazily towards him, kissed him and murmured fondly that he stank of booze, before falling back asleep. Ned set his alarm, took a Modafinil and lay his head on the pillow. Within two minutes his head was spinning, shoots of saliva were moving from the back of his gums, and he knew that he was going to throw up. In the toilet bowl the white pill floated, partly dissolved and fuzzy at its edges, on a bed of undigested rum. He brushed his teeth, drank a glass of water and took another Modafinil to replace the wasted one. He needed to feel sharp in the morning.

By seven thirty he was in the office. He knew this was going to be a big day, and wanted to make sure he was the first in. But now he felt like he had overshot the mark. None of his colleagues was likely to arrive for another ninety minutes – or longer, after the late night. He sent some emails, then looked at as many Twitter accounts for Berlin news sites as he could manage, to see if Abdel's body had been found. What would the headline be? *Underworld kingpin found dead . . . Hitman murdered in Neukölln . . .* Ned found that his German vocabulary was insufficient to guess at the wording. Probably they would make a big deal of the details – shot in the head, hidden under a rubbish bin. It would make for a good, melodramatic story. But he couldn't find anything. It didn't look like the body had been found yet. It might take days, weeks even, for it to be discovered. Ned was pretty sure he hadn't seen anyone else in the street, neither when Abdel first confronted him, nor when he went back to the car park to finish the job. Would there be CCTV recordings? It was unlikely, he thought. He had no idea who owned that car park. It didn't seem to be in use, and there was no meter for public parking. The wheelie bin must have belonged to someone. Maybe he could check on some sort of land registry? But doing that in German, with a hangover and so many other things to think about, was more effort than he was capable of.

By the time the security guard rang the buzzer at 08:45, Ned had planned the speech he was going to make to the team. He told the guard to come up to the fourth floor, and opened the office door to a gangly, dark-haired young man. The guard's name was Kevin – one of those names that seemed inexplicably funny to Ned when it applied to a German person. He didn't speak any English. Ned made him a cup of coffee and asked him cheerfully if his parents had been fans of Kevin Keegan. He looked at Ned blankly. He didn't seem the most physically intimidating person in the world, sitting there sipping his cappuccino in his white shirt-sleeves and blue trousers. He looked to be in his early twenties. At least his presence would be symbolic.

Ned knew he needed to get it right when he told the team about Kevin and the fire at Folasade's apartment. He needed to hit his mark. He had to make it seem unalarming, a random incident unconnected to anything else. The cause of the fire wasn't yet known, he would stress, and the security arrangements were simply a precaution. At 09:07, Ned heard the lift doors being hauled open, delivering the first of his colleagues.

IN THE TIME IT took her to walk from the U-Bahn to the office, Alice had reached a decision. After the news about the Fox Pop deal and Ned's bizarre behaviour last night, she had to disincorporate Gliss from The Thing Factory immediately, and she had to present Ned with the buy-out as soon as possible after that. She let herself into the building – four, eight, six, six – and the idea grew on her that she ought to do both things simultaneously. Yes, why not do them both now?

'Morning,' she said. It was a surprise to find Ned in the office before her. And who was this? There was a handsome man sitting drinking coffee. He looked as if he were dressed as a bus driver: smart trousers, black leather shoes and a white shirt with black piping.

'Alice, this is Kevin from Olympus security,' Ned said. 'Kevin and his colleagues are going to be doing some work for us for the next few weeks.'

Kevin stood and offered her his hand. Alice shook it limply and said to Ned, in a deliberately neutral voice, 'Can we speak in the meeting room?'

'Sure.' Ned followed her in and shut the door behind him just as Heather and Jaki were arriving in the office. Alice thought Ned looked odd, agitated and on edge. 'We ought to be quick,' he said, not looking at her. 'I want to address the whole team once everyone's here.'

'What the fuck, Ned? Why have you hired a security guard without consulting me?'

'We hardly consult each other on everything we do, do we? Anyway it all happened very quickly. It was one of the things I needed to sort out yesterday. I didn't say because I didn't want to spoil the party.'

'You did a pretty good job of that anyway.'

'What I didn't want to tell you was that the night before last, after Tristan's gig, Fola went home and there was a fire at her apartment.'

'Oh my god, is she okay?'

'Yeah, she's fine. She got out unharmed. She's been staying with me since it happened. The police think it was probably just kids throwing a firecracker through the window, but given that people have been worried about those weird emails we received, I thought I'd get some security around the place just to put their minds at rest.'

'My god. That's so awful for Fola.'

'She's a bit shaken up, but no harm done. I think her place was pretty gutted though. They said she might be allowed back in later today to see if anything has survived the fire.'

'So what's this security guard going to be doing? Just sitting around the office all day?'

'I thought we could station him on the door. Either in the hallway or downstairs. He can check who's coming in and going out. Then there'll be a couple of guys on twenty-four-hour call to accompany people home or come out in emergencies.'

'How much is it costing us?'

'About six hundred euros a day. But it depends how often we have to call them out.'

Alice looked at Ned. It seemed to her as if he were over-compensating, putting on a show of confidence that he didn't truly feel, shoulders thrust back in his chair and legs stretched out. 'It's a lot of money to commit to, just to put people's minds at rest,' she said. 'Didn't you want to wait until you saw whether people actually *were* worried or not? I mean, if the police say it was just a random arson attack?'

'I thought it would be better to be proactive.'

Pause.

'Ned, are you sure you're telling me the whole story?'

'Of course.'

His foot was tapping out a rhythm on the floor.

'Fine,' Alice said. 'I'll leave the explanation to you.'

'Thanks.'

'One more thing, though. You never told me last night where that blood on your cuff came from. Or why sorting out this security guard kept you out of the office all day.'

Ned hesitated. 'I was looking after Fola for a lot of the day. She didn't get to mine until like four in the morning after dealing with the police, so I let her have a lie-in, made her breakfast, made sure she was okay.'

'Fine. And the blood?'

'I'm a bit embarrassed about that. The truth is I went out for some drinks because I was so on edge. With Fola and Dad and everything. And I got into this stupid fight in a bar. Playground stuff.'

'That doesn't sound like you.'

'Well, I haven't really been feeling myself lately.'

'I can imagine. Just don't make a habit of it, okay? With the Fox Pop deal in the works, we need to make sure we're totally spotless. We can't have a CEO going around getting into bar fights.'

'Roger that. I came off worse, to be honest. That blood was from my own nose. So I'm not keen to repeat the experiment.'

Alice smiled. 'I remember you said to me once: *Don't worry, love, I can handle myself* . . .' (She had slipped into the voice she used to tease Ned – what she thought of as her 'common' accent.) 'Hopefully you've learned your lesson.'

Ned grinned wonkily at her.

Alice looked through into the office. 'It looks like there's a good crowd now, if you want to explain about our new doorman.'

Ned excused himself to go to the bathroom first, and Alice sat in the meeting room alone for a moment, looking out across Kottbusser Tor. In a way it made sense. Of course he would be liable to go off the rails a bit, with his father dying. If anything, it was remarkable how much he seemed to have been holding it together until yesterday. That probably wasn't good for him. No one should keep their emotions as thoroughly nailed down as that. If he needed to get drunk and get into a scrap in a bar to get something out of the system, fine. But still, there was something off about the whole thing. The security guard, the story about Folasade, Ned's absence all day yesterday. It didn't quite make sense to Alice.

THERE WERE MANY QUESTIONS after Ned had told the team about the security arrangements. Was Folasade okay? Had she inhaled much smoke? What had the police actually said about the fire? Were there any signs of a link between the fire and the emails? Was Kevin armed? How quickly would the other guards come out if they were called? And when would Folasade be back in the office?

Ned did his best to keep the mood positive. Since they were scaling up with the Fox Pop deal, he said, it was normal that they'd need to take more security precautions. He saw Alice make a face, presumably at his attempt to harness Kevin to her success on social, but he didn't think anyone else thought it strange. Kevin was sitting at the front with him, and people asked him a few questions, but came up against his total lack of English and his startling inarticulacy in German. He didn't seem to have been briefed on the job at all. There was some discussion as to whether it would be better to station him in the hallway or downstairs, and they decided on the hallway. Several minutes of fussing around followed while Kevin was set up in front of the mural with a chair, a small table, and some bottles of water. He took a selfie in front of the picture of Mesut Özil. He didn't need any reading material, he said, but was it okay if he played the radio from his phone? And what was the *Wifi-Netzwerk Passwort*?

Once he was set up, things settled down. Ned took himself to a hot-desking spot in the annexe and tried to gather in his thoughts. He checked Twitter again for news of Abdel's body. Nothing. What did that mean? It was possible that no one had found him yet. The car park didn't look like it saw much use. The wheelie bin didn't seem all that heavy when Ned had dragged it over to cover the body, so perhaps it wasn't due to be emptied for a while. How often were collections? And had anyone heard the gunshot? It had seemed shockingly loud to Ned, in the silence of the empty car park. But it was near a busy road, and in a place where the bins would often clatter about, trucks would perhaps be driven in, deliveries unloaded. It might not have seemed remarkable to anyone who overheard it.

It struck Ned how foolish he had been to carry on wearing the same hoodie, the entire same outfit, all evening. He needed to get home at once, retrieve it from the laundry bin and dispose of it, somewhere it would never be found. Yes, he should do that at lunchtime.

And then what? He realised he had no concrete plan, in

the face of outcomes that had the potential to be overwhelmingly trying. What if Al-Zein knew already that he had killed Abdel, and were coming straight for him? What if the police had found the body, and knew Abdel had last been seen leaving the casino in pursuit of Ned? He could be dead, he could be in a prison cell, by this evening.

Ned felt uncontrollably drowsy. The Modafinil he had taken last night and this morning was only making him grind his teeth.

ON FRIDAY AFTERNOON, WORD came from Fox Pop that they would sign the contracts on Monday. The news brought Alice's immediate concerns into focus. She felt at first that she had so much to do that she didn't know where to start. Then she took a block of blue Post-it notes, put each matter she needed to deal with on to a separate note, and arranged them on her desk; she started a block of smaller yellow notes on which she broke down each item into tasks. Soon she had a clear structure in front of her, with five discrete but related blue projects each putting out a fantail of achievable yellow goals. One thing at a time, and it would be manageable.

Ned had his denim jacket on. Alice caught his eye. 'Off to lunch already?'

'Something like that.'

'Have you got a minute? I could walk with you if you like. I might get a falafel wrap.'

They walked past Kevin in the hallway, went down in the lift and out across Kottbusser Tor. It was a gorgeous day, sunny and breezy against a blue sky. Alice told Ned that Fox Pop were signing on Monday, and he asked if he could do anything to help. She tried to think of something, but came up blank. It was almost four months now since he had shifted focus on to Gliss, and so much had changed on social that it would be pointless trying to get him involved now; she would have to spend so long explaining how things worked that she might as well do the thing herself. 'It's all ticking over okay at the moment,' she said. 'But there is something we need to work out.'

'Oh yes?'

'You remember I mentioned the idea of disaggregating Gliss and incorporating it as a separate company? With the Fox Pop deal having come together so fast, we really need to move on that.'

Ned didn't reply immediately.

'Does that sound okay?' Alice said.

'Are Fox Pop put off by Gliss?'

'As far as I'm aware, they don't know about it. And I don't want them to. There's so much money at stake.'

'How would it work then?'

'I spoke to Daniel about it and he says it would be simple. We just register a new company and make over Gliss and all its assets and IP to that. He says he could put it in motion today and get a new business account and an office early next week.'

'You want us to move out of the office?'

'Not immediately. But it does need to be registered at a different address. And soon social's going to expand so much, it will make sense to move the whole operation.'

They were halfway up Adalbertstraße, close to the falafel place. Ned was looking distractedly from side to side, across the street and down the sidewalk. Alice carried on: 'My thinking was that since Gliss has really been all your initiative, we make you sole owner of the company. That seems fair.'

Ned turned to her. 'You don't even want to keep a share in it?'

'To be honest, no. I thought it was a good idea at the time, but with everything it involves, it's – not my cup of tea, let's say. And with all this security stuff, online threats and worrying about firebombs . . . No. It needs to be totally separate.'

'It won't be that separate if I own one company and half of the other.'

'It will be as separate as we can make it for now.'

They ordered two falafel wraps, Ned's with extra halloumi, and waited in silence while they were made. Walking back down Adalbertstraße, Ned tore open the paper around one end of his wrap, took a large bite, and said, 'Okay, let's do it. I need to pop home now for a while but if you set it up with Daniel, I can sign off on it this afternoon.'

At Kottbusser Tor they parted, Alice going back into the office and Ned heading south towards the bridge. It was surprising to her how well he had taken it. But he didn't seem to be fully present. He seemed so glazed over, Alice wondered if she could have said anything to him and he would have agreed. She couldn't believe it would be this easy to remove Gliss from the business.

Back upstairs, the atmosphere seemed charged. Five of the team were crowding around Daniel's laptop, trying to read the same webpage. Alice looked over a shoulder and saw a news story on the *Berliner Zeitung* website.

'What's *Clanmitglied*?' said Heather.

'A clan member,' Daniel said. 'They call these organised crime networks *clans*, which is maybe not the best word for it.'

'And *erschossen*?'

'Shot. He was right next to where he lived, it says.'

'That's near me. I must have walked down that street.'

'In broad daylight.'

'I never understood that phrase. What's "broad" about daylight?'

No one answered Tristan's question.

'He was thirty-five,' Daniel said. 'Abdel Haddad. A wife and four kids. He was a very *berüchtig*, ahh, notorious . . .

violent offender . . . believed to have links to the Al-Zein clan of Neukölln.'

'Shit, are they the ones who sent us those emails?'

'It is not so clear. But possible. They are definitely involved in prostitution in Berlin. This article says that authorities think this may be a killing of revenge for the one in Hasenheide. That we received in the web link.'

People started to wander back to their desks. It was weird, Heather was saying to no one in particular, to think of these things happening in Berlin when it seemed so peaceful in general. Alice suppressed a smile at the confidence with which Heather could hold forth on what Berlin was like, when she had lived here for about five minutes. Then Daniel, his eyes still locked on his screen, began to tell her about the recent history of organised crime in Berlin. There had been much public debate about the clans in recent years, he said: some people thought the police had treated them too lightly from fear of not wanting to seem to discriminate against a minority group; others were worried that they were now recruiting new members among the refugees. But the situation was difficult for them, he said, because many of them were undocumented immigrants who weren't allowed to work legally or to receive benefits. It made sense that they became involved in criminal activity.

'That's no excuse though, is it?' said Heather. 'Lots of people don't have much money and they manage not to get involved in crime.'

'It depends what you mean by "involved". If you ever have bought weed from one of the boys in Görlitzer, in a way you have had an involvement with the clans.'

One of the interns working on Gliss had been hovering by the desk, nervously waiting for her moment to ask Daniel something. Alice drifted away into the annexe, and over-heard the intern saying that there was a problem they needed to deal with. A sex worker in the UK was saying she'd been robbed in her own apartment by a client who'd come to her through the app. She'd had all the earnings for the week taken. Daniel asked if she had gone to the police, and the intern didn't know the answer. It really should have been Ned and Folasade dealing with this, Daniel said, sounding annoyed. Neither of them was here. The intern was saying that they ought to be seen to act quickly, because the woman was writing a thread about the incident on her Twitter account, and lots of people were engaging with it. Daniel said he would phone Ned . . .

Sat at a desk in the annexe, Alice consciously tuned all this out. Nonsense about gangsters, more trouble arising from Gliss: it really wasn't what she needed right now. She transferred her arrangement of Post-it notes on to a sheet of A3 paper, set it in front of her and was still for a minute, breathing in for a count of four, holding it for the same time, and breathing out slowly. She had a sense that the current moment, today, was one of the moments in which her actions would decisively affect her future. If she got things right, if she made the right calls, her life could take a path of striking success and reward. It was rather extraordinary to be in a position to realise this. Most people never faced such moments, or never knew they were facing them until much later. But here she was. She could shape her future.

She set to work. Within two hours she had set in motion the furtherance of her plans to disaggregate Gliss, to open new offices for The Thing Factory in London and New York, and to change the management structure of the company.

At four o'clock, as if she had willed it to happen, a reply from David Singh arrived: a deal had been agreed in principle, he said. Could she come to the bar of the Ritz-Carlton at five to hear about it?

THE FALAFEL WRAP WAS just the thing – carbs and fat and salt – and Ned had finished it by the time he reached Kottbusser bridge. He felt better now. The feeling of constricting anxiety that had played across his body when Alice told him about making Gliss into a separate company had passed. Of course, that was no problem. Why would it be? Now that he thought about it clearly, it was surely a good thing from his point of view. Gliss was more or less self-sufficient now, and he would be the sole owner as its profits started to grow. If anything, Alice was doing him a favour in giving up any claim to the equity.

He was home within five minutes, bounding up the stairs two at a time. He was glad to find that Folasade had gone out. From the cupboard beneath the sink he took a white bin liner and dug down to the bottom of the laundry bin for the fluorescent hoodie he was wearing yesterday. That went into the bag, followed by all the other clothes he'd been wearing, followed by his trainers, finally followed by everything else in the laundry bag – it had all come into contact with the bloodstained hoodie, he reasoned, and it was best not to take any chances. It made for a bulky bin liner. Ned remembered that his mother had given him some vacuum storage bags last year. One of those mysterious gifts that always suggested to Ned that his mother really had no idea what sort of person he was. But now it would be useful. He bundled everything from the bin-liner into the vacuum bag, hauled out the vacuum that only his cleaner had ever used, and sucked the air out of the bag, leaving a compact, solid mass of cotton and polyester, surprisingly lumpy and hard. Then he put the vacuum bag inside the bin-liner, knotted the top and headed out with it.

He was on the bus when he took his phone from his pocket, ignored two missed calls and several messages from Daniel, and found the news about Abdel on Twitter. *Auf offener Straße erschossen.* Shot in the open street. Or maybe a better translation, Ned thought, would be shot in plain sight. Out in the open. It seemed strange that they'd gone for that headline – it was a bit overdramatic – and it was a surprise to learn that it was the street where Abdel lived. It provoked in Ned several thoughts at once. On one hand, it could support the idea that Abdel had chanced upon him by the building site: he had simply been on his way home from the casino, he hadn't been sent to follow Ned, and therefore Ned hadn't been recognised in the casino at all, only afterwards, when he had removed the baseball cap.

The other clan members might have no idea that Ned had been in the vicinity when Abdel was shot. On the other hand, the fact that Abdel had been heading home, shot on his own street, must significantly increase the chances of someone having seen Ned around at the time. Mustn't it?

The funeral was happening next Friday, the report said. Police expected it to be very large. When Ned reached the part about Abdel's wife and four children, he contemplated whether he felt guilty. He imagined what they would be doing right now: the mourning rites, the hushed household disrupted by wailing children. It was certainly a shame. But no, he decided, he didn't feel guilty. The guy had pulled a gun on him. And look, here it said he had a track record of more than a hundred offences – robberies, assaults, sexual assaults, witness intimidation . . . That was just what the police had managed to pin on him. Ned was pretty sure there would be a few killings on Abdel's CV that they'd never got him for.

When the bus reached the bottom of Stresemann Straße, Ned alighted. After checking that there was nobody around to watch him, he moved to the backyard of a building that housed a convenience store and a restaurant, and deposited the bin liner into a large wheelie bin. He wondered if the rest of the team had seen the news yet. If Folasade had seen it. She was still off work, and had probably been on Twitter all day long. It was likely she had seen it. What would she think of a member of the Al-Zein clan being killed, so soon after the attack on her apartment? Ned could imagine her taking a certain satisfaction in it, taking it as revenge. But it could also be frightening. How serious it seemed. There was no way of knowing how she would take it. In any case, she had seemed to accept the police's version of events, that it was most likely to be a random act of arson. He would have to wait and see whether she said anything about it.

They ought to go away this weekend. Yes, they should go out to one of the lakes for the day at least. Ned felt like it would put more distance between him and the Abdel situation.

ALICE WALKED AWAY FROM her meeting with David Singh in a floaty mood of elation. It was remarkable, it was incredible, she almost wanted to break into delighted glee in the faces of random passers-by. And then she felt a moment of near-panic, her heart racing. Was she doing the right thing? It was *so* much money, an amount she hadn't remotely imagined as a real possibility – maybe she ought to sell her half of the company too? Cash out and live forever on the proceeds. What if the bubble burst in six months and her half of the company became worthless? Could that happen?

She got on the U-Bahn at Potsdamer Platz. The instant the train doors closed, music began to play, a recorded backing track blaring from a loudspeaker built into the rucksack of a scruffy-looking middle-aged man, who then took up his trumpet and played the vocal line with great gusto. What was this song? *Doodle-oodle-oodle-ooh-doo-doo* . . . yes, it was that song 'Price Tag'. It seemed suddenly delightful to Alice, as she met the man's gaze and he communicated to her his joy in playing, even while the effort was making his eyes bulge. As the train approached the next stop, the man started tootling down the length of the carriage, jiggling a Subway cup that hung from his belt loop. One person gave him a coin. When he came to Alice, she reached into her pocket and pulled out ten euros. He saw her slip it into the cup and bowed elaborately to her, before coming to the end of his phrase at the precise moment that the train doors opened and he stepped out.

No, she was definitely doing the right thing. Everything was converging and coming into place, just as she had planned it. She could have walked back to the office, but she was glad to have taken the U-Bahn. The song lingered in her head.

THE NEXT MORNING, NED was walking to Folasade's apartment, the one he had found for her on Airbnb, and looking at information about the different lakes on the outskirts of the city on his phone. There were a lot to choose from: some with sandy beaches, some with nudist areas, some with the forest on their edges, some with a party atmosphere. He couldn't remember the names of the ones he'd been to before. Ned was weighing up the choice when he noticed that a police car had stopped at the traffic lights next to him. He froze, fully ready for a squad of officers to jump out, guns trained on him. But no, it was a normal stop for the lights; in a few seconds the car pulled away and was gone from sight.

Folasade's apartment had candles and miniature Hindu statues on every surface, polished wooden floorboards and lots of rugs. It looked like a yoga studio, Ned had said when he first came round. Folasade confirmed that the woman who owned it had several yoga DVDs in her collection, along with the complete box set of *Sex and the City*, dubbed into German. Folasade was working her way through it.

Ned was on his knees, packing a bag for their trip to the lakes. He called over his shoulder: 'I spoke to my mum the other day and she's coming out to visit in two weeks.'

Folasade, who sat on the sofa looking at her phone, didn't answer at first. Ned turned to look at her, and she said, 'Have you seen this? About this gangster who got shot?'

She was angling the screen towards him. He narrowed his eyes from across the room and saw a follow-up story about the killing. Abdel's face stared back at Ned, dour and handsome. Ned went back to rolling up the beach towel he had in his hands and said, 'God, yeah, I saw it yesterday. Grim, isn't it?'

'It's scary. Weren't these the guys that we thought those messages came from?'

'That was Jaki's theory. Daniel wasn't so sure though, and he knows Neukölln really well.'

Folasade's hand came down to rest in her lap and she stared ahead, looking thoughtful. Ned could see her trying to add it all together in her head. He felt like a teacher watching a bright pupil in the middle of a maths test he had set. He put the towel in the bag and came to sit down next to her on the sofa. 'Do you want to go to the cinema tomorrow?' he said. 'I could see what English-subtitle screenings they have at the Babylon. Or we could go to Il Kino.'

She looked back at him. 'Do you think it *might* have been

those people who blew up my apartment? I know the police said it was unlikely, but that was just one officer, and he hadn't even investigated yet. He didn't know the details of the emails.'

'Have the police not been in touch yet?'

'No. I would have told you, of course.'

Ned thought he heard a note of annoyance in her voice. 'Of course,' he said. 'I mean, it's possible that they bombed your apartment, isn't it? But those messages definitely looked like prank emails to me. Anyway, we should get our skates on if we want to get a spot on the beach before it's too busy.'

He hoped it didn't seem too obvious that he was trying to change the subject.

Folasade stood up and returned to the task of packing the cool-box for their picnic. 'It's nice that your mum's coming here,' she said. 'Will you introduce us? Just as your colleague, I mean.'

THE REST OF NED'S weekend passed uneventfully, but not exactly calmly. Folasade had seemed captivated by the Abdel story; at the lake she kept on looking at her phone, reading new stories about it, and sharing them with Ned, who gritted his teeth and gamely pretended to take it as a curious local news item. He spent Sunday alone, unable to keep his thoughts from shooting off along the same anxious tangents: what if Al-Zein knew it was him? And what if the police were on to him? And so on. By the evening he was exhausted. He slept poorly, stayed in bed late on Monday morning and dealt with some messages about the sex worker who'd been robbed. Daniel had given the guy's IP address and the messages he'd exchanged with the woman to the UK police: he seemed to think that was okay in terms of the data protection. Ned hoped he was right.

In the afternoon, after a long struggle to drag himself out of bed, Ned found himself back in the office of Nocerino, the private investigator. It seemed strange that four days had passed since he was last here – sitting in the same seat, with Nocerino seated in the same spot across the desk from him, it felt like five minutes ago. Nocerino even seemed to be wearing the same tie, a red number patterned with yellow lions. It looked like he had bought it in Venice.

'You have asked of me to do something a little bit difficult,' he said. 'If it is indeed the Al-Zein criminal organisation that has been sending you these messages and making the attack on your colleague's residence, they are very closed and secretive in their operations.'

Ned was ready to be disappointed in Nocerino. He seemed rather worn out, for a man who couldn't be much over forty, but there was an alertness in his manner that gave Ned cause for optimism. If Nocerino could give him some useful intelligence on Al-Zein, if he could give him a sense of how they might respond to Abdel's killing, he would feel more in control.

'I have, however, managed to use a contact in the police service to help me build up a picture of the current situation for the Al-Zein clan. I have not yet finished writing my report, but I could brief you now.'

'Please do. Anything would be helpful.'

Nocerino shuffled a sheaf of papers and laid them on his desk. 'There has been one interesting development since we were last meeting. Rather amazing, in fact. Have you seen it? The evening after you came to see me, it seems that an important member of the clan was murdered.'

'I saw it online. Who was he?'

'Abdel Haddad. Thirty-five. My police friend is telling me that he was a soldier for the clan, possibly a hitman, but certainly someone used for intimidation and violence. He was for ten years in prison, and then he was, ahh, the authorities were trying to deport him, but they did not succeed.'

'Do the police have any idea who killed him?'

'Now, this is interesting. It is strongly suspected that it was this Abdel who carried out a killing of a member of the Miri clan in Hasenheide last summer—'

'Yes, I saw that in the news—'

'It was big news. And so the strongest theory is that this was a revenge killing by the Miri clan. But there is one problem with this interpretation. It is also known that the Miri and Al-Zein have recently made friends again. They are using the same lawyers now, and they have even some joint business ventures. So this timing would be very strange indeed. The police have questioned the head of the Miri and he says he knows nothing about it.'

'How odd.'

'Of course it could be someone else. Perhaps the Hell's Angels, or perhaps a Turkish gang. But they normally are very much afraid of the Lebanese clans, who are more powerful. So this is really a mystery.'

'He must have had a lot of enemies,' Ned said. 'He sounds like a pretty bad guy.'

'This is true. But it is not so normal for a member of the most dangerous criminal organisation to be shot in his own neighbourhood. I think that jealous husbands are not so often doing this.'

Ned smirked. He was growing to like Nocerino, his steely little jokes. The guy was seriously bright.

'Let me tell you about Al-Zein anyway,' he continued. 'At the centre of the clan are the Haddad family, and it is the eldest of them, Abbas, who is the head. A very powerful man. He came to Berlin from Lebanon in the 1980s. The clan has strong involvements in drugs – most of the cocaine and cannabis in Berlin is coming through them – but also in real estate, in offering protection to local businesses, and in gambling and prostitution. And this is where their interest in your organisation comes from, I believe. They have already suffered a significant damage to their work, when the law changed and the big megabrothels were allowed to open. Al-Zein have not been able to open a large club yet because of licensing difficulties, so already they are angry about this loss of income, and now it seems that your website is making them angry as well. They are of the old school, small brothels in the red light districts and all this sort of thing, so you can perhaps understand why your new technology is upsetting to them.'

'Last week you said you didn't think Al-Zein had sent the messages or carried out the fire. That it wasn't their style. Is that still what you think?'

'On that, my view has changed somewhat. When I looked back over the messages you received, they seemed authentic to me, and that also is what the police are thinking—'

'Hang on, the *police*?'

'Yes, they are looking into these messages, my friend tells me, and they are finding them to be consistent with other methods of pressure that Al-Zein had used on rivals and competitors.'

'But how did the police know about the messages?'

'You are reporting these messages to the police yourself, no?'

An emotion that Ned couldn't quite identify surged through him. Hadn't they all sat there in the plenary and specifically agreed *not* to pass the messages to the police? Wasn't that the whole point of going to a private investigator in the first place, to keep the police out of it? Or was he going mad? It must be that one of his team had gone against the decision they had taken together, and made a police report in spite of being told not to. It was unbearable. If the police knew the Al-Zein clan had sent threatening emails, if they authenticated them, they would immediately connect that to the firebomb attack, and it would be only natural to wonder if there was a connection between that and Abdel's killing the very next day. The police might be closing in on him right now, and Ned didn't even know it. They might be about to arrest him as soon as he left Nocerino's office. The situation was much worse than Ned thought.

'All is okay?' Nocerino said.

'I'm just confused as to how the police knew about the emails. I wasn't aware that we had filed a report with them.'

Nocerino raised a finger to ask for a moment, then leafed through some pages on his desk. 'I perhaps have the information here, ahh . . . No, that is . . . Ahh, yes, the report was being made by Jakob Eckstein on the 3rd of June. Last Wednesday. You know him?'

Jaki. Of course. He had been the one to take the emails the most seriously from the beginning. And that date must have been when they discussed the matter at the plenary. Still, Ned was surprised that Jaki would go behind his back like this, when they had agreed a strategy in the meeting.

A T LUNCHTIME THE NEXT day, the whole team had assembled, sitting on three rows of beanbags and chairs in front of the big screen in the annexe. They started eating while Jaki fiddled around trying to connect Alice's laptop to the display monitor.

'While we're waiting,' Alice said, 'I might as well start. I haven't really prepared anything to say, but this is *Tooting* – it's a short film that was shot in 2012, mostly in a studio but a little bit on location as well, and, umm, it's set in a social work department of the council. In London. How's it looking, Jaki?'

Alice had been meaning to watch the film again over the weekend in preparation for today, but something stopped her from doing so. Several times she'd had it open on her laptop, all ready to begin, and found that she was drawn into other tasks. She wasn't sure what was holding her back. It was in The Mint Gun Club on Saturday evening that somebody pointed out how the tradition of the Hype Session had lapsed in the last month, with everyone so busy. Alice had never led a session until now. When the film was ready,

Alice walked to the edge of the room and turned the main light off, then stood in front of the group, feeling like a police inspector about to brief her officers on a case.

'So this comes from a few years ago, but I hope it will stand up. I play the character of Rose, who's a social worker, and I suppose this was the biggest screen role I ever had, along with a pilot that I was in at the same time that never got picked up for a series. As many of you know, I went out to LA after this to try to get my career going over there, but I ended up mainly working as an extra, before I gave all that up and came over here and founded the company with Ned. So I didn't know it at the time, but this short was probably the climax of my acting career. And I hope you like it.'

She turned to her laptop, full-screened the media player window, and pressed play while a brief round of applause faded out. She felt unexpectedly emotional. As she sat down, Ned caught her eye and smiled. She couldn't quite read his look. She hadn't given much thought to the fact that they'd still been seeing each other when she got this part. It must have been the last few weeks before Ned left London for Berlin. A few months before she went to LA. She didn't know if he'd ever actually seen it.

The opening shot showed a swanky cocktail bar, plate glass and waistcoated waiters. Alice's voice was heard, talking to a man who told her fondly, *You're looking well.*

As the conversation carried on it became clear that they were exes, having a stilted meeting. The camera slowly zoomed, and then cut to a close-up of Alice. *How's Clapham?* she asked. The camera cut between the two of them. *As salubrious as can be expected*, he replied. *How's Tooting?*

Alice looked out towards the night sky above the lit-up buildings. *You mean my houseshare with four total strangers? Let's just say that the area is up and coming.*

They both sipped from their large glasses of red. Alice looked down for a moment, turned her head back towards the bar behind them, and said, *This is fancier than the places we used to go to.*

I had a promotion, the man said. *Elizabeth is happy.*

I bet she is.

Yes, well . . . The man reached down to take up a brown leather document wallet from beneath the table. Cut to Alice fiddling with her ponytail while he said, *I've got the things here*, and handed her some papers. Alice addressed herself to the pile of pages in front of her. *Application for a decree nisi*, she said. *Shame I never did Latin in school.*

The man watched over her awkwardly while she read the document. *How's work?* he said.

Really good, actually. Ah, unreasonable behaviour . . .

It's just a legal formula. To establish the grounds. Otherwise we'd have to wait two years to do it on separation.

Whereas you were always a model of reason.

Well, I—

Just fucking with you, Alice said, then handed him back the papers and chinked her glass against his. *To us.*

To us, he said.

The shot cut to the man leaving the bar, then to Alice swilling a sip of wine around her mouth and looking out of the window sadly. A throaty-voiced American country song played as the word *Tooting* appeared on screen in white capitals. Then it was the grey light of morning, an exterior shot of a large office building, red brick and dull grey windows. Then an interior, a dingy office, desktop computers and coffee mugs on the desk. Alice with her head down. *Good weekend?* asked a woman's voice from outside the frame.

The real Alice, the Alice standing at the back of the room watching her colleagues and employees watching her on screen, couldn't watch anymore. She crept softly out of the annexe into the main office, and heard her own voice saying, *Not bad. I got divorced and did my hand-washing. You?*

Alice thought she had put on weight since it was filmed. It was shocking to see how skinny she had looked. And something about her performance seemed naff, twee, to her now. Maybe she hadn't actually been a very good actress at all. There seemed to be something coarse in her gestures, something brittle about the way she delivered the lines that were meant to be witty. It was disconcerting to watch herself, at this remove. Was that how she spoke now when she was pitching to clients? And in meetings? Was she still that person? She had the idea that she had changed.

Well, it wasn't for her to judge her abilities as an actor. She had never enjoyed watching herself. The staff all seemed pretty rapt. They hardly touched their lunches while the first scene played out. And now she heard the first laugh coming from the annexe. It seemed genuine and unreserved.

EVERYONE WENT BACK TO work after the screening. The Fox Pop deal had given them lots to do. They busied themselves finding new influencers to bring in on retainer, analysing data, planning strategies and content themes, and working on reports for existing clients. The mood in the office became slightly manic; the music from the Bluetooth speakers grew louder, and people's voices grew louder and more strained in response.

Just after three o'clock, the landline in the office rang. An intern answered it, and Ned, who was drinking a cappuccino, listened from a few feet away. 'Jakob? Oh, Jaki. No, he's not in the office at the moment. I can take a message if you like . . . No, yeah, okay, I could give you the CEO. He's just here . . . Hang on.'

Ned knew what it would be. He had prepared for this moment. The intern's serious voice when he came over and said, 'Ned, it's for you,' confirmed Ned's guess before the intern added, 'It's the police.'

Ned said he would take it in the meeting room, and

carried the handset through with him, steeling his nerves as he went. He stood with his back to the door, and said quietly, 'Hello?'

'Hello. I am speaking to the boss of The Thing Factory company, yes?'

'That's correct.'

'This is Police Captain Stefan Kohler of the fifth *Direktion* of the Berlin *Landespolizei*. I am calling to make some inquiries about a recent complaint made by one of your employees, Jakob Eckstein. Are you familiar with the substance of this complaint?'

'Yes, I think so. It's about some unusual email messages that we received, no?'

'Just so. Have there been any more messages since the report was filed?'

'I'm not sure. I'd need to check.'

'Please do that. I am wondering if you will come to the station to talk about this matter in person. We are also making inquiries about a deliberate starting of fire at the residence of another employee, Folasade, ahh—'

'Awoniyi,' Ned said while the man stumbled over the name.

'Just so. So if you will come to the station, we will like to get more fully the details of these incidents.'

Ned felt a strong resistance, but couldn't think of a way of getting out of it that wouldn't look suspicious. 'Okay, that's fine.'

'Could you come today?'

Back in the office, Ned told Alice that he had to go to Neukölln to talk to the police. She looked agitated. He told her it was about the messages they had received, and she was as surprised as he had been to hear that they had been reported to the police. 'Just make sure it doesn't become anything protracted,' she said. 'Or dramatic. We don't want anything getting in the papers that connects us to this sort of thing.'

'I'll try. It's not like I've got anything to tell them beyond what they already know, anyway.'

He asked an intern to make copies of the emails for him, and headed out. An hour later, after popping home, he was walking towards the station of the Neukölln north-west division. He knew he wasn't far from where he had confronted Abdel, though for the moment he couldn't have said exactly which street that was on. The Al-Zein clan were operating right under the nose of the local police station.

He announced himself at the station and waited for twenty minutes on a bench in the foyer until Captain Kohler arrived. He was a tall, slender man of about forty. He took Ned into an empty office, a nondescript room with white walls and blinds and a beige, tiled floor. He sat down behind a desk in the middle of the room, and gestured for Ned to sit down opposite him. The manila envelope he had carried under his arm lay between them on the desk.

After preliminary questions about Ned's name, occupation, and place of residence, all of which Ned had told to the man at the desk already, Kohler said, 'So I understand that your organisation received five unusual email messages from this address.'

He was pointing to the address busj28ey8r@hushmail.com on a printout of one of the emails.

'I believe it was actually six messages,' Ned said. 'Another must have arrived after the report was made.'

Kohler noted this down. 'What did the additional message say?'

Ned passed him the final sheet from his own set of printouts. Kohler said that he would need to take a copy of this message.

'These messages were reported to us because of their threatening nature, yes?'

'I myself didn't consider them threatening,' Ned said. 'I thought it was probably a prank.'

'What is this prank?'

'Like a joke. A hoax.'

'Ahh. But you indeed reported them to us.'

'One of my staff reported them. I thought it was unnecessary.'

Kohler paused a moment and looked directly at Ned. Ned wished he knew exactly what Jaki had said to the police. How much did he tell them? Did he say that they'd been debating the authenticity of the messages in the office, researching the clans? Did he mention that Ned had put on a posture of defiance towards the threat? That he had said 'Fuck the haters'?

'In this case,' Kohler said, 'I think it was your colleague who showed the better judgement. We now believe these messages to be genuine threats issued by the Al-Zein criminal organisation. Does that name mean anything to you?'

'Not very much. But one of the messages contained a link to a news story that mentioned them, so that's how I've heard of them.'

'And you were not worried by this link to a story about a murder?'

'No. As I say, I assumed it was somebody playing a joke on us. We receive a lot of strange messages. We're quite a well-known company for a start-up.'

'Indeed. It was after the launch of the Gliss website that these messages started, yes? Did that attract much publicity?'

'It was a fairly high-profile launch.'

'And why do you think this criminal organisation wanted to threaten you?'

Ned paused. He was aware that so far Captain Kohler had only asked questions to which he already knew the answer. 'Gliss is an app that disrupts the sex-work industry by empowering sex workers,' he said. 'I suppose they didn't like the idea that we would improve on their business model.'

'But you did not take the threat seriously, even though your employee was enough concerned to take the messages to the police?'

'Correct.'

Kohler made a nearly imperceptible frown. He nodded, then took a new sheaf of paper from the envelope. 'The next event that interests us is the attack by fire of the residence of your employee, Folasade – how are you saying?'

'Awoniyi.'

'This took place in the early morning of Thursday the 4th of June.'

Ned didn't respond. The guy could ask him an actual question for a change.

'Is that so?' Kohler said finally.

'Correct.'

'And you had been with the young woman earlier that evening?'

'Yes. Most of my staff went to a comedy club in Wedding. I left around eleven and went home.'

'And she phoned you after the attack?'

'She asked if she could come to my apartment and I ordered a taxi for her.'

'What did she say when she phoned you?'

'She was upset. She said she'd woken up to find her apartment full of smoke and had rushed out. And she said the police thought it was probably boys throwing a firecracker through the window.'

'What is firecracker?'

'*Feuerwerk.*'

'Thank you. And what did you do, when you heard about this incident?'

'As I say, I called a taxi for her. She came to my apartment, I looked after her and she went to bed. It was very late at night.'

'And the next morning?'

'I just made sure she was okay. And I went online to find her a new apartment to stay in temporarily.'

'And then you went to work as normal?'

'No, I stayed at home, all day, then went to a work function in the evening.'

It was the first outright lie he had told Kohler. Ned wondered if it was the right thing to do.

'But you did not, for instance, contact the police?'

'The police already knew about the fire. Folasade called them out when it happened.'

'And you did not think it was relevant to inform us of the connection to the threatening messages?'

'I didn't think there was a connection. As I say, Folasade told me the police said it was a random arson attack.'

Kohler paused for a moment, shuffled the papers in front of him, and seemed to be reading something on one of them. 'Okay. So you were not concerned by these threatening communications and links to stories about killings, yes?'

'There was only one link.'

'Just so. And also you were not concerned about one of your employees being the victim of a fire attack?'

'I was concerned. I allowed her to stay in my home, and took the day off to make sure she was okay. But I believed the police when they said it was just a random event. Just kids messing around, they said.'

'So tell me, when did you start employing a private security guard at your office?'

Ned tried to conceal his surprise that Kohler knew this. How did he know? Had they sent someone round to the office and met Kevin? 'Last week,' he said.

'Why did you make this step?'

'Just to reassure people.'

'After the fire attack?'

'Yes, I suppose so, but—'

'You have said that you were not concerned by the threat from Al-Zein.'

Ned hesitated. 'Look, there are several factors at play. The Thing Factory has become a very successful business. Very high growth. We're looking at turnover in the millions, in our first year. So it's normal that we would have some security measures in place. First we have very valuable intellectual property that we need to protect, and second, part of the business is involved with sex work, which is often controversial.'

'So you thought that you might be attacked by – who? Radical feminists? Prostitution has been legal in Germany for many years.'

'I'm aware of that.'

'I am experiencing confusion around this question. On one hand, you say you are not at all worried about these threats from Al-Zein, and on one hand you are hiring a private security firm in the same week. You cannot explain this, yes?'

'I have explained it. The security measures were part of the normal programme of expansion for the company, to protect our assets, our staff, and our intellectual property, which are all very valuable.'

'Ahh, you must be very wealthy then.'

'I'm a successful entrepreneur.'

'And with that kind of money it must be easy to pay people to do anything you want. To deal with inconvenient factors.'

'I don't know what you're talking about.'

'You know, I am sometimes with the feeling that technology companies think they are outside the law,' Kohler said musingly.

'Again, I don't have the faintest idea what you're talking about. The Thing Factory is a fully registered, tax-paying business.'

'Ahh . . .' Kohler sipped his coffee, and slid an A4 colour photograph from his manila envelope. Ned recognised Abdel's mug shot, the one that had been circulating online, at once. 'What does the name Abdel Haddad mean to you?' Kohler said.

'I don't know it.'

'This is the name of an important member of Al-Zein. He was found dead last Friday. Did you hear about this?'

'Okay, I did see that in the news.'

'What did you see about it?'

'It was all over the internet. I live in Kreuzberg, so everyone was talking about it.'

'Do you know what happened to him?'

'I heard that he was shot dead in a car park by a rival clan.'

Kohler paused, looked at Ned for a moment, and nodded thoughtfully. 'Do you think this is an everyday event in Neukölln?'

'I have no idea.'

'So why do you think somebody would have wanted to shoot this man?'

'No idea.'

'Can you take a guess?'

'He must have had an enemy.'

'Indeed. But you are not his enemy, yes?'

'I didn't even know who he was.'

Kohler held up the photograph, looked at it a moment, then slid it across the desk to Ned. Abdel's unsmiling face stared up at him. He couldn't prevent the image of how it looked when he'd last seen it – purpled, misshapen and partly missing – floating into his mind. 'Do you recognise him?' Kohler said.

'No.'

'For sure?'

'For sure. There are a million people in Berlin who look like him.'

'You do not like the Lebanese? You think they all look the same?'

'I think shaven-headed men with black beards all look like shaven-headed men with black beards.'

'Very good.'

Ned glanced at his watch. 'If you don't mind, I have a lot of work to do today, and I've been here for forty minutes already. Was there anything else?'

Kohler spread his palms open. 'You are free to go.'

'Thank you. And if you want to speak to me again, you'll have to go through my lawyer. I don't appreciate being quizzed as if I'm some sort of suspect, when I came in voluntarily to help you.'

Kohler creased his brow. 'Why would you think you are a suspect?'

'That's not what I said.'

'Just so. But one final question. How tall are you?'

'How tall?'

'Yes. Around 181 centimetres, is it?'

'I'm five foot eleven. I don't know what that is in centimetres.'

'We can work that out,' Kohler said, noting the figure down.

He told Ned that he could leave. On his way out, Ned stopped at reception to tell them that he was leaving, but the man at the desk barely took any notice. Ten seconds later, he was outside on the street, feeling suddenly at a loss for what to do with himself. Kohler's last question had thrown him. Why on earth did he want to know how tall he was?

N ED WENT FROM THE police station straight to Folasade's apartment, turning the conversation with the police over in his head. She buzzed him into her apartment block, and when she opened the front door he was surprised by the silence; she usually had the radio playing continuously. As soon as he was inside, she asked him what the police had wanted.

He told her what they had asked him, and what he had said.

'Was that all?' she said. She seemed tense to Ned.

'I guess with that guy getting killed,' he said, 'they're just going over all the recent reports about the crime clans. Here, let me sit down and get my shoes off.'

Folasade was still standing, watching Ned as he undid his shoelaces on the sofa. 'They phoned me,' she said.

'What?'

'The police phoned me.'

'When?'

'About an hour ago. When you were with them, I guess.'

'Which officer was it?'

'I don't remember his name. Something German.'

'What did he want?'

'He asked me if I'd had any further contact from the Al-Zein. And then he asked what you and me were doing last Thursday.'

'What did you say?'

'I said that we stayed in all day, and then you went to the party.'

Ned looked at her. He felt the pressure of her thoughts on him like a laser beam. She had lied to the police for him. She had said he didn't leave the flat. That meant she must suspect there was something she needed to lie about.

'Ned,' she said in a whisper, 'was it you?'

She fixed her gaze on him for one second, two seconds. Something in Ned cracked. 'You did the right thing,' he said, 'saying I spent the whole day with you.'

Folasade looked away from him towards the wall, then glanced around the room for a moment. 'Oh my days,' she said to herself. 'Is this for real?'

Ned nodded.

'Oh my god.'

She came and sat down next to him on the sofa, looking straight ahead.

'I know it must sound awful,' Ned said, 'but it was . . . it was just a really fucked-up situation.'

She turned to him and he saw her brown eyes widen. 'It's really fucked up,' she said. 'What the hell happened?'

Ned hesitated. 'Well . . . there are things I haven't told you about. Just before we had that team meeting where we discussed the messages, I started to think I was being followed, but I didn't think there was anything in it at the time.'

'By those organised crime people?'

'Yeah.'

'Christ, why didn't you tell any of us?'

'I didn't want to panic anyone. And I didn't know for sure it was them until later. I figured it was just a half-hearted attempt to scare me. And I suppose I felt . . . it got my blood up, somehow. It made me think fuck you, I'll sort this out myself and show you that I'm not intimidated.'

Folasade stared at him in a way that Ned couldn't read. He carried on: 'But then when I heard about the fire – the attack – at your place, I knew that it was really serious. So on Friday, after I'd found this place for you and seen that you were okay—'

'And had sex with me,' Folasade said.

'Yes, after we'd had sex, I went out to sort out the security guard for the office and to see a private investigator.'

'What for?'

'To look into who might be behind all this. So I'd have

as much info as possible, and feel more in control, I suppose. And it was after I'd done that that I realised the same guy was following me again.'

'This was Abdel Haddad?'

'I didn't know his name at the time, but yeah. So I tried to lose him. I went and sat in a bar for a while and he was hanging around on the street outside, but then he gave up and left. Then when I left the bar I saw him again, looking like he was on his way home. And I decided to follow him.'

'What were you planning to do?'

'I don't know really. Just find out where he was going. See if he gave anything away that might prove useful. Maybe turn the tables on him, scare him a little. Let him know that I could do to him what he'd been doing to me.'

It sounded nutty, now Ned heard himself say it aloud. Folasade was sitting forward, staring at him.

'So I followed him, and eventually he went into this casino. This is in Neukölln. And these five other Middle Eastern guys followed him in.'

'Fucking hell,' Folasade said.

Ned was on the verge of telling her about disguising himself, going into the casino, listening in on them, but it suddenly seemed too much. He didn't want her thinking he was truly unhinged. 'So I had a quick look through the window,' he said, 'and I saw them all sitting around a table, and I thought this must be their base. I could see which one looked like the boss. And then I headed home, and I was just around the corner when the first guy, the one who'd been following me, grabbed me from behind and pushed me down this side street. We were in this sort of car park, like a vacant lot, and he started telling me how we had to stop doing Gliss, blah blah blah, or if we wanted to carry on we had to give them a cut of the profits. And I said, basically, fuck you, and then he pulled his gun on me.'

'Fuck.'

'I know, right? He had it aimed right at my forehead. I'm sitting on the ground by this point, where he's pushed me down. And I really thought . . . I don't know what I was thinking, I was thinking all sorts of things, but it was definitely a possibility that he was going to shoot me there and then. Then finally – it seemed like ages he had it trained on me – I managed to distract him, I made him laugh and he turned away for a second, and I jumped him.'

Folasade had her hand over her mouth.

'I knocked him down, and then . . . the rest is a bit vague, I must've blacked out with anger, but I smashed his head into the ground, and . . . well . . .'

'You shot him with his own gun,' Folasade said.

Yes, Ned thought. That will do for a story. Best not to mention that the shooting happened when he had gone back, and that Abdel was definitely unconscious, possibly dead already, when he was shot.

'I shot him. I did. I mean, he was still moving after I'd smashed his face in, he was trying to throw me off his back, so I shot him before he attacked me again. Then I tried to disguise his body a bit and got the hell out of there.'

Folasade was staring at him, looking shocked and puzzled. Eventually she spoke. 'That's like the definition of self-defence, isn't it, if he had a gun pointed at your head?'

'I guess. Though the police might wonder if it was excessive force. I don't know if they have that idea in German law. And it's my word against his that he pulled his gun on me, except that he can't give his word anymore. And if it was self-defence I ought to have turned myself in. I'd rather not risk it, anyway. They basically have nothing linking me to him except for those messages, which must be pretty dubious evidence.'

Listening to himself speak, Ned realised how incoherent he sounded.

Folasade swallowed some Club-Mate, and said with a frown, 'So you went straight from that to the fancy party for social?'

'It was a bit of a blur. I don't even remember how I got away from Neukölln. I went and had a drink first, I was feeling so wired and crazy. My hands were shaking like mad.'

Folasade took Ned's hand in her own. 'Poor you. I can't even imagine it.'

She fell silent for a moment, then something in her seemed to kick into action. 'We need to get our stories straightened out properly,' she said. She sounded practical and cool-headed.

All Ned could say was 'thank you'.

Over the next few minutes, Folasade talked Ned through the details of the previous Thursday. They had slept in late together and had sex, before they spent an hour looking at Airbnb apartments on Ned's computer, and the rest of the day watching television on her laptop in bed, before Ned cooked a risotto in the evening and washed up, then headed to the party at Panoramapunkt. They had watched five episodes of *Parks and Recreation* and three of *Game of Thrones*, season five. Ned deleted the parts of his browsing history that contradicted this story – the searches for private investigators and security companies – then opened an incognito window to read episode summaries for the programmes he was supposed to have seen. Folasade quizzed him on how they had spent the day. He got every question right.

Ned cooked some linguine with parmesan, lemon juice and fresh basil. He felt that the conversation had gone well. Folasade had taken it better than he could have hoped. It looked like she was onside. In fact, his position now was much stronger, surely, than it had been this morning. He had an alibi, a rock-solid one, and he felt better, freer already, for having shared the story with somebody. Or at least most of the story. He knew he could never tell the whole truth to anyone.

'SO YURI AND AYTAN can definitely come tomorrow?'
Alice said. She was in the meeting room with the
door shut, looking out over Kottbusser Tor, anxious that
nobody overhear her phone conversation.

'Looks like it. They're in Seattle at the moment. But if
they think this is worth spending that much money on, it'll
be worth rearranging their diaries for.'

David Singh sounded triumphant. He and Alice had
agreed on Thursday as the day to take Ned out for lunch
and present the buy-out to him. They'd agreed that Yuri
and Aytan should be there, to make it seem more finalised.
Alice stretched back on her chair, enjoying the patch of
bright sun that pooled over her bare ankles through the
window, and switched her phone from one hand to the other.

'I think it's looking good with Ned,' she said. 'The way
he accepted the arrangements with Gliss so easily, it looks
like he'll go along with everything. I guess his mind is
elsewhere.'

'Hmm,' David said thoughtfully. 'How long is it since
his dad died?'

'It must be more than a month now.'

'Yes. I wanted to ask if you wanted one last chance to reconsider the whole thing.'

'How do you mean?'

David paused and there was a sound of rustling down the line, then he said: 'I shouldn't say this really when it stands to cost me a large payday on the success fee, but I think you should be sure in your mind about whether this is the right thing to do. It's a big thing, to cut your co-founder out. And it could cause bad blood. Bad publicity, if he wants to be awkward. There's also the chance that he might not accept.'

'Well . . . I've really got so much leverage on him, I don't see how he could refuse.'

'Okay. But I just want to be certain that you've considered all possible eventualities. I assume you've thought about the fact that Ned will probably never speak to you again.'

'I have.'

'And you're okay with that?'

'I am.'

'Okay. I've said it now, so I won't mention it again.'

They went over the details for Thursday one more time. When she had hung up the call, Alice sat in the meeting room and pondered the conversation. How did she really feel about the situation? Ever since she'd first broached the idea with David, it had taken on such a reality in her mind that she'd long ceased to consider whether it was the right thing to do. But she hadn't been sleeping well recently, it was true; she'd found herself waking from hideous dreams in which she was shamed and humiliated, though Ned hadn't featured in any of them. In the most recent dream, she was on holiday with her family somewhere and had vomited in a hotel room and not told anybody, and her brother had discovered it . . . Was it like her, to be doing this to Ned? Wasn't it too ruthless, now she thought about it? What kind of person did it make her?

She thought back to what her therapist in LA had told her when she was trying to get her shit together to split up with her boyfriend last year: that she had a tendency to diminish herself, to downplay how formidable she could be, as if she was afraid of outstripping the man in her life, or of outstripping her father. Alice shocked herself with how much she'd cried in therapy that day, but she realised it was true, and that she needed to try not to do that anymore. And it had worked. It had brought her to where she was today, running her own company, and living the life she was supposed to be living. No, she couldn't turn back on the plan now. She had to cut Ned out.

To ALICE, NED SEEMED ill at ease in the car on the way to Potsdamer Platz. She had slept terribly last night, thinking about how the meeting with Aytan and Yuri and David would go. When she texted Ned to tell him he had to come to lunch with some important potential investors, he had agreed almost too easily: there had been no resistance, almost no curiosity from him, and none of the persuasive tactics she had planned were called for. She'd been anticipating him saying he didn't want to come, that he had no interest in meeting investors. But he didn't say anything. He barely asked her anything about it that morning, as if he didn't care, and when she told him they were having lunch with these guys Yuri and Aytan, the venture capital people she'd met with in March, it didn't seem to register at all. He seemed distracted to Alice, as if he were speaking to her from across a distance in space and time. He was staring out the window when she said, 'Have the police been back in touch?'

'Only once since I spoke to them. Just to check a detail.'

'What detail?'

'They asked again how tall I was.'

'Why?'

'I think they're just trying to freak me out. Make me feel like I'm under suspicion or something. It's really fucked up.'

'That's crazy. Why would they do that?'

'I guess they know that Al-Zein sent us those weird emails, and they're trying to put two and two together. Trying to pin it on someone.'

'How tall are you, like six foot?'

'Five eleven.'

'I thought you were taller than that.'

'It would round up to six foot.'

'Half the men in Berlin must be five foot eleven. What would it prove?'

'I don't know.'

For an instant, Alice pictured herself visiting Ned in a German prison: he had killed a Lebanese gangster, she was visiting him out of conflicted loyalty to her disgraced former business partner . . . But no, it was ludicrous. She couldn't imagine it. That wasn't her life.

'What happened with that woman who got robbed?' she said.

'Which one?'

'On Gliss.'

'Oh, yeah. Nothing happened in the end. The police

thought there wasn't enough to press charges. We blocked the guy's phone number and laptop from the app.'

'God, I hope she's okay,' Alice said. Ned nodded.

The car was stuck in traffic near the corner of Stresemann Straße. 'Do you know what this street used to be called?' Ned said.

'What?'

'Hermann-Göring-Straße. I think it's this street anyway.'

'Wow,' Alice said softly.

They fell silent. Alice knew she didn't have long now. She had to say the right thing, to lay the ground for David's offer. She had gone through it so many times in her head, but something held her back now. Her phone pinged in her pocket. A text from David: Yuri and Aytan couldn't make lunch because their flight had been delayed. No matter: David would still have all the details. There was no going back now. She needed to do it.

'You must feel under a lot of pressure,' Alice said.

'Hmm.' Ned was still looking out the window, either picking at his teeth or biting his nail.

'Ned, I wanted to ask you something.' That got his attention. 'Do you ever worry that anything from the scam sites will catch up with you?'

'How do you mean?'

'That someone will connect the steroids or the diet pills or the Amazon thing to you?'

Ned looked down at the footwell for a time, thinking. Finally he spoke. 'Sometimes, yeah. Once or twice it's made me a bit panicky. And now this police thing . . . I wouldn't want them sniffing around, let's say that. I'm confident that all the security and encryption on those projects was up to scratch. But Christ, I don't know . . .'

'What?'

Ned hesitated a moment, looked out the window, then spoke: 'To be honest, I'm increasingly thinking I might as well cash out. With The Thing Factory. You know? We never made an exit plan or anything, but I'm sure now I could sell my share in the company for a tonne of cash. I guess . . . well, I've been thinking about it, but I didn't want to tell you yet. I didn't want you to think that I was abandoning you or going behind your back or anything.'

'Gosh,' Alice said.

'I mean I'd consult you, obviously. I wouldn't sell up to anyone who I thought you wouldn't have a good working relationship with. But I'm thinking now that it might be the best step. There's just too much heat on me at the moment. And to be honest, you're blatantly better at running the business than me. You'd probably do better without me. You could get a proper board of directors.'

Alice felt the moment travelling through her body. It felt as if the world were shifting on its axis, suddenly reconfiguring itself around her. She felt sick. She found herself compelled to bow her head. She shut her eyes.

'Hey, are you okay?' she heard Ned saying.

'There's something I need to tell you,' she said.

THREE HOURS LATER, NED was at home, padding around the apartment, and considering what it felt like to have been offered such a crazy amount of money for his share in the company. Was it a joke? But no, Alice and that guy David seemed to be totally serious. The deal seemed to be well advanced. Alice must have been putting it together for weeks, without him even knowing about it. It was as if she'd guessed that he wanted to sell up, without him even needing to say it. If the due diligence all went okay, it would happen. They had gone over the documents, shaken on it and toasted it with champagne. It was no joke.

The buzzer went. It was probably nothing, Ned told himself. He was in the middle of a huge city: there were delivery men, meter readers, neighbours needing favours. The buzzer went again, and Ned realised with surprise that it was someone at his front door, not the door into the courtyard downstairs. Through the peephole he saw Captain Kohler, in uniform this time, with another officer standing next to him. They rang again, the noise now shockingly loud in Ned's ear. He waited a moment and opened the door. 'Hello?'

'Hello again. We have met before, of course, and this is my colleague, Officer Vogt. We are wanting to speak with you again about our friends, the organisation known as Al-Zein. Will you come to the station?'

Ned sized them up. Vogt was a huge blond-haired guy in his thirties. He looked like a caricature of a German. 'Am I under arrest?'

'You are not. But it would be much preferable for you to come with us voluntarily. We have a car outside.'

It occurred to Ned that he had failed to find a lawyer for himself. It had been on his to-do list, but so much had happened this week that he hadn't got around to it. He could get Daniel to come, but that might cause further difficulties – Daniel would have his own version of their interactions with Al-Zein, and of Ned's arrival at the Panoramapunkt party. Daniel might have noticed the blood on his hoodie, or heard Alice mentioning it. Silently Ned turned to take his denim jacket from the cupboard in the hallway. 'Let's go then.'

It was a long walk down five flights of stairs, through the courtyard, and down Dieffenbachstraße to where they had managed to find a parking spot. Back in the station fifteen minutes later, Ned knew his way around the place. They sat him down in the same interview room, asked if he wanted a coffee. It seemed they were being excessively friendly to him.

'So,' Kohler said. 'We have last time discussed your

relations with Al-Zein. Emails they have sent your company, and a probable attack on the home of your colleague. You still say that these were not of great concern to you?'

'At the time, no. But I didn't know that the fire was anything to do with the emails. That's what the police had said.'

'Ahh, yes. Do you have the name of the officer who was telling you this?'

'No – well, he didn't tell it to me, he told it to Folasade on the night of the fire.'

'She does not remember the name?'

'She didn't tell me. I should have thought you would have a record of which officer attended the scene.'

'Just so.' Kohler took a sip from his coffee, wincing slightly at the temperature. 'Could you tell me again what you did on the day of Thursday the 4th of June?'

'Sure. I slept in late, because Folasade had come around very late at night. Then I looked after her, I made her breakfast, and we looked on the internet for an apartment for her to stay in temporarily, and we watched television.'

'And you did not leave the apartment?'

'Not until I went out in the evening after dinner, to go to a work party at the Panoramapunkt.'

'What time was that?'

'Around nine thirty.'

'And the early evening?'

'I stayed in with Folasade. We watched more TV. And I cooked dinner.'

'It sounds like a very pleasant day.'

Ned said nothing. After a moment, Vogt spoke to Ned for the first time. 'Do you own a bright green hooded sweatshirt?'

'I don't.'

'Have you ever owned such an item of clothing?'

'No. That wouldn't be quite my style.'

'We are interested in talking to a man who in many ways fits your description. Same height. White. Mid-thirties. Not a native German speaker. He was in the neighbourhood of the killing on that day, wearing this unusual sweatshirt and a baseball hat. The man who has the shop in the neighbourhood says that he bought these items and immediately was removing the . . . *wie heißt das*?'

'The labels,' Kohler said.

'Exactly. What do you think this behaviour means?'

'He must have been cold,' Ned said.

'It was a very warm day.'

Ned shrugged. Vogt carried on: 'It sounds to me like the action of somebody who wants to disguise their appearance. Is this so?'

'I have no idea.'

'Please excuse us for one moment,' Kohler said, and he

and Vogt stood up and walked out, leaving Ned on his own. This must be a technique, Ned thought, to try and make him nervous. He determined to treat it lightly. He forced himself to hum a tune.

After a time, Kohler returned alone. 'In our last conversation,' he said, 'you have told us something rather interesting. Do you recall what that was?'

'Try me.'

'Excuse me?'

'I mean, no, I have no idea what you would find interesting. Tell me.'

'When I mentioned Abdel Haddad, you gave a detail about him.'

'I didn't know his name. When you said he'd been killed I said, oh yes, I saw that in the news.'

'You also said something else, that was not mentioned in the news.'

Ned shrugged.

'You said that he was shot in a car park. Do you remember saying this?'

'Not particularly.'

'Where were you hearing that it happened in a car park? All it said in the newspapers was that it happened on the street where he lived.'

'I don't know. I must have heard it at the convenience

321

store or something. Everyone was talking about the killing, and news travels fast. I live right next to Neukölln.'

Kohler was staring at him thoughtfully. 'That is your reason for knowing this information?'

'Yes. Someone must have told me.'

'But you don't remember who?'

'No.'

'You said it was at the convenience store. Is that on Dieffenbachstraße? We might need to talk to the owner of this store. He appears to have access to very confidential information about criminal cases.'

'I don't remember where I heard it. I just meant someone in the neighbourhood must have told me.'

'To us it is somewhat strange, because this information about the car park is known only to a small number of people. Only the direct family of Abdel Haddad. They did not want it known, because they considered it humiliating for Abdel's memory.'

'As I say, the information must have travelled quite far. Probably someone put it on Twitter after they had seen the police at the crime scene.'

'Yes, that is probably it,' said Kohler with a tense smile. 'I wonder, would you be willing to provide a photograph for us? This is to help with identification of the man in the hooded sweatshirt. Are you willing to do this?'

'Do I have a choice?'

'In theory, yes.'

'I refuse. In practice.'

'Very good then, I will arrest you and you will not have a choice to participate. That will be worse for you, I think.'

'Fine,' Ned said. 'Let's do it. I'm ready.'

Ned sat grim-faced against the blank wall as they took a photograph of him, then sat alone in the room for half an hour. He felt suddenly exhausted, as if his legs and feet were sunk in thick mud. He felt emptied out. Maybe he should just give himself in, tell them the whole story, say it was self-defence. After all, the guy was a gangster; he pulled a gun on him. It *was* self-defence. But then he knew he would have to explain lying to them, and hiding the body, and throwing the gun away. And they might be able to tell that Abdel was unconscious already before he was shot. Could a medical examiner work that sort of thing out? And it would surely ruin the buy-out, the Fox Pop deal, everything. It would ruin everything Alice had worked for. No, he had chosen this course. He had to see it through. And what did they really have on him, even if he was identified in this line-up as the man in the bright green hoodie? The fact that someone who looked like him had been in the neighbourhood at the time? What did that prove?

THE STREET WAS BUSY with pushchairs, shoppers, and boys on bicycles; with golden retrievers walking off the lead; with people eating shawarma from greasy paper wraps. Alice looked vaguely into a window displaying men's clothing, with a short stack of beautiful-looking blue sweaters piled on a low wooden shelf. They cost almost three hundred euros. She wondered if Tristan would like them, or if it might be a bit excessive for a spontaneous gift; then she walked on past the shop and forgot about it before she had really made up her mind either way. She crossed a busy intersection, came to a bridge, decided not to cross it, and turned back. She realised then that she felt bad about how she had treated Ned. She had a hollow feeling in her stomach, a tightness in her head. How could she have been so disloyal, so untrusting, so selfish? To have found out that he *wanted* to sell up, that he was actively proposing it himself, then to have to admit to him that she had in fact already made the arrangements, that they were on their way to receive the offer right now, that she had been preparing this for months behind his back: it felt humiliating to her to have done this. It was humiliating to her sense of who she was. And Ned had been so happy to accept the offer. Why hadn't she just been open with him all along?

It occurred to Alice that she hadn't taken a proper day off in months. Not when she was hungover, not when she had her period. She phoned Richard and asked whether he could hold the fort for a day if she and Tristan took a break, and gave him a list of the things that needed addressing, then she texted Tristan and asked if he wanted to go to one of the lakes tomorrow. He did.

By eleven the next morning they were on the beach at Orankesee. It was beginning to get really hot, and the beach was filling. The sand curved a half-moon around the blue water, backed up by green woods. In the middle of the strand was a huge looping water slide made up of tubes in a dull chrome that caught the light when the slide rounded a corner. A spiral staircase led up to the slide's entrance; already a queue of children ebbed and flowed at the top of the stairs, most of them running back around to join the queue again when the slide deposited them gawping into the water.

'Did you remember the snorkel?'

Tristan checked in the bag. 'Here it is. Oh, shit.'

His rustling in the bag had caused an open pack of *Schwarzbrot* to fall on to the sand. He blew on it.

'I'm going to swim,' Alice said.

'The water will be warmer in an hour,' Tristan said.

'I'll brave it.'

She took the snorkel and the goggles. The rubber strap was tight around her skull, but she liked the feeling of the goggles pulling tight into her eye sockets. Nothing would be getting in or out. On her bare feet the sand was hot already, and sharp between her toes. She walked into the water, aware of being leered at by a trio of teenage boys off to her left. When the water reached the top of her legs, she squatted into a sudden crouch so that she was submerged up to her shoulders, then kicked her legs out behind her and put her face in.

The water was marvellously clear, though there wasn't much to see except the bottom of the lake, with a few pieces of murky plant life. She swam in a purposeful front crawl, making an effort to keep the timing of her breathing relaxed and regular: in for four strokes, out for four strokes. Soon she moved above a group of whitish-silver fish, and felt her heartbeat rising slightly. She couldn't see the bottom of the lake now. It was fine: the fish were tiny, they were minding their own business. She turned over on to her back, trod water, and looked back to the beach where she could make out Tristan sitting on the blanket halfway up reading his book. At that moment he looked up and waved at her. She waved back.

Something had changed in her relationship with Tristan in the last week or so, she thought. Or perhaps something had changed in her. When he rang her, she felt a slight reluctance to pick up, though she always did pick up; when a message from him appeared on her phone, she felt vaguely irritated in anticipation. She had stopped looking forward to spending time with him. It's not that she didn't enjoy spending time with him; but she didn't look forward to it. She knew too that this was hypocritical of her, because at other times she would want his company, she would text him, and if he wasn't busy he would always cross town to come and see her.

They had had their first argument last week. It was after they'd had sex. Alice had been saying to him, 'Fuck me, fuck me'; she had enjoyed it, but he seemed quiet and withdrawn afterwards, and when she asked him what the matter was, he said that it made him feel weird, being told to go harder. Alice said that she wanted him to want to fuck her, she wanted him to find pleasure in her body, and that she liked it that way sometimes. He said that he found it difficult. It seemed disrespectful to women. It seemed like it was objectifying her. Something in this chimed with Alice. Although their fucking had been enjoyable, in the first rush of starting to sleep together, she felt that there was something slightly prim and regretful about Tristan's relationship to his own physicality. Alice sympathised with him on this, but she also wished he wasn't quite so feeble. Their conversation took an unexpected turn, with both of them drunk and arguing positions which they hadn't really thought through, until it ended with Alice saying much more forcefully than she had meant, 'It's not fucking feminist to treat women like they shouldn't enjoy sex!' They had got over that row, had laughed it off, but since then they had been more inhibited with each other. It felt like he wasn't telling her something.

After a few stretches of front crawl and back stroke, Alice headed back for the shore, pleased that she had swum so steadily, with no moments of panic over how deep the water beneath her was, and that she had held her nerve when water got into the snorkel.

T HE AFTERNOON WAS LOVELY, with a soft breeze taking the edge off the bright sunshine. Folasade was out picking up some supplies for an early supper, and Ned looked forward to her returning with food from the deli: he imagined roast artichokes and anchovies in oil, breadsticks, and slices of bresaola. He sat on his sofa, unsure what to do with himself while he waited for her, but content to do nothing. He wondered if he should tell her now about the buy-out. Tell her that he was about to become extraordinarily rich. He felt as if he might burst into tears. On Twitter, every picture of a dog or a baby, every retweet about someone finishing their exams, seemed lovely. He felt rather spaced out, giddy and high.

When the police had come back into the room and told him he was free to go, because he hadn't been identified from the photograph, and because in the meantime another organised crime group had made a credible claim of responsibility for the killing, it felt like it was happening in another reality. As if his life had skipped track into a different, parallel world. Of course, it was still possible that the police would question other members of his team; that they would find out that he had turned up at Panoramapunkt later than he had said, and drunk, and wearing a bloodstained fluorescent hoodie. It was possible they would find that he had gone out to arrange a private detective to report on the crime clans that afternoon – especially since Nocerino had been asking questions of someone in the police force on his behalf. But the look of resignation on Kohler's face when he said that Ned hadn't been identified from the photograph suggested that Kohler was closing the book on him, giving up the lead. And he did, after all, have a rock-solid alibi in Folasade. And now it seemed, impossibly, that somebody else had claimed the murder. It really seemed that he was completely in the clear.

He was hungry but the fridge was almost empty. He took a cracker from the cupboard and spooned a slick of peanut butter on to it, followed by a drizzle of honey. He thought of texting Folasade to ask her to pick up some paprika crisps, and went back into the front room, balancing his cracker on fingertips so the honey didn't run off. The moment he reached for his phone on the sofa, the buzzer went off.

It annoyed Ned that people never shut the door that led from the street into the courtyard; anyone at all could walk all the way up to his front door. 'Hang on,' he called out as he fetched a plate from the kitchen to put his cracker on.

With his nose up against the door, Ned saw the bearded man from the casino. Abbas, the older brother. Head of Al-Zein. He was wearing a black suit and a white shirt, open at the collar. Ned was still staring when Abbas's image, distorted in the convex lens of the peephole, lunged forward and knocked at the door, causing it to resound against Ned's hand as he leaned his weight on the other side. Abbas took a step back, spread both his palms, then pulled open the breasts of his jacket to show his fitted white shirt. He was showing Ned that he had come unarmed. Ned opened the door.

Abbas said in German that he believed Ned knew his name already. Could he come in?

He seemed tired and heavy. It occurred to Ned that today was Friday – the day of Abdel's funeral. Abbas must have come straight from there, to be wearing the suit on such a warm day. He reminded Ned of one of his lecturers from university – softly spoken, with the carefully modulated phrases of a scholar. But perhaps it was just the beard, the dashes of grey at his temples, the hunched and disappointed bearing that gave that impression. Ned stepped aside and signalled towards the sofa. Abbas walked past him into the apartment and sat down heavily, with his hands clasped between his knees. Ned pulled a chair out from under the table and sat facing him. He liked the feeling of being higher up.

Abbas said that he had come from his brother's funeral, following it with a sentence whose meaning Ned didn't catch. Ned said nothing for a moment, then said that he was sorry to hear that, and asked if Abbas would like a peppermint tea. Abbas nodded. Ned went and made two cups. When he came back, Abbas was standing up, looking out the window. He owned a building two streets away, he said vaguely, while he looked for it across the rooftops of Dieffenbachstraße. He turned back towards Ned, accepted his peppermint tea and put it down on the coffee table with the air of a man getting down to business, and said that Ned didn't need to be afraid of him. Even if Ned had been involved with the death of his brother, he had no desire for revenge.

Ned asked why.

Abbas paused for a long time, then spoke. Ned didn't understand all of what he said, but he seemed to be saying that Abdel had been causing a lot of trouble. The situation was complicated. He had been acting in very unstable ways, and challenging Abbas's authority. The shooting in Hasenheide last year was a direct challenge to his authority, which had caused very many problems for the family. He had been told not to do it, and he did it anyway. Abdel had done some other things that Ned couldn't quite make sense of, but it was clear that Abbas was still very angry about them. He was becoming worked up. It seemed that Abdel had been acting out of turn. The threatening emails, the stalking, the firebomb attack, Abbas said, these were also things Abdel had done on his own initiative. And when he had run out of the casino, shouting that he was going to kill the man who had been sitting there playing the *Automaten*, they had all thought he was mad. They had told him to calm down, it was just an American tourist, but he had gone anyway. So when he had turned up dead, shot in his own backyard, with his gun missing, Abbas assumed he must have done something pretty crazy to bring it about. *Verrückt*, he said, for crazy – the same word Abdel had used about Ned in the car park.

Ned looked down at his tea. His life was changing so fast that he felt like he was scrabbling to keep up with it. Now he thought about it, it made sense that Abdel was an unstable person: that explained the recklessness of following Ned so overtly, of the firebomb that could have burned down the whole building, of pulling his gun out just because he'd been insulted.

Ned asked Abbas if he would like to know what happened in the car park. Abbas shook his head.

Ned asked how they had found where he lived. Abbas

said they had known his address since they first became aware of Gliss, after one of the early publicity pieces. They had kept the information from Abdel because they were afraid of what he might do with it. Abbas presumed that Abdel had found out his colleague's address on his own.

Ned asked why another clan had claimed responsibility for the killing. That was the thing that really puzzled him.

Abbas smiled to himself, sipped his tea and placed his mug back down. It was his idea, he said. It was a way of solving a problem. He had asked his colleagues in the Miri clan to claim responsibility because he knew the police would want to close the case as simply as possible if they thought it was between clans. If it was just inter-clan violence, it was simple. They wouldn't investigate any further. The Miri would choose one of their younger members to take the prison sentence, and in a few years he would come out of prison and be a hero. In the meantime, the Miri and the Al-Zein clan could continue to work together. It was his idea as well, Abbas said, to tell the man from the hoodie shop that he had to pretend not to recognise Ned when they showed him the photograph in the police station.

Ned asked him why. He did things differently from his brother, Abbas said. He wanted to deal with this problem, he wanted the police to leave Ned alone, because he thought that Ned might be useful to him. He wanted to put an idea to Ned. A business proposal.

Ned was really listening now. Abbas sipped his mint tea and paused, thinking. Al-Zein used to have an important role in the sex industry, he said. They used to be powerful there. But they had fallen behind the times. Since they had been competing with the megabrothels, they had no possibilities for making real money. And now Gliss looked like it might overtake them as well. It was a new idea, it was intelligent. It was exactly what he wanted the clan to be involved with. That was why he hadn't wanted Abdel to start threatening them. He wanted to do business with them. His organisation would be interested in investing in Gliss, he said. He could see that it was a great business.

Do you mean *der Schutz*, Ned asked him. Protection.

Abbas shook his head. No, no, he said, these days the clan was a business organisation. They did things properly, legally. They had several companies. Officially the directors of the companies were respected German lawyers, since Abbas was banned from being a company director. But the lawyers worked for him. One of these companies owned rental properties, shops and casinos. And they wanted to buy into Gliss.

Ned stood from his chair and paced a few steps back and forth in front of the window. He found himself irresistibly breaking out in a smile. It was extraordinary, how things were falling into place. Yesterday the buy-out for The Thing Factory, today this. People were queuing up to throw money at him. He laughed to himself, and looked back at Abbas, who was staring at him with a look of curiosity. Yes, why not, he thought. Why not?

He asked Abbas if he would be interested in buying Gliss outright.

B ACK ON THE BEACH with Alice, Tristan seemed in a reflective mood as he ate the black bread with slices of plasticky cheese and sweet cherry tomatoes. 'How long will the due diligence take?' he said, still staring out to the horizon.

'David says it could be months. They have to go through everything. It's good that we moved Gliss out before the process started.'

'But could it be quicker than months?'

'I don't know. We're not the biggest company in the world, so it can't be that complex.'

Alice took a cornichon from the jar and pressed it between her lips. She hoped the due diligence would go quickly. David kept telling her to stay calm, not to rush things, but she felt ready for the next phase now. She wanted to have a new board, to launch in the US, to be sole CEO. It was a little maddening, to be in this interim period, when the battle had been won but the results hadn't been seen yet. It made her restless. She had a mustard seed caught naggingly in one of her teeth, and worried at it with her tongue for a few seconds.

'I don't know if this is really the right time,' Tristan said, 'but there's something I ought to tell you.'

'Oh yes?'

'I don't think I'm going to become the new COO. I've had another offer, and I think I'm going to accept it.'

Alice stared at him. 'An offer from whom?'

'Facebook.'

'Fuck. Is it big?'

'It's pretty big. It's to work on their video on-demand plans. They want to start producing original content themselves, or getting partners to do it for them. And, you know, it's California . . .'

'They'll love your British accent,' Alice said.

'I need to go out for a formal interview still, but they've basically offered it to me. I met with this guy.'

'When was that?'

'Umm . . . last week.'

Alice heard in his voice the tetchy defensiveness of someone who knows they've brought unwelcome news. She didn't want this to become a row. She found herself crossing and uncrossing her legs while she worked out what to say. It hadn't remotely occurred to her that Tristan might not be running the company with her. He might have told her.

She wanted to ask how long this had been in the works: did he know this was a possibility when they were discussing manoeuvring Ned out of the picture? Did he already know it that night when they first kissed? But she held her tongue. She didn't want to seem bitter. 'Congratulations,' she said, and came to give him a kiss. 'That's really exciting news, and you deserve it.'

'I'll be sorry to leave you in the lurch for a COO,' he said.

'We can advertise. Or maybe Folasade could do it.'

'I think she'd be great actually. You'd want a separate creative director under her, but she'd be great at running it. And it would be better for her than running Gliss.'

'Indeed,' said Alice.

'Indeed,' said Tristan in an impression of her voice. She told him to fuck off, and poked him in the ribs, making him roll back on the sand in laughter.

They left the beach at three o'clock, when it had become so crowded and hot that it was irritating. On the S-bahn, Alice felt like she was on horseback, striding thirty feet above the cars and pedestrians. Tristan had his headphones on, and Alice sat in silence. It was strange to think that they wouldn't be working together. The fact that Ned wouldn't be around anymore had only just started to feel real to her, but the idea that Tristan would go too had really thrown her. She tried to examine her feelings. She felt afraid, and oddly guilty. She tried to think what her therapist would have said. (It occurred to her that she really needed to find a new therapist; it was ridiculous that she'd been in Berlin for a year, and not sorted it out.) Of course, it wasn't rational for her to feel afraid. They could advertise for someone to replace Tristan, and they'd get brilliant applicants. They could headhunt someone. So maybe she was feeling fearful now, doubting her ability to run the company on her own, as a way of downplaying herself, trying to protect herself from admitting the scale of what she'd accomplished. But she shouldn't do this. She'd had this before. She shouldn't feel guilty about her achievements. It was fine for her to succeed; it was good. It was good for her to outstrip Ned and Tristan. She had done it already. She had to grow into that fact.

Alice felt better for thinking it through. Back in her flat in Prenzlauer Berg, she took a cool shower, threw all the windows open, got the fan going and lay wet-haired on the cooling cotton of the bedsheets. Soon Tristan joined her from the shower. His fluffy hair made him look like a solemn little boy.

They lay in pleasant doziness, listening to 6 Music and looking at their phones. '*The Martian* looks like it's going to be good,' Tristan said, with his eyes on the screen. 'Oh my god, this labrador has adopted eight ducklings that were abandoned by their mother.'

Alice had only been half-listening. Now she shifted her head into the crook of Tristan's arm, to watch the ducklings crowding in for a spot by the belly of the dog as he lay on his side. Soon she had fallen into twirling her fingers in the hair around Tristan's belly button, and they were kissing and stroking each other. She moved slowly down his chest in a line of kisses until her face was next to his half-erect cock, which was lying at a jaunty angle across his thigh. She shuffled round on her knees so she faced him between his legs.

'What would you like me to do now?' she said.

It felt cruel and enjoyable, to put it to him directly. She knew how excruciating he found it to talk about sex in that way, even though he could talk about it in the abstract in a bar with friends for hours.

'Umm, what you were doing just then was nice.'

Alice grinned, took his cock in her hand rather firmly, and said, 'You didn't answer the question. What do you want me to do?'

Tristan giggled.

'Come on. This is your chance.'

He was jiggling his legs nervously. Alice kept her gaze on him, and tightened her grip so that it must have been on the verge of being painful. 'Come *on*,' she said. He had rested his head back on the pillow, with his forearm covering his eyes. Then she saw him refocus. He shifted his shoulders up on to the pillow so he could look at her, and he said, 'I'd like you to suck my dick and make me come on your tits,' in a new thickened voice that was not his normal one.

'I T's JUST THAT EVERYONE'S so young,' Ned's mother said.

Ned looked around him at the people in Zitrone. 'What about that guy?' He was pointing to a man wearing a leather jerkin with no shirt underneath, with hoops the size of wrist bracelets dangling in his distended ear lobes, who looked to be in his fifties.

'Well, he's dressed in a very young way.'

Ned smiled. 'It's true, there are a lot of young people here. Probably because there isn't enough money to be made. If you eventually want to get a proper job, you have to move to Frankfurt or somewhere. That guy just didn't get the memo.'

'Poor but sexy, is that what they say? I saw that in the guidebook. Although you seem to have found a way to make money here, so well done on that.'

'Thank you.'

'And you're selling your company?'

A week had passed since Ned had accepted the buy-out offer. Last Wednesday, Alice had gathered the whole team together. They had discussed the search for new office premises for Gliss, the question of which staff would have their contacts moved over to Gliss from The Thing Factory, the development stage for the Fox Pop campaign, and the state of the deliverables for the other social clients. Ned had hardly spoken at all. She had talked them through the plans for the New York and London offices, which weren't really news to anybody; the proposed new board of directors, and the new posts that would be created. Then she said, the most important news was that Ned had accepted an offer for his fifty per cent share in The Thing Factory from a venture capital firm called Eccola. Tristan, Folasade and Daniel knew about it already, but to everybody else it was a surprise. Ned improvised some remarks about how much he had enjoyed working with them all, and they responded with tributes to him. Folasade cried. A huge bouquet of flowers appeared, some bottles of champagne, and a tray of flutes . . .

'Yeah, I'm selling my share to this sort of investment firm,' Ned said to his mother, 'but Alice will keep hers, and keep on running it.'

Ned's mother nodded, and said, 'Thank you by the way for putting all those little tabs in the guidebook. It gave me lots of ideas for places to see.'

'There's a lot to see,' said Ned. 'You know, if you wanted to stay longer I could easily find you another place. I was wondering if you'd like to do something while you're here, maybe take a beginner's German course.'

'Yes, you mentioned—'

'I found it a good way of meeting people when I first arrived. And it was fun, being back in the classroom.'

'What sort of people were in the class?'

'All sorts. Some students, but some people who came here for work. Spanish, Polish, Indian, Israeli – all sorts really. I suppose they were mostly in their twenties. But not all of them.'

'I don't know, Edmund. Let me find my feet for a few days first then I'll think about it. I suppose it's the sort of thing I should do, now I'm on my own. Dad and me never travelled as much as we wanted.'

'It's difficult, isn't it, when you're tied down with work and things.'

'We always wanted to visit Berlin actually. He'd been here before we met, when it was still – you know, East and West and whatnot.'

'I remember him telling me. It's such a shame you didn't come out sooner.'

'Well, you always seemed very busy.'

Ned detected the note of reproach in her implication. 'I'm sorry,' he said. 'I was never very good at making time to talk to you.'

'Oh no, don't worry about that. Your dad was ever so proud of you. Whenever we spoke to you on Skype, he'd be talking about it all day afterwards. And you were with him at the end. That's what counts.'

Ned found his eyes suddenly full of tears. He reached across the edge of the table and held his mother's hand. 'I'm really glad I was there.'

'I think we gave him a good send-off, didn't we?'

'We did.'

Ned's mother pointed to a line on the menu with her free hand. 'I think I might have the chicken strips. Now how on earth would you pronounce that word?'

Ned leaned over, and said, '*Hühnerbruststreifen*. Good choice.'

The waiter came, and they ordered. They spoke about her Airbnb apartment, how smoothly the collection of the keys had gone and how smart it was. Ned showed her how to use Citymapper on her phone. They spoke about how she was going to spend the next few days: the first thing she wanted to do was to see Nefertiti, she said, she'd always wanted to see her, and Ned admitted that he had never been to the Neues Museum, even after living here for two and a half years. He would go with her. 'And how is Alice?' Ned's mother said.

'I think she's well.'

'You haven't had a falling-out, have you?'

'No, nothing like that. I guess our ambitions have gone in different directions. She's done amazingly well at running the company. She's turned it into something huge.'

'I'm sure you played your part,' Ned's mother said.

Ned nodded thoughtfully. 'I wanted to say, Mum – since you and Dad did so much for me, if you ever need anything now, you just have to ask.'

'Like what sort of thing?'

'I don't know. A cruise trip. A holiday home.'

'Don't be ridiculous, Edmund, you can't buy me a house!'

'Well, the fact of the matter is that I could, if you wanted one.'

'Anyway, the mortgage is paid off, and I'll have Dad's pension now too. I'm fine really. You should enjoy your earnings.'

'I'm just saying, if anything comes up, or if you want to do any work on the house . . .'

'It's very kind of you to offer. Now, where's that waiter? We've been waiting for ten minutes.'

Ned smiled indulgently at her.

O N SUNDAY MORNING, NED and Folasade were sitting up in bed. He had just told her that he was going to sell Gliss as well, though he didn't tell her that it was Al-Zein he was negotiating with. Folasade seemed to take the news quite neutrally. The rest of the team would be told when the deal was agreed.

'I've been thinking,' she said.

'Sounds serious.'

Folasade smiled. 'It's been a few weeks now since we started sleeping together, and obviously it's all been a bit intense. So much has happened.'

Ned nodded. He found himself somewhat distracted from the moment by how lovely her bare breasts looked as she sat with her back propped against a pile of pillows.

'I don't know if she's told you this,' Folasade said, 'but Alice spoke to me last week about applying for the COO job, now Tristan's going to Facebook.'

'I thought she might do that.'

'And I think I need some time away. I probably came back to work too soon after the fire and everything. But I'm going to take the job, if she offers it to me. So I probably won't be working for Gliss anyway.'

'I think you should take it. You'll be great at it.'

'Thank you,' Folasade said, and unexpectedly kissed him on the mouth. 'It's got me thinking, though. About the future. If I take it on, I want to go into it knowing where everything stands.'

'How so?'

'I want to feel like it's a clean slate. Like I know what I'm doing, and what my goals are. And with everything that's happened, I think it would be best if we cooled things off. You know? I know we're not, like, a couple or anything, but I just think it would be a bit too complicated. And if I'm staying in Berlin, taking this job, I want to feel like it's a fresh start. No unfinished business.'

'No skeletons in the closet,' Ned said with a laugh in his voice.

'I didn't say that exactly . . .'

They hadn't discussed Abdel's killing since the day they worked out the details of the alibi. Ned wondered what Folasade really thought about it. It seemed strange that she hadn't mentioned it at all. After the initial shock, when she'd gone very quiet, she had seemed to come to terms with it very quickly. It didn't seem to have changed their relationship – if anything, it might have intensified it.

Ned was surprised as well by how little it seemed to have affected his own life, day to day. No nightmares, no cold sweats. He didn't seem to feel guilty about it at all. He could rationalise it to himself: Abdel had pointed a gun at his head, and the previous day had tried to kill someone he was very close to; if anything, Ned was doing everyone a service by taking him out.

But he knew that his lack of guilt was strange on some deeper level than this, and that no good would come from probing into it. He had learned that introspection told one very little. If people treated you like a good or kind or otherwise valuable person, as Folasade was treating him now, then you probably were one. It seemed to Ned that the more he did whatever it took to win, the more people seemed to like, respect and value him; he concluded from this that he was acting in accord with some basic truth about life that it had taken him until his thirties to discover: that it was simply better to be a winner than a loser. But surely there must be limits to how far one should go? Clearly he hadn't yet come up against them. In any case, he knew that he wasn't someone who wanted to cause suffering to other people, at least not unnecessarily.

He turned towards Folasade, who looked a little tearful. She really did have lovely breasts. He had a brief moment of gratitude, at the wonder of being where he was, of being in bed now with this remarkable, talented, gorgeous woman. But yes, she was probably right: they shouldn't let the relationship become too serious.

'Baby,' he said, 'that's fine. I can see your point of view. I think it makes a lot of sense. You're right, if you're starting a new job, you don't want to be hanging out with your old boss in the evening. And for me . . . well, I don't really know what I'm going to do. I need to work that out.'

'I guess you don't really need to do anything for a while.'

'I'm not sure I'd be very good at that.'

'Do you think you'll stay in Berlin?'

'I'm thinking no, to be honest. Clean slate and all that. Or maybe I'll keep an apartment here. Come and see the old gang sometimes.'

'That would be nice.'

Ned hesitated, then thought he would just say it. 'You know, if you didn't want to take the COO job right now, you could join me in doing nothing for a while. We could do – whatever people who have time and money do. Go to Borneo to hang out with the orang-utans. Scuba diving in the Alps. That sort of thing.'

Folasade laughed. 'I think you should probably do that with someone else. I'm not the outdoor type.'

'No, me neither,' Ned said.

Pause.

'You know,' Folasade said, 'I never said it at the time, and I'm still getting my head round it really, but I think you did an amazing thing with that guy who tried to kill me. I'll always be grateful for it.'

'Thank you,' said Ned, and squeezed her thigh under the covers.

N ED DECIDED TO GO shopping on Sunday afternoon. Why not? He couldn't think of the last time he had bought any new clothes. His first instinct was to head to TK Maxx in Alexanderplatz, or that place in the Potsdamer Arkader where they had good sales. But now he was on the verge of being incredibly wealthy. He needed to come to terms with it. He was about to be rich beyond anything he had imagined. And his Amex card already had a limit of fifteen thousand euros. Where did rich people go to shop? He decided to walk up Friedrichstraße, with a vague sense that there were lots of designer stores at the north end. Yes, he would do that. Why not buy himself an entire new wardrobe? Throw away everything he owned and replace it with something better. He wouldn't need a lot of things, just the right number and the best quality. Well judged, tasteful things – nothing showy, just clothes made of the best materials, cut to perfection. He didn't know quite what they would look like, but he believed he would recognise them when he saw them. Yes, that would be his afternoon.

It felt like being another person. The easy credit, the

promise of millions to come, were putting distance between this new person and the old Ned, the person who had sat alone in his apartment working on websites that first winter in Berlin, who had conned a few gullible people out of some small change to give himself a head start. That person was gone. Now he was Ned the self-made start-up millionaire. He had seen the whole thing through, from vision to exit. It occurred to him that he should start going to the gym again, get a personal trainer, stick to a regular work-out routine. He would have the time now.

As he walked through Kreuzberg and Mitte, the city's atmosphere seemed to have changed. All the things Ned had cherished – the bar-cafés with their tables out on the sidewalks, the jaunty thrustingness of the Ampelmännchen, the TV Tower looming above it all – they all seemed less vivid to him now, as if their charm had gone. It occurred to Ned that his time in Berlin was coming to an end. Or maybe the change was in him, not in the city. He had spoiled Berlin, he had fouled it up with his blunders and excesses. But he had got away with it. That was the important thing.

After his shopping, Ned had one more piece of business to attend to. He sat in Zitrone with an iced coffee. On an encrypted cloud storage account linked to a Hushmail address, he still had the spreadsheet with the contact details of every person who had paid him money for the fake steroids, the slimming pills and the rainforest land. He drafted a message inviting them to give the details of a Western Union branch or a Bitcoin wallet address, in order to be refunded the money that they had lost. Ned worked his way down the spreadsheet, adding the correct name and the amount owed into each email. He knew that many of them, perhaps most of them, would never reply. But everyone who did reply would get their money back. After two hours, he had contacted them all.

As he walked back down Dieffenbachstraße towards his apartment, it felt as if everyone were watching him now, as if he were famous and people knew it but were keeping a respectful distance. It felt as if nobody could touch him. As if he had truly come into his own. He felt absolutely confident that this was his moment. He had earned this, he had planned it and made it happen, and it had all gone perfectly. From now on, he would do everything right. Now he would definitely go straight.

I would like to thank Lisa Baker and her colleagues at Aitken Alexander for all of their help; Niamh Mulvey, Rich Arcus, Jon Riley, Sharona Selby, Milly Reid and everyone else at riverrun who worked on this book; Tom Marks and Jon Day for their comments on the draft; and Katherine Angel.